I0612322

Consensual Conquest

T.A. Kemons

DEEP DESIRES PRESS

Winnipeg, Canada

Developmental editor: Margaret Larson
Proofreader: Francisco Feliciano

Published February 2023 by Deep Desires Press, an imprint of Story Perfect Inc.

Deep Desires Press
PO Box 51053 Tyndall Park
Winnipeg, Manitoba R2X 3B0
Canada

Visit http://www.deepdesirespress.com for more scorching hot erotica and erotic romance.

Subscribe to our email newsletter to get notified of all our hot new releases, sales, and giveaways! Visit deepdesirespress.com/newsletter to sign up today!

Consensual Conquest

Chapter One

What the fuck is Jack doing walking over to me? If he's looking for a seat, they're scattered all over the dungeon inspired study lounge, even empty ones next to his friends, but he walks to my table. *Oh, fuck! Why is my pulse jumping out my neck?*

"Is this seat taken?" Warmth pours from his honey-brown eyes and classic movie star smile.

I look deep into my textbook, a desperate ploy to obscure my burning cheeks.

"No," Aub jumps in to answer for me while tucking her straight, black hair behind a heavily pierced ear.

Aubrey's been my best friend since we met in middle school, but if she's going to egg Jack on, I might have to beat her ass.

We've always considered Jack a side crush since he wasn't our style of guy, and we didn't know him except by reputation and having a few classes with him over the years, but that didn't stop us from making up little fantasies of him every once in a while.

He's always been one of the heartthrobs of our class, and I'll begrudgingly admit, easily so. After being held back in second grade when his mother died, he epitomized the idea of never letting a good tragedy go to waste. According to legend, Jack kicked his life into high gear after her death. Bulking up when puberty hit till his body looked like a six-foot-five tank, he became a national wrestling champion our sophomore year in high school. He's likely to go All-American here in our freshman year of college.

Like Aub and I, he took college courses his junior and senior years of high school. I question why he chose Mercyhurst out of all the other schools I'm sure he was offered wrestling scholarships to. Aub and I accepted since it's our school of choice with its wonderful forensics program. The fact it's in our hometown doesn't hurt, either.

If Jack's brains and body aren't enough to wet a girl's panties, he has money from somewhere that isn't his parents, and a lot of it, or so the stories go. The only evidence of the money, besides some of his closer friends saying it exists, are his clothes. He always wears tailored suits. Today it's grey slacks and waistcoat over a light purple shirt.

Oh, God, he has the sleeves rolled up! Both Aub and I agree that he is his absolute hottest when his sleeves are rolled up to show off his rock-hard forearms. *Oh! He even has tattoos, now.*

His dark brown hair is cut like a 1920's mobster with the sides cut so short it fades into shaved halfway down, while the top is slicked back. He rocked a mohawk our senior year, and the year before that his hair hung all the way down to his mid back. I didn't think he could look any sexier but each year I've been proven wrong.

"Happy birthday," he says as he leans back in his chair.

Fuck, I mentally growl. *Why the fuck is he talking to me?* When I glance up, his smile hasn't changed but his eyes expect a response, threatening to stay locked onto me till he gets one.

"Uh, thanks." I force a smile. Nineteen is a filler year. I figured no one would give a shit. *I guess not.* "It's not a big deal."

He laughs, a deep and rich sound that vibrates through the wood table and up my arms. "Of course, it is. Birthdays are always a big deal. It's *your* day. The day all your family and friends get to appreciate you, even if you don't want them to," he adds with a bright smile.

As nice a smile as it is, it makes me boil inside. Jack is used to getting what he wants with that smile, and chipper attitudes are not my cup of tea. Good looks can only get you so far in my book, but gleeful smiles and happy-go-lucky well wishes are where I draw the line.

"Yeah, well, whatever." I go back to my book, scooting my chair forward as if that'll lock me into reading.

"I got you something," he says.

Like a fish with a lure in my mouth, my head shoots back up to regard him. His hulking shoulders lean forward, and his smile makes me hot again, but rather than boil I feel as though I might melt. A sigh escapes me. *Damn it. Why do I like that cocky smile?* I would smack it off the face of my ex-boyfriend. *Why does it make me want to pinch his cheeks?*

Completely shocked that he would have even thought about my birthday, let alone get me a gift, I can't help myself. "You got something for me?"

After a moment of hesitation, he grimaces. "Unfortunately, no, but you were suddenly very into having a birthday there for a second."

I scoff. "Jerk." While I appreciate his little logic trap, I don't enjoy being the one to fall for it.

Aub's blue eyes catch on fire. "That's a real dick move, you know?"

"It was." He holds his hands up as if being caught. "I'm sorry. I'll make it up to you. I'll bring something for you on Wednesday."

A gift from Jack? How many times have I imagined him giving me my heart's desire with all his mystery money? Luckily, my mother taught me the value of my heart, and no amount of money can buy me. "Don't."

"Y-yeah," Aub agrees, though I can hear the confusion in her voice. It's nice to have a friend back you up even when they probably disagree. "Too late, jerk."

"It is too late," Jack says, as if they're both in perfect

agreement. "I've already thought of a great gift. Consider it wrapped."

I eye him sharply. He doesn't flinch like my previous boyfriends would, but I don't let that take the heat from my voice. "Then unwrap it and take it back."

"Only you can unwrap your birthday present." He folds his arms as he sits back in his chair, an overly smug grin stretching his clean-shaven face.

Don't engage. I've seen him work over others in the past. He's the kind of guy who always has a response. Best thing is to back away and let him stew in silence. If he even can.

"You heard her!"

No, Aub! Back off, now!

"She doesn't want your stupid gift." She raises her book to cover her face and mouths, 'right?'

"I wouldn't want a stupid gift, either." Once again, he acts like he's agreeing with her. "But this one is actually very thoughtful."

I scowl at him. "How could it be thoughtful if you came up with it, in like two seconds?" *Shit! Fucking idiot! Why did I do that?*

"Well, maybe I've thought of it before, Abby."

I pick up my book to block my face. If my cheeks aren't as red as a stop light, then my whole face is! Jack is cute, but this is ridiculous! *I never let guys get to me like this. What the fuck is going on?* I question as two separate heats war inside me. The scintillating heat begs to let Jack do whatever he wishes with me, while the scalding heat demands control. Is this some special gift Jack has? Some magic power to get under a girl's skin? I've never let a guy frustrate me this much. If anything, *I'm* the one used to teasing and taunting. Kevin, Otter, Cid, Raul, I've had every rocker, skater, and brooding boy in our class eating out of my hands at one point or another. Sure, they're not built like Jack, no one is. *Am I just a horny girl for muscles?* The question pushes the boiling heat over the top, and I relax in hatred.

My relaxation seems to transfer over to Aub as her cold eyes hold Jack. "Only her friends call her Abby."

"This is our fifth year as classmates, and she always corrects the new teachers into calling her Abby. But you're right," he concedes.

I know better though. Jack Billard doesn't concede.

"Maybe I should start at square one and work my way up. Miss. Abigale Bethany Charleston."

My heart skips when he says my full name, forcing me to tumble from the safety of my hot fury. *Why did he have to say each name like he enjoyed it?* And how the hell does he even know my full name? *Shit!* How could I forget? He was a teacher's assistant for English last year.

"May I call you Abby? Or should I stick with Miss. Charleston?"

"Call me whatever you want." I shrug, still pretending that I'm reading my textbook. I'm not going to play his games. He twists every girl he talks to around his little finger. Despite a growing desperation to be wrapped around him in any way possible, I'm not going to let him do it to me.

"Abigale, then," he says with the weight of finality, as though his choice has somehow sealed my fate.

Aub's brow rises with suspicion. "Why not just call her Abby? That's what you said the first time."

Aub! I'm begging you, stop!

"I thought that's what she wanted. Turns out, she wants me to call her whatever *I* wish. I happen to think her name is very pretty. I like the way it feels on my tongue."

What in the actual fuck? This is not the same fucking person from high school. *Why is he saying all this?* I shift in my seat and realize I'm slick between my thighs. *No! Don't fucking turn on me now, fucking traitor! Hate him! Hate him!*

"Hey, Jack," Colin Peterson calls from across the room.

Some other girl shushes him.

Colin and Jack exchange head nods and then Jack stands. I don't want him to go, but I also don't know if I can handle him staying.

"See you two later." He pushes in his chair and leaves.

I can't help watching his large, muscled back walk off. *Oh, those pants make his ass look so good!*

"What the fuck just happened?" Aub asks.

"I don't know! I didn't ask him to sit with us," I whisper.

"You think it was a joke? Like his friends dared him or something?"

Oh my god! What if that's it? What if it's all a joke? Jack is known for keeping a straight face when he's joking.

I place my book down and feign reading as I let my hand casually cover my face from Jack's direction. "Why would you think that?" I ask, wanting her to say all the terrible shit I'm thinking.

"I don't know." She follows my lead and pretends to read. "But he scratched his neck just before Colin called for him. Maybe that was like a signal."

"Are you serious?" The heat boils inside me once again and I embrace it like a cherished friend.

Would he really do that? He always seems like such a nice guy. A bit of a smart ass, but he's not ever overly mean. Well, except when wrestling. He's apparently very mean in wrestling but that's just a testosterone competition. He's always been nice to girls. A real turn of the century gentleman. Just another one of the things every girl gushes over him for.

"I don't know, Aub. Maybe he was having fun, but I don't

think he was doing it as a joke." At least I hope not. If it turns out to be a prank, I'll cave his balls in.

We decide to get some work done, looking over the music selection Mrs. Cenna handed out in orchestra. As we talk about which pieces are going to be easy and which will prove challenging, I look over to Jack a couple of times. He's chatting with his friends, all of them whispering and snickering.

When our next class is about to start, Jack holds the door for everyone leaving after him. This is nothing new, he always did it in high school, and college is apparently no different.

"Bye, Abigale," he says as I pass.

"Fuck off, loser," Aub shoots back with a smile.

"Bye, Aubrey." He grins.

Chapter Two

"It's not *us* he was interested in. It was *you*," Aub whispers with a sly smile as we sit in Physics. "He wants those juicy ta-tas."

"Shut it!" I snap. I hate when she calls them ta-tas, and part of me hates them as well. So many guys come up drooling on themselves looking at my boobs rather than my face. The fact I wear corsets desn't really help either, but fuck those idiots for all I care, corsets feel better than bras, they just pump up the girls more than I care for. "There's plenty of women for him to go for with just as big of tits."

Aub scoffs. "If you say so, Madam F-cup. Besides, maybe he's already run through them all."

"No way. He's a good little Christian body. I mean boy!"

Aubrey roars a laugh at my slip up.

Ms. Lekser directs a sharp eye on the both of us, quickly shutting Aubrey up. The woman is as hippy as Woodstock, but the knives that shoot from her eyes remind us she doesn't take kindly to being interrupted. We had her while we took a few college courses our senior year of high school and she reminds me of Dr. Jekyll, Mr. Hyde. The woman keeps an eye on us rest of class, keeping us from our conjecture on what Jack's deal is.

"Christian body!" Aub laughs as we leave class, finally able to rub my Freudian slip in my face. "That's so perfect, I love it."

"Shut up. You know I didn't mean that!"

"Seriously though, he and Vanessa were dating most of senior year then stopped out of nowhere in April. Makes you wonder why he lost interest all of a sudden."

"So? That doesn't mean they had sex and he dumped her." Then again, Les is my ex because of sex, or lack there-of.

"But it doesn't *not* mean that," Aub suggests. "Oh shit."

I follow her shocked gaze. Jack stands at the door to Romanticism, greeting people as they enter.

Jack tested out of English as a freshman in high school and has taken college courses since then. There's no way we're in the same class.

"Hey there. Good to see you two again." A big, eager smile paints his face.

Is he puffing out his chest? It's hard to tell, given it's so overly large to begin with. He's like a brick wall with a fashion sense.

"Hi." I don't smile or scowl. Simply an automated response.

"Sup, bro!" Eric Fecklin says as he walks up, holding his hand out.

A wrestler back in high school that most certainly hadn't been offered all the scholarships Jack would have been. Even though he graduated three years ago, he gives Jack their old team's four clap greeting. Each low-five increases in volume, the last seemingly exceeding the legal limit for decibels in a single location.

I roll my eyes. "Men." *Fuck! Why did I open my damn mouth?*

"Hear that?" Jack asks. "First time a woman called you a man, Eric. You should be proud."

Eric gives Jack a light punch to the shoulder and laughs. He turns his attention toward me, his shit-brown eyes sparkling with overconfidence. "How about it, little lady? You want to give me a shot at them titties?"

"Watch it, Eric," Jack warns, his face as hard as his words. "That's way over the line."

"You wouldn't know what to do with a woman if she gave you fucking instructions," I snap. "And I can take care of myself, thanks," I add, scowling at Jack.

The class laughs at Eric's rejection, but Jack just holds his hands up and shrugs.

I sit down at the double desk Aub picked out for us. She raises an eyebrow as one side of her lips pulls up.

"What?"

"Jack Billard wants to *bone you*." She falls into a sing-song voice halfway through.

"Stop, you're being gross!" I whisper.

Jack comes into the class, followed by Mr. Faulst. They walk over to the teacher's desk where Mr. Faulst hands Jack a folder and he walks to the podium.

Oh, fuck! He's a fucking teacher's assistant? How the fuck is that possible? He's a goddamn freshman. Or freshman-esk. He might be like Aub and I where we're sophomores by credit count even though it's our first full semester at the college.

Jack calls out names and looks around the room. "Abigale, I know you're here. Oh, and happy birthday," the bastard adds with a smile that reminds me of my four-year-old cousin whenever he does something sneaky.

The whole class turns to me and starts wishing me a happy birthday.

While I seethe at Jack, I'm actually fine with the attention till Eric starts to sing *Happy Birthday* and everyone joins in.

He stands up and claps the tempo like a brain-damaged seal with a shit-eaters grin slapped across his face. He's getting me back good for what I'd said a few minutes ago.

I turn my death glare back to Jack but he's not even looking at me. He's talking with Mr. Faulst, pointing to something on the teacher's computer screen.

When the singing ends, I begrudgingly thank everyone.

"Very nice of you, Eric." Jack's focuses on the computer for another moment before returning his attention to the class. "A little over the top for my taste but that was very nice. Kevin

Danielson? There you are." He keeps prattling off names as if he hasn't just helped embarrass me on my first day in college.

I'm gonna kick his balls into his throat!

"Aubrey Silt, we all know you're here."

"What the fuck is that supposed to mean?" Aubrey shouts.

"Language," Mr. Faulst lazily admonishes.

"*That* is exactly what I mean," Jack says with another winner's smile. "Your charm is impossible to miss. Sharmella Smith. Hey, good to see you."

"What a dick!" Aub whispers.

The rest of the period goes the way I expected it, mind numbingly boring. As we leave, Jack holds the door again. I walk past him, expecting some kind of smartass comment, but he doesn't say anything. Once Aub and I walk in step down the hall, I peek back over my shoulder to find him staring right at us.

He's not going to act weird all year, is he? There's no way he can keep this up.

Psychology is just a syllabus overview like the other classes, so my mind only lingers on Jack, but when class comes to a close, this strange, horrid day turns into an all-out nightmare. First, only a couple people wish me a happy birthday, nothing I can't handle, but then the hallways to Forensics becomes a gauntlet.

"Happy birthday, Abby," Amber Litch says with a smile and a wave. Her flock of friends she's had following her since junior high all echo her warm wishes.

"Hey, Abby, happy birthday," some guy I don't know says. He's a baseball jock with a letterman's jacket, but I've never seen him before in my fucking life.

I get the same from nearly a dozen others before we reach our class.

"You think Jack put them up to this?" Aub asks.

"That's it," I nearly shout, causing a few heads to turn. I

lower my voice as we enter Forensics. "This is all because of my birthday! He's been playing with me the whole time. That insufferable ass!" I slam my books down on the nearest desk earning me more stares, but when they see me boiling over, they quickly turned their attention elsewhere.

The lab is set up with four stools to a desk, and as people come in, they stay clear of Aub and me. Mostly me.

The last girl to come into the class is Cinthia Zwit, our high school's valedictorian, barely edging Aub and me out. Aub and I know her fairly well since she was with Aub in Mathletes and with me on the debate team. She wants a career in law enforcement like us, but given that she suffers from a bone disorder, forensics might be her only option.

Quick to keep most people at arm's length, she's never told anyone exactly what she has. Kyphosis is certainly part of it given the exaggerated curve in her spine, but as her condition also leaves her walking with crutches and even sending her home on occasion, I suspect brittle bone disease is part of it. I feel a little bad for using her to test my diagnosis skills, but I can't help myself. She also has a speech impediment, but it only shows up when she's nervous, which in math or science classes is never.

"I guess I'm with you," she grumbles as she sits next to me. "Don't expect me to do everything."

"I'm not here to have other people do my work," I snap back.

Maybe it was the competition for valedictorian, maybe it's because I was chosen as captain of the debate team over her, whatever it is, we've never gotten along, and we likely never will.

"Yeah, we earned our way in here, just like you," Aub says with the same satisfied smile she had when she made captain of the Mathletes.

Cinthia scoffs. "*Earned*?" She jerks a fist next to her mouth as she pokes her cheek with her tongue to give the impression of giving head.

My jaw drops. "Excuse me? You did not—"

In walks Bastard of the Year.

"Fuck!" I hiss. *There's no fucking way! What the fuck is he doing in this class?*

"You'll have to take a seat in the back," Ms. Meav says. "Three lovely young ladies. Don't let yourself get carried away."

"Hi, lovely young ladies." Jack sits down across from me. "Thanks for saving me a seat, Cinthia."

"An-Any-Anything for-for-for you, Ja-Jack." Stars flash in Cinthia's eyes as she gazes up at Jack.

"Cinthia helped me out a lot last year," Jack says to the two of us. "I probably wouldn't have done well enough to make Forensics this year if it wasn't for her."

"Oh, you-you-you're too modest. You-you-you're really smart."

"A little too smart." I give him my best stare down. Still, I take that complement seriously.

Cinthia isn't known for calling anyone smart if she doesn't believe it. Maybe she'd make an exception for the glowingly handsome Jack Billard, but I doubt that.

"I don't think there is such a thing as too smart." He smiles.

"It's only a bad thing if the person thinks they're being cute, but really, they aren't." I restrain myself from shouting at him. "They're being an obnoxious jerk!"

His fierce, honey-brown eyes are too intense to keep staring at for long, like looking a wild animal near pouncing, and I pray that he caves first. When he nods and looks down for a moment, I let go of the breath I hadn't realized I've been holding.

"That would be bad," he agrees. "Look. I didn't think Eric was going to start the class singing to you. I just wanted to wish you a happy birthday and get the class to do it, too. I thought it would make for a nice first day of college. I'm sorry I brought it up."

He has the audacity to act like I'm talking about Eric? I stand on the footrest of my stool, lean across the table, and whisper as violently as I can get away with. "I'm talking about you! You had everyone wish me a happy birthday. Not just in Romanticism. Up and down the halls. In my Psychology class. Everyone just suddenly remembered my birthday." I jab my finger at his face. "I know you put everyone up to this. People I didn't even know. You're an ass, Jack! You think you can just come talk to me for five seconds and I'm going to motorboat you." I shake my dangling chest. "You're just like every other guy, except you're worse. You hold the doors, you go to church, you act like you're a saint and then everyone in your shadow grovels at your feet. I see right through you!"

He stares at me for another minute as I slide back to my stool, only because Aub pulls me back by my studded belt. He keeps eye contact the whole time, and I realize he'd even held my eyes when I shook my breasts. Points for him on that, I guess, but nowhere near enough to make up for this other shit.

"I'm really sorry to hear that." He pulls out his phone, taps in his code and flicks around for a moment. He has the new iPhone. Of course, he has enough money for one of those. He puts the phone on the table and slides it over to me.

I barely manage to catch it, partially with my lap at that. Already pulled up on the screen is a text.

Delphi Kingston: Hey Tigers! We took over West Point, let's take over Mercyhurst! We just had our first birthday!! If you see Abby Charleston (the smart, sexy goth girl), make sure to wish her a happy birthday! But no singing, we already hit her with a song.

There are several smiley faces after the message and a shit load of replies.

"I had a feeling you didn't want any more attention after the birthday song, given how pissed you looked. But Delphi sent that out. I have the same message forwarded about four more times." He holds out his hand for his phone and adds, "I didn't mean to embarrass you. I swear."

I slide the phone back, but it goes way off track and over the edge. Thankfully, he manages to catch it by standing and reaching with his long arm.

"Sorry," I mumble.

"You don't need to be sorry, Abigale." He puts his phone back in his waistcoat pocket before sitting.

"How much money do you have to not even bat an eye at an iPhone falling off the table?" Aub asks.

I wonder the same thing.

"I have three—"

"What?" Aub nearly shouts. "You have three, freaking iPhones?"

"Three *more*," Jack corrects with a grin. "You didn't let me finish."

"Give me one." Aub scoffs. "I still have this shitter Nokia."

"Nokias can fall off a cliff and still work. If I cough on my phone, I'll break it." Jack chuckles. He folds his arms over his chest and jerks suddenly. "Oh. I think I just heard the screen crack."

All three of us girls laugh, but I'm quick to stop. I'm still mad at him for some reason. It's not his fault that people wished me a happy birthday. It's not some grand conspiracy to make fun of me or to toy with the goth girls. Just good-natured people trying to brighten my day, and here I am thinking I'm about to rip the next person's head off. So, what am I mad at him for?

Because he started all this happy birthday mess? Because he's giving me so much attention? Why does this burning feeling of unrest linger in my chest?

The rest of the class goes by semi-quickly. It's just an introduction and syllabus read. Nothing else. When we leave, Jack holds the door for everyone like he always does. "See you tomorrow, Abigale," he says as I walk by, that confident smile back on.

I want to squeeze it off his perfect little face! Damn boys! Why do they have so much power when they really want it?

Chapter Three

When Aubrey and I get back to my house, my sisters are in the living room. My older sister, Deanna, can pass as my twin, but she recently shaved one side of her head and cut the rest to her shoulders. She also added two more bottom lip piercings which made me consider adding to the one I have in the center. Other than those, we have all the same piercings: four in each ear, one nose, two on the left brow, and one in our belly buttons. Black eyeliner and darker eyeshadows make our green eyes pop, and our lips have only ever seen either black, white, or red lipstick. No lip gloss in this family.

Our little sister, Zest, looks like a clone of Deanna and me from ten years ago. Her long black hair hangs in the same loose curls we all received from our mother, but her face is clear of the warpaint Deanna and I wear.

"Sup, bitches," Deanna calls. She stands in the door frame leading to the kitchen, watching some cartoon that Zest has on.

Zest jumps up and down on the couch. "Sup—"

"*Don't* say it," Deanna snaps. "You must be this tall to cuss." She holds a hand up to her head, smiling at Zest's pout. Her emerald eyes return to Aub and me. "So, how was your first day?"

"It was kinda nice, and kinda screwed." I want to say, "absolutely fucked," but Zest's within earshot, so I hold back.

Deanna sighs. "Yep. Pretty standard."

I'm about to let it slide when Aub says, "Not even close to standard."

"Oh?" Deanna walks across the room to join us in the foyer. With one last look over her shoulder at Zest, she turns to us with a greedy smile. "Do tell. What did the day hold for you little doves?"

"Jack Billard." Aub shoots me a wicked smile over her shoulder.

"The wrestler?" Deanna grimaces. Her face scrunches for a moment and then shrugs. "I figured he would have gone on to wrestle somewhere."

"That's what I thought, but there he was in the study lounge." Aub proceeds to recount the whole day to Deanna, class by class.

About halfway through, Deanna wants to see what Jack looks like now. She'd only seen him his sophomore year in high school. They move the conversation to Deanna's room, but I stay downstairs and make a late lunch for Zest and myself. I'm cutting the peanut butter and jelly sandwich in half when a scream and *thump* of feet running through the upstairs hall causes me to jump from my skin. Knowing my sister as well as I do, I fly to Zest and cover her ears just in time.

"Are you fucking serious?" Deanna shouts from the balcony looking over the foyer.

"Are *you* serious? Zest can hear, you know? We're in the kitchen if you want to have a normal conversation."

Feet *thump* again. "Hell no, I'm gonna get off on this guy's pics." Deanna laughs from the top of the kitchen stairs.

"I'm sure Curtis would love to hear that," I shout back.

"He'd understand."

Zest raises a brow and scrunches her face. "What does she mean, 'get off' to his pics?"

"Don't ask me." I shake my head and start packing all the ingredients away when a thought dawns on me. "Don't ask Mom, either. Just don't ask anyone."

A few minutes later, they come down the kitchen stairs. Deanna jerks her thumb to the narrow staircase. "Okay, Zest.

You're not tall enough for this conversation. Take your sandwich upstairs."

Zest takes her plate and the bag of chips.

"I said your sandwich, not the bag of chips."

Zest turns around with a devious smile. "I guess I'll just ask Mom what you meant by getting off to a guy's pictures."

Traitorous little bitch.

"Okay, okay. Take the damn chips. Maybe ask Mom what an extortionist is." Once Zest is up the steps and her door closes, Deanna graces us with a playful smile. "So, what do you think he's going to bring you tomorrow? I'd be happy with one of those iPhones, but I'd take a pack of condoms, too."

"*Ew*," I groan.

"What if it's a pair of panties?" Aub asks as she sits at the table and takes the other half of my sandwich.

A thick, sickly slime runs down my spine picturing that. "That might be even worse. If a guy I barely knows bought me underwear, I'd vomit."

"If *that* guy got me underwear, I'd get changed right then and there." Deanna laughs.

"That's because you're a degenerate." I frown.

"Okay, okay. Enough, teasing." Aub looks back and forth between Deanna and me. "What do you think he's really up to? No jokes. No sidesteps. I want to hear real answers."

Deanna's gaze falls on me. "You haven't done anything with him in the past, right? Like, nothing. No playful rubbing, no batting of eyelashes? Absolutely nothing, right?"

"Yeah. We've never said more than ten words to each other. I've never even been partnered with him for class assignments."

"It's your body," Deanna says plainly with a frown. When I glare at her, she shrugs. "What? Are your prude sensibilities shocked? Don't make me laugh." She slides her hands down her curves. "All guys want from women are hips and tits, and we Augustia women have those in spades."

Invoking Mom's last name makes her point. Mom is just as shapely as the two of us. She claims good genetics, proper diet, and exercise which is why she forced all her daughters into after school athletics. While Deanna had kept in shape playing soccer, I'd used track and field, but we both ended our not-so-stellar athletic careers in our junior years when we just couldn't keep up with the girls who didn't have to carry nearly as much chest. My last day of pole vaulting ended without a single clear as my chest hit the bar every time. I'd never cried from shame till that day, and I don't plan on doing so ever again.

"Guys will do anything for it," Deanna continues. "They'll suffer for it, and trust me, bitches, *make* them suffer for it. They don't deserve us." She tilts her nose into the air and adds with a haughty tone, "We are goddesses among men and they should worship us.'"

Her impression of Mom makes me laugh but it doesn't make sense for Jack. "But there are others. He could have any one of them. Why me?"

"Why not you?" Deanna asks. "How many women look like you? Like Mom says, 'The girls attract all the boys.'"

He's not like that. *What do you even know about him?* the nasty side of my mind whispers. *You don't know him at all.* "No, no. Wait. He's dated girls with smaller chests."

"All the more reason." Deanna shrugs. "He's upgrading, figuring out that he like them big. Maybe he's got a thing for the dark girls."

What? There's no way. "Who says he's into goths?" The walls creep in and soon I'm stuck behind the counter, pressed between Jack's interest and Jack's scheme. *It was just a joke. He's not interested and he's not scheming. There's nothing to any of this!* "He doesn't hang out with us! He's never even looked at me."

"He's *never* looked at you?" Deanna's face morphs with a heavy dose of skepticism. "Are you sure about that? Maybe he's just never *talked* to you. Maybe he was too nervous before, and now that he's hot shit, he has enough confidence to approach you."

"*Eh.* Even I have a hard time believing that." Aub finally comes to my rescue. "Jack was crazy popular our senior year. He definitely doesn't have any nerves when it comes to girls."

"Sorry B-cup," Deanna says, pouting her bottom lip. "This is a problem only us Fs have to deal with."

Aub clutches her breasts in offended shock. "I'll have you know I'm starting to fill out C's now, thank you very much. And I've had a lot of guys say they had to work up the courage to talk to me."

"That's because you're pretty, hun, and you have a stellar ass. But for every guy you have come up to you, there's ten more who can't get it together, and those numbers double with every cup size. You've had, what? Four boyfriends? While Abby here had one? Barely," she adds with a scoff. "Men are always scared of what they want. They need a woman to give them courage. When they're young, it's their mothers that give it to them. But what teenage boy is really asking his mommy for help with girls? All these guys are just lost little puppies, not sure what to do."

"No." I shake my head. "It's not about my chest. I shook them at him, and his eyes never left mine. And he looked really concerned when I was berating him for making my day hell. Almost like he was hurt that I was accusing him."

Deanna gives a dismissive wave. "That's just the frail male ego. Men can't take being called out."

"But he wasn't being called out. It wasn't his fault. He

looked like...I don't know. Remember when Dad forgot Mom's birthday when we were Zest's age?"

"Mom was apocalyptically pissed." Deanna laughs.

"But Dad felt like shit." I remind her. "He was so sad for having messed up. That's kinda what Jack looked like. Like he really felt bad that I was upset."

Deanna's brow raises and she looks away for a moment. "You sure you haven't done anything to him? Even accidentally? Maybe brushed up against him at a gym assembly or something?"

"No. At least I don't think so."

"Definitely not," Aub says. "I *for sure* would have remembered that. I would have made a whole day of teasing you out of it."

As Aubrey laughs, Deanna eyes me with suspicion. Just as I'm about to call her out on it, she shrugs. "Well, maybe he's just a little bitch and got worried he ruined his shot. I don't know. I still say he just wants a taste, but you know what Mom says, 'Don't let them taste if you aren't willing to dish it out.'"

I mouth the words along with her as I've heard them so many times since hitting puberty and Mom gave me *The Talk*. I'm not about to let Jack any closer till I figure out what game he's playing. Mom also says, 'There's no man in the world a real woman can't burn.' If Jack really is toying with me, I sure as fuck won't let him get away without a few scorch marks to remember me by.

Chapter Four

After all of Tuesday wondering what the fuck is going on with Jack, Wednesday starts with Orchestra, nice and calm, but when Aub and I come into the study lounge, we find a large box on our table with a ribbon and bow tied to the lid. A small card dangles from a string.

To: Abigale. From: Jack. Happy Birthday, Abigale. I'm sorry I didn't have it yesterday.

"Holy shit! It's huge," Aub whispers. "I bet you he doesn't even get me a card for my birthday."

My heart races as I lift the top. Inside, several tubes of acrylic paint and a number of brushes lay on a glass pallet that protects a canvas on the bottom. I give him points for not buying the ridiculously priced brands, but these are still expensive. The whole box probably costs somewhere in the mark of five hundred. *Is this fucker trying to buy me?* I place the lid back on and turn to his friends' desk, but he's not there.

"Colin," I call.

Colin's long blond hair swirls around his head as he turns to me.

"Where is he?" I ask.

"Who?" He leans back in his chair with a smug grin on his face.

"Jack! Where is he?" I ask again, not letting an ounce of the fire in my chest go to waste.

His eyes shoot wide and he catches himself before he falls backward. "I-I don't know. The fucking gym where he always is? He probably hit the showers or something. I don't know. I swear," he adds when my stare shifts to a scowl.

"He definitely didn't 'hit the showers.' How else did he get the present here?" Aub asks in a whisper.

Aub and I get out our Physics books and work on our homework for next Friday. We want to get ahead in our schoolwork since we'll eventually get behind if we don't start early. Not because we're bad at math, but we intend to have fun during college. That's going to cost us a lot of nights where we should be studying.

About halfway through the hour, Jack comes in, speaking with the wrestling coach for a moment before walking over to us. Today is light grey again but no waistcoat, just a light blue shirt that has the sleeves rolled up along with a fucking bowtie and suspenders.

Before he sits down, I push the box of paint supplies over to his side of the table. "It's too expensive."

"It's the thought that counts." He sits and pushes the box back over to me.

"I don't want it." I try to push it back, but his sturdy arm holds it in place.

"Well, I can't use it. I don't know how to paint. Might as well give it to someone who knows what they're doing with it."

I use both arms against his one but get nowhere. *He's not even fucking struggling!* "Well, it's really easy to learn. You can start with your fingers!" I push as hard as I can, but my chair slides back instead. "Damn it." I huff.

"If she doesn't want it, she doesn't want it," Aub says in my defense.

"That's true." Jack shrugs his bulky shoulders, but still doesn't let go of the box. "Does she *actually* not want it? I mean, I was told these are quite nice and that *any* painter would love to have them."

"Who told you that?" Aub's sapphire eyes narrow on Jack.

"My sister. She dabbles. I showed her some of your work, so she knew what kind of supplies you'd like."

I stop pushing as questions spiral in my mind. "My work? What do you mean?"

"You were part of last year's art show. I still have pictures from the event."

Damn it. I remember him being there now, and how I'd grown irritated at how he took people's attention from the art with his all-too-pleasant conversation.

"I thought photos are school property." A satisfying gotcha smile slides across Aub's lips. "What are you still doing with them?"

"Yeah! Why do you have pictures of my art sitting at home?"

"Admiring your skill." His smile morphs into a sly grin. "Photos taken with school equipment are property of the school. All of my photos were taken with my camera. That's the medium I dabble in. The photos that ended up in the school yearbook were donated." He sits back. "So, technically, I own them."

I take my chance and shove the box across the table at him.

It hits him in his abs that are wider than most guys' chests. The vertical lines of his suspenders emphasize his width. He frowns at the box. "I guess she really doesn't want them. Well, maybe next time." He mumbles something as he pushes the box to the side and reaches down to grab his backpack.

"Don't leave that here." I nod at the box.

"I'm not going anywhere." His eyes pop up as the *zip* of his backpack steals my breath.

"You— You're not going to go sit with your friends?" Fear slides through my veins like ice water but I can't tell if I'm more scared of the idea of him staying or leaving.

"Nah." He pulls out his math book along with a notepad and

pencil. "I won't get anything done if I'm over there. I don't even know why they come down here."

I look over to Aub with wide eyes, asking what we should do, but she just shrugs.

I glare back at Jack. "Okay. Just don't distract us from our work."

"No, problem." He pulls out his phone and plugs in headphones.

For a moment, I wonder what he's listening to, but I shake the thought. The rest of the hour goes by quick. I glance over at him a few times to find him working, sometimes massaging his temples. Math isn't his strong suit, apparently.

When ten rolls around, I make sure Aubrey and I are out the door before he has a chance to hold it open for us. I hope to avoid him as much as possible, but I have two actual classes with him, and he's going to be one of my lab partners for the rest of the semester!

After our hour reprieve, he holds the door for Romanticism. "Hello."

Aub and I walk to our desk to find his present sitting there again. I put my bag on my chair and walk back to him, fury in my veins and I hope my eyes as well.

"Hey, Abby," Eric says as he strolls into the class. When I look at him, he jumps to the side. "Shit! Never mind."

Good.

"Jack!" I snap as I reach him. "I told you I didn't want your gift."

"Right, but you said it was because it was too expensive. I took out all the paints, so now it's much less expensive."

"That's—" I grit my teeth and squeeze my eyes for a moment as one of my eyelids twitch. *How can he be so infuriating?* "The brushes are what cost the most! It doesn't even—"

"I can switch the brushes for the paints if that would make you happy. That's really all I'm going for here. You're real cute when you're mad and all, but you have an incredibly beautiful smile that I'm hoping to see."

Holy shit! He said I have a beautiful smile! He really said that. Oh, fuck, I'm standing here like a fucking idiot! I turn around and walk as calmly as I can back to my desk, even though all the heat I was going to use to sear Jack's backside turns inward to melt me like a candle under a blowtorch.

"What just happened?" Aub asks as I sit. "You look like he just grabbed you or something."

Worse. "He said I have a beautiful smile."

Aub pulls out her textbook and then mine when I don't follow her lead. "Hold this, dummy!"

She shoves the book in my hands, but pages don't register on my fingertips.

"Well? Open it."

"No." As if my mother's hands grip my shoulders and straighten my spine, I grab the heat in my heart and turn it back out toward the world. "Fuck him. I won't let him see me hiding."

"Everyone's here," Jack says as the teacher tries handing him the attendance folder.

"Fine." Mr. Faulst sighs. "Open your books to chapter two. Chapter one is a waste of time. We're going to be talking about hyperbole, you all know what that is by now. Read the chapter and then write me a page long poem or short story with at least five uses of hyperbole. Easy stuff. Just warming your lazy summer brains up."

I start to write a poem about killing a guy but then scrap that. I end up writing about an old man who dies alone in his home with no wife and no children, that is deeply hated by everyone in his life. Hopefully, Jack will be the one to grade it.

I don't look at the man on our way out. I leave his present on my desk. If he wants it, he can pick it up, or else the next person to sit there can have it. I think I'm done with it till we get to Forensics. He sits there, casually talking with Cinthia, acting as if he has nothing to do with the present in front of my chair.

"I thought I was clear." I slide the box over to him.

He nods with a pleasant smile I want to smack off his face. "You were. It was too much with the brushes. So, I took those out and put the paint back in. It's perfect now."

"They'll be perfect back on the shelf from where you got them!"

"Why don't you wan-want them?" Cinthia asks. "I thought you loved to paint."

Cinthia also presented at the art show last year. She programmed a robot arm to paint and her, or its, art was at the show. We talked about different paints and how I enjoy the process to relax. Something I desperately need now.

"It's not about whether or not I like to paint, or that he got really nice supplies, or that I'd really like to have all of it."

Jack perks up at my slipped confession. "You—"

"It's inappropriate." I harden my jaw along with my resolve to stop those honey-brown eyes from melting my heart.

His thick eyebrows rise. "I see." He takes the box and moves it out of the way.

Finally!

"I hope you know, that was not my intention. But I can see your point. Maybe next time," he adds under his breath.

"Last time you said that, the box was on my desk in our next class." I scowl. "I had better not see that waiting in the fucking study lounge."

"Next time as in your next birthday." Jack chuckles.

"There won't be a next time."

"You're right." He nods his head in solemn agreement. "Of course."

Something tells me he isn't being serious, but I leave it alone. I take my victory and sit down across from him.

"If she doesn't want them, could I-I-I have th-them? My robot uses the same supplies she does. Just less black."

She gives me a deadpan stare alongside her jab, but I don't care. I have my victory.

"I've actually already decided what I'm going to do with them," he says with a cheery tone.

Aub frowns with skepticism. "What's that?"

"Well…" He looks over his shoulder and leans into the table. When all three of us lean in with him, he whispers, "…It's a secret."

We all groan and sit back in our chairs, disgusted with ourselves for falling for it.

What a dick!

"You're a complete ass." Aub giggles.

"If I co—cou—could lift my crutch, I-I-I'd hit you in the h-head." Cinthia says with her deadpan stare, but there's a slight curve to her lips that wants to smile.

"You need a lobotomy." I pull out my textbook so I won't start laughing.

The rest of class goes on the same way, with Jack willingly playing the fool to make us laugh, but he's surprisingly smart when it comes to lab work, knowing which chemicals to grab and the right measurements without even looking at the assignment sheet twice. When we leave class, he holds the door for everyone like he always does. He gets asked a few times about the present in his hands, but he dodges the questions with jokes.

After a quick trip to the restroom, we find Jack in the parking lot putting my gift in the trunk of his car, an old, light blue piece of shit. Not like a classic that can one day be restored; it's junk on wheels.

"What's with the shitty car, Mr. Monopoly?" Aub teases as we walk by.

He laughs. "It's not shitty. It's my first car."

"Your first car? You get your license as a graduation gift?" I snicker.

He grins at us, leaning back on the trunk, his massive arms crossing his chest, tightening the fabric around thick muscle. "No. I've just taken care of the old girl." He gives the car a slap and the Chevy emblem falls off the trunk." He picks it up and presses it back in place while Aub and I howl with laughter. "Hey, everyone's first car is a junker."

"Not mine." I smile as I press the button to unlock my car a few spaces down. It's Mom's second car, but she lets me use it since she and Dad are rarely home and get taxis to the airport.

"Your parents got you a Lexus? Those must be some high insurance rates. I didn't want to pay out the nose, but guys get it worse than girls, so I went with something a little more practical."

"No girl would be caught dead in that thing." I smirk at him as I open my door.

Jack's grin spreads like a wolf's, confident and dangerous. "We don't have to get caught."

He slides into his car and the door shuts before I can say anything back, but I don't have anything other than crimson splashed across my cheeks.

When I sit in the car, Aub plops down in the passenger seat and sighs. "I'm super fucking jealous, bitch. You get to flirt with a hot boy all day."

"I'd rather slap him." I growl as I grip the wheel hard enough to kill it.

"Anything to get your hands on him."

"Damn it, Aub. Not you, too."

Chapter Five

The next few weeks allow me to relax to a certain degree, at least in the sense that Jack isn't shoving a birthday present down my throat. When Aub's birthday comes around, a little gift bag sits in front of her usual chair. Inside is a bar of soap that a silly birthday card says is for her potty mouth. What kept her mouth clean for the rest of the day was the hundred-dollar gift card to our favorite shop, Kastle Boutique.

He's nice to be around when he isn't flirting. I've had classes with him in the past, and if I'm completely honest with myself, those classes were better because of him. His take-charge attitude is a plus, and his goofy antics are a great way to end the day. Yet, being this close is something different than just being in the same room. He's always been the class clown, but this feels like a private show, tailored to me.

The only downside is that his constant attention is hard to bear at times. It makes me feel like I have to live up to him, as if I have to earn his attention, as if I *owe* him something in return. That raises my fucking blood pressure. My last boyfriend made me feel that way, and after I dumped his ass, I promised myself; never again.

While Jack never says any of the things Les said, it makes me wonder if he would, if he ever gets me alone. So far, we've been in public, with Aub close enough to hear everything. Would he change if it's just the two of us?

His flirt game is a clean notch above other guys, as his confidence is clear in another stratosphere, but when he turns on the charm, it also feels hard to handle, almost like I'm supposed to be won over by him, like I'm supposed to have the same stars in my eyes as Cinthia and so many others. I often find myself bouncing between wanting to knee him between his legs and giving him sultry winks. He's gotten neither, despite his best efforts.

One thing I will give him credit for, he doesn't reserve his flirting tones and innuendos just for me. Aub gets her fair share, as does Cinthia. Though, I notice, I'm the target of most of his eye contact, no matter who the teasing is meant for, once again leaving me to wonder what he'll do if he gets me alone. Those thoughts leave me crossing my legs in an attempt to smother the growing heat.

He shows up in the study lounge late again, dressed in a black suit with a bright red shirt under his waist coat with the top two buttons open, showing a little bit of his chest. I'm immediately reminded of a vampire character in one of my favorite book series. *If they ever make a movie, Jack could play Amir.* He sits and waves with a smile before pulling out his textbook and getting to work.

Part of me wants to say something, just to get him to say something, but the room is so quiet I won't be able to whisper without being overheard, and he has his earbuds in a moment later anyway. I keep working but can't get my mind into it. All I can think of is wanting him to talk, to joke, to laugh. I look up at him to find he's massaging his temples. A quick glance at the clock tells me it's already nine-thirty-two.

Twenty minutes! How could I daydream for twenty minutes?

"Hey, you okay?" Crouched next to me with his math book in his lap, Jack places a light hand on my arm.

I nearly jump from my seat. *How the hell did he get there?*

"I was going to ask for some help, but maybe you're just as stuck as I am." A soft chuckle escapes him.

I jerk my arm out from under his strong, firm hand. That fire that makes me boil shoots through my body till it clashes with the fire that melts my core. *Should I just let him? Should I quit trying to run from his unexplainable interest? No*, I growl in my mind, letting the scalding heat take over. *I do want him, but on my terms, not his. When I say, not when he says.*

"I was thinking of something else." I hiss. "Are you really stuck? Or is that just some lame excuse to harass me?"

"Nope. I am very stuck, and I'm not ashamed to ask for help from someone smarter."

"That's the first true thing I've ever heard you say." My eyes flick to Aub and I smirk. "Why not just ask Aub? She's way smarter when it comes to math than I am."

If he really is after me, he'll have to admit it. While I help Aub in certain classes, she helps me just as much, and Math is her domain. *Let's see you worm your way out of this one, Jack.*

"Yeah, you're right." He nods. "I think you'll make for a better tutor, though. You come across as someone who likes to give instructions." His honey-brown eyes flash with hunger no food can satiate.

I stare at him while images of us roleplaying as teacher-student play through my mind. I can easily use some of my mother's corporate outfits to play the part of a slutty professor.

"Move your chair over here," I order. "And if you try to make this anything other than math, I'm kicking you in the balls."

He grabs his chair, barely having to lean over to reach it with his tall frame. "I consider my balls perfectly safe then."

His smile almost makes me smile but I'm set on making him suffer for it. This guy has everything handed to him. I'm not going to offer myself on a silver platter. *If he really wants me, he's going to have to work for it like any other guy.* Any other guy that's cut from stone and has eyes soft enough to make my pillow jealous.

"I wouldn't count on it." I check what part of the book he's in. Chapter seven. *So, he's also working ahead.* He's in Calc two, but still, good for him. "Explain to me how you're working through B."

"I can't get past A." He laughs.

"B is easier, I promise. Show me."

As he works on the problem, his scent moves over me. He wears a cologne of spiced wood with undertones of... *What is that? Citrus?* My tongue glides along my dry lips as I become quite thirsty for a glass of orange juice. As I watch his hands move over the paper, my eyes drift up his forearms. Muscles like coiled ropes slide under his skin. I wonder what it will feel like to be tied up by those thick arms. *He could take me however he wanted...if I just let him.*

"Abigale?"

I gaze up at his questioning face.

"Is that right?" he asks.

My eyes dash from his back to his paper. "All wrong." I lean back to put some much-needed distance between us.

He slouches in his seat. "Oh...shit. That sucks."

I take a deep breath and stretch my back with my hands over my head till I feel a satisfying *pop.*

Jack stares down at his lap while fiddling with his pencil. Perhaps I'm being too harsh.

"You're not beyond my help, dumb-dumb." I pat the back of his arm. "Come on, I'll show you. We need to find the slope first."

The rest of the period, I walk him through chapter seven. He gets the hang of it mostly, but he'll probably need more help, which I'm willing to give as long as he continues to behave himself.

As Aub and I walk to Psych, she's overly quiet but her eyes hold that same bristling energy that came after her first kiss or the first time she got head. When we finally get to class, she sits on the couch in the back of the room and pulls me down with her.

"You gave Jack a *gigantic* boner," she squeals as she stomps her feet in excitement.

Before I even have a chance to respond, Lacy and Presley pull chairs up next to us.

The two girls graduated high school with us, so we know them well enough to share class notes, text party invites, and gossip about boys. In between sharing notes and drinks at parties, Aub has let slip that Jack took an interest. All the girls from our old school wanted to keep tabs on Jack, and these two are no different.

"You suck his dick?" Lacy asks as she flips her big brown hair over her shoulder.

"What? No!" I turn to Aub. "What are you talking about?"

"Remember when you did your little stretch act." She reenacts my simple back stretch as a chest wiggling orgasm.

"I did *not* do it like that!"

"Do it." Presley grins, her hazel eyes studying me. "What was it really?"

I put my arms up and stretch my back. "It was like that," I say with the innocence of a wide-eyed doe.

Aub guffaws. "But you moaned."

"What? No, I let out a sigh because I popped my back. It wasn't a moan!"

"Girl, I want to stick a twenty in your panties, cuz you just gave us a show." Presley bursts into laughter that the others join.

"What did he do?" Lacy asks. "Was he all like?" She leans forward to look at my boobs with wide eyes while she licks her lips like a fiend.

"He was so fucking cute." Aub's sadistic grin belies the

sweetness of her words. "His eyes went big and then he looked down and just waited till she was done. When he stood…" She pauses, biting her lip. "*Ooh!* I swear to god, his pants came out like a fucking foot!"

They all laugh but I can't believe I did that. How could I be so stupid? In sophomore year they really started growing and fucking Philip Black pointed at them when I bent over to tie my shoes. Since then, I've always been so mindful of how I move, especially around boys.

"I'm honestly scared for you," Aub says, still laughing. "He's going to split you in half!"

They all roar with laughter which gets the attention of Aaron and Jessie, the only two guys in the class.

"What's so funny?" Jessie asks.

"We were talking about Jack Billard's dick." Lacy shrugs like it's nothing.

"Abby gave him a boner." Aub smirks and gives me a light elbow in the ribs.

"I did not! Shit." I sigh, giving up the fight. "I didn't mean to! I was just stretching my back out and…*Ugh!*"

"It's huge, huh?" Jessie asks, but the rhetorical tone to his voice make all the girls hone in on him.

"Wait, do you know?" Presley asks.

"Yeah. Like every guy knows." He laughs. "He doesn't want the girls to know, so he's always been like, 'Keep it to yourself, please.' Or, 'It's not something you should talk to a lady about.'" He deepens his voice to sound more like a neanderthal but doesn't get close to Jack's timbre. "But what really keeps all the guys quiet is if they talk about his dick, not only are they talking about some other guy's junk, but they have to talk about how it's *way* bigger than their own."

Aaron rolls his eyes hard enough he might be having a

seizure. "I'm not going to sit here and talk about Jack's dick, that's gross."

"Oh my god." Lacy stands, her butt wagging like an excited puppy. "You've both seen it, haven't you!"

"No," Aaron shouts. "Nope! Never seen it, never want to!"

"Jack comes in at like five or six in the morning." Jessie glances over his shoulder and lowers his voice. "His first real class isn't till ten-fifteen. He wrestles, runs the track, lifts weights, all of it. You can imagine all of that could work up a sweat for such a big boy. So, he uses the showers every day. Every. Single. Day. Every guy who's passed through the locker room between eight and ten has seen his dick."

"Nope! Fuck this, I'm out," Aaron shouts again as he walks over to his desk.

"It's flaccid, of course." Jessie continues with a shrug. "But it's fucking huge. Like, guys make jokes about him being a porn star."

The girls all brake into laughter as Aub shakes my shoulders. "He's going to destroy your pussy!"

"No! Gross," I shout.

"How big?" Lacy leans over the table. "How big? How big?"

"It's like seven or eight inches." Jessie holds out his hands, measuring the length.

"Oh, that's it?" Lacy's shoulders slump. "Xavier has a seven incher. It's not bad, you'll get used to it. I think it's perfect, to be honest. A little bit of a challenge but not overwhelming."

"That's flaccid, bitch," Jessie says. "Your man, Xavier, is probably like two or three inches flaccid. I'm seven inches, too, but my dick looks like a tootsie roll when its soft."

Lacy folds her arms over her chest. "He could be shower, not a grower."

Jessie smiles wide. "He's a grower and a shower."

The look on Lacy's face goes from confusion to realization to horror in about three seconds. "Oh, I'm so sorry, Abby. I'll be at your funeral."

Everyone laughs but me.

Jessie frowns. "I wouldn't be worried about his dick. I'd be worried about his secret."

Aub and Presley jump to their feet to stand with Lacy. "What secret?" they all demand in near unison.

"I don't know." Jessie gapes. "Fucking crazy bitches. I just know he's an altar-boy-wrestling-legend with a dick as fat as his bank account. Something's got to be wrong with that boy."

"True." Presley turns to me and smiles. "Well, keep me posted. Let me know how that dick feels, and then let me know how he likes his diapers changed."

"You're all disgusting," I say as they all laugh. "Perverts! Every one of you!"

We all continue to joke about it, but I keep thinking, *What if Jessie's right? What if there's something seriously wrong with him?* Girls used to joke about him probably having a small dick, but if Jessie's telling the truth, a tiny dick is not it. *He can't be perfect.* So, what's wrong with him? Having a diaper fetish might be favorable to whatever it really is.

Chapter Six

When Romanticism starts, Jack is suspiciously absent from holding the door. He's managed to be at that door every day of the semester. I growl at the ache in my chest. He strolls in ten minutes late and I hold my jaw from dropping. He's wearing grey slacks and matching waist coat with a light blue shirt.

"Holy shit, he changed his clothes." Aub's voice is electrified with excitement. "Do you think he fucking jizzed his pants?"

"Shut up. I don't know." I cover my face for a moment and take a deep breath. "Fuck! Did he? Would he really..." I can't say the word, or any other that means the same thing. It'll make it too real. "Just from me stretching my back?"

"Maybe *this* is his secret. I told you how Austin was a premie. Guy ran a fucking hand up my leg and came." She rolls her eyes with a disgruntled frown. "Maybe Jack's like a super-ultra premie. Look on the bright side," she adds with a smile. "That means he won't have to stick it in."

"Stop talking about that! He isn't getting close to that unless I say so."

"You know you're going to bone him at some point."

Scalding heat rises in my chest. Aub never caused this fury to explode in me before, but I'm not going to be told by *anyone* what I have to do. "I don't have to fuck anyone just because I had a little crush on them in the past. You regretted even making out with Austin."

"Yeah, fuck that prick." She frowns.

"I'm not going to let a guy take my virginity just because he's hot," I say more for myself than for her as I whip out my folder a little more aggressive than needed.

"Fine." Aub pulls her notes out with matching frustration.

Mr. Faulst starts lecturing about the new resurgence in contemporary literature, pulling our attention to the front of the class. While Mr. Faulst rambles on, my eyes scan the room, but Jack is nowhere in sight.

"What, is he fucking Batman now?" Aub scoffs.

The sarcastic comment hits a chord of truth. Strong, rich, mysterious. Maybe that's exactly who he is. Batman's dark secret isn't that he's Bruce Wayne, it's that *Bruce* is the mask. Is that Jack's secret? Is his Bruce Wayne exterior just an act?

At Forensics, Jack stands at the door with a big smile, welcoming everyone. "Hey, you two."

We both say "Hi" as we pass him, making sure to sound annoyed. Once I hear him greet another couple people, I glance over my shoulder to see him smiling at me. Not with his big silly smile he normally puts on, but a sly winners grin.

I scowl at him to make sure he knows he's not winning, but it only makes him smile more. *Bastard!*

"Good afternoon, ladies." He sits down but the winners grin is replaced by a polished smile, the type that the Hallmark love interest always sports. "I have our blood work here. I think it's going to be suspect A."

"Y-y-you're absolutely r-right," Cinthia says.

"And how would you know?" Aub asks. "You didn't look at the answers, did you?"

"I-I-I-I-I wo-wou-wou-"

"Come on Aubrey." Jack places a reassuring hand on Cinthia's back. "Cinthia doesn't cheat."

"Thanks, Ja-Jack." Cinthia breathes a deep sigh as she gazes up at him like a dog that wants her master's love and affection.

"Could you two make out somewhere else?" I groan.

Jack laughs and goes to get the microscope but Cinthia glares at me as if she's going to bury me.

"Jealous?" A pleased smile slides along her lips. "A guy like him isn't interested in girls like you two, all looks."

"Fuck you, *Deputy*." Aub spits the last word, reminding Cinthia that she was only Deputy Captain of the Mathletes. "Why the fuck are you even here? You took this class last year."

She glances over to Jack and then turns back to us. "The two of you in your slutty fishnet and corsets are nothing but a distraction to his baser male instincts. I *know* him. Like all men, he gets sidetracked by exposed skin, but he doesn't really want it. He wants a good, wholesome woman. He likes girls with brains, not big, fat, disgusting b-bo-boo-"

Jack sets the microscope down as Cinthia continues to stutter what has to be 'boobs.' He gives her a reassuring smile, the way he always does when she stutters but doesn't know what to say for her.

Her shoulders turn in as she shrinks in place. She gazes at him on the verge of tears, unable to stop her stutter, but unable to finish without Jack finding out what kind of viper hides behind the innocent little shell.

As much as I like the idea of Cinthia getting what she deserves for practically calling us sluts two seconds ago, something in me needs to yank her out of the fire. I turn to Aub for help, but the vicious grin on her face tells me I'm on my own.

"Books," I shout. "We were talking about our books." I grab mine and hold it up.

Cinthia gasps for air, finally able to stop, but tears continue to well.

"Come on, Cinthia." I walk over to her, positioning myself between her and Jack. I push her crutches into her hands before grabbing her arm as gently as I can. "Let's go. Aub, help Blockhead with the lab."

"Wh-where are we g-g-going?"

"We're going to the bathroom, hun. You need to go really bad."

Once we're in the hall, I let go of her arm. I hold the door to the bathroom for her. We stand in front of the mirrors, and I hand her a tissue. As she dabs under her eyes, she looks back and forth at our reflections.

"Tha-thanks for saving me back there."

"Yeah. Don't mention it."

Even after she finishes, we stand there in silence for a minute. A snake of uncomfortable revulsion slides down my spine. I've never felt intimidated or jealous of another woman before. I'm not even sure if that's what this is. Something about the way Jack treats her, the way they laugh and smile at each other. It's like she's ahead of me in some way. Out of all the women in school, I never suspected I'd be challenged by Cinthia but despite her physical disability, she's a powerhouse in her own way. Like Jack, she held several state titles in high school. She shares one with my name for debate team and one with Aubrey for Mathletes but she has three science awards all to herself. Aub was right, she didn't need this class.

'I probably wouldn't have done well enough to make Forensics this year if it wasn't for her.' Jack's words play in my head as my eyes narrowed in on Cinthia.

Like a slap to the face, all the times she's looked up at Jack flash before me.

"He's why you took this class again," I say. "Isn't he?"

She regards me through the mirror, her back still turned to me. "Are you in lo-love with him, too?"

"What? No!" A rush of heat shoots through my chest to

splash my face. I turn back to the door to make sure no one's coming, but also to hide my face from the mirror. "I barely know him. You probably know him better than I do."

She turns to stare with hard, focused eyes and a curl to her lips that borders on a snarl. "Yeah, I do. Thanks for helping me out back there, but don't think that we're best friends now. Jack is mine! I've known him for years now, and he's always been a good guy that sluts like you want to take advantage of."

"Sluts like me?" I growl. I saved her from fucking up in front of her crush and this is the thanks I get?

"Yes! But you're even worse with all your black magic whore clothes. Acting like some modern-day witch. He's a good man, and always showing off half your body with your tramp friend isn't going to win him over." She steps forward to put us toe to toe. "You keep flirting with Jack and I will end you."

Flirting with Jack? When have I ever flirted with Jack? I take a deep breath and suppress the scalding heat that runs through my veins so I won't kick this girl's crutches out from under her.

"I don't flirt with Jack, bitch! He flirts with me. He's not after my fucking tits. If you weren't so blinded by him, you would have seen that by now!"

"He likes—"

"He likes *me* because I'm fucking smart. Fuck this! I don't even care. Jack means nothing to me."

"Then stop trying to tempt him with your slutty body!"

I lean forward till our noses nearly touch. "I'm glad it bothers you. If you ever end up with Jack, just remember, I can take him whenever I feel like." Knee bending heat moves up from between my legs to fuse with the scorching heat in my chest and words fall from my mouth as if I was born to say them. "I own him."

I walk out the door, my boots thudding on the hallway floor as I go back to class. Cinthia's light foot falls and the taps of her crutches echo behind me. When I come to the door, I hold it open for her and she glances up at me as she passes. Her eyes hold what I mentally force in my own. *We are not friends, but we will be civil, and we will keep this grudge silent.*

When we reach our table, Jack adjusts the slide. "Oh, good. You're back just in time. I have the slide ready, if either of you want to look first."

"You go," Cinthia says. "I know what it looks like."

I walk over to the microscope and look in to see the blood cells. I'm looking for a dead virus we found from the crime scene sample when spiced wood and a touch of citrus wafts over me. My eyes drift to my right to find Jack standing there. He's close enough I can hit him with my hair if I flip it over my shoulder. Granted, he is just standing next to his own chair but given that he placed the microscope, I have a feeling he planned this. I let him stay so I can revel in his scent a little longer.

I can't grasp what makes it so enticing. Other guys I've hung out with smelt good, too. I thought Les had the best smell in the world for the six months we dated. I chose to date him over my other options because of his cinnamon and lime fragrance. Jack's scent makes mincemeat of Les'. It's so much deeper, so much stronger. It coats my tastebuds, making my tongue long for the actual thing. Since he can't see my face, I allow myself to bite my bottom lip and smile at the thought of unzipping his pants— *No! Fuck. What am I doing? Why do I like this so much?*

My eyes eventually slide back to him and down to his pants. *Is that a bulge?* There is a lump there but nothing like what Aub described. I decide it's time to teach him a lesson in personal space, before that intoxicating scent pulls me into his fucking pants.

I jab the butt of my fist into his crotch. Something heavy gets in the way at first, but as I follow through, I connect with something else that I'm positive must be his balls. With it all under the table line, I'm pretty sure no one sees it happen.

He goes rigid and grunts as if something's caught in his throat before taking a short walk on stilted legs. He handles it much better than I imagine he would. I've knocked a few guys to the floor with crotch shots, but here he is walking it off like a... Well, I guess he is a literal champ after all.

He coughs one last time, then says, "Okay, Aubrey. Your turn. *Uhmm!* You know, I think I'm going to head to the restroom."

"Got the shits?" Aub asks as he hustles from the room.

Cinthia watches him leave with big doe eyes. "I hope h-he's okay."

Tears form in the corners of my eyes while I hold back my grin. I motion for Aub to look at the microscope as I cover my mouth to hide my spreading smile. A deep breath helps calm me before I whisper, "I just punched his dick."

Aub blows out a laugh that made the slide move. "Oh, shit! Don't make me laugh." She fumbles the slide back into place.

"It's like a metal slinky," I whisper as she gets the slide back in place.

She bursts into laughter again and steps away from the microscope, waving her hands. "Oh, I can't." She wipes tears from her eyes, then fans herself. "A slinky!"

Chapter Seven

My little love tap seems to teach Jack the importance of personal space, but it doesn't keep him away. That Wednesday, he sits next to me in the study lounge again. Even though he's not asking for help, his mere presence constantly pulls on my attention. I put in earbuds in the hopes that music will distract me enough to get back to work. He taps my book to get my attention and I pull an earbud out.

"What?" I snap, feigning annoyance.

Ignoring my harsh tone, he smiles. "What are you listening to?"

"Does it matter?"

"It's just, you're crazy smart. So, I was curious as to what music you use to study."

"Death metal," I lie. It's Bach. I always listen to Baroque when I study. It's like nothing else ever works.

"I suppose that fits, but I have a feeling that's not the case."

"Oh? Why do you think that? You think my music wouldn't be good enough to study to?"

"No, it's not that. You're a cellist. I mean, usually when I listen to anything heavy, I end up focusing on the guitar and bass rifts, not my work, but maybe you have more control than I do."

"Trust me." I lean in close to make sure he gets the message. "I will *always* have more control than you."

He scrolls through his phone. "Well. If you won't tell me your superpower music, I guess I'll have to go back to my own."

"And what is that?"

He lifts his phone to show the screen. It's the Kingdom Hearts Original Soundtrack.

"You played Kingdom Hearts?"

I played that game every day over my summer break just before our high school freshman year. It was a good game, but I can't see Jack playing something where the story revolves around cartoon characters and the love you have for your friends. It was even a little much for me, but hey, what can I say, I've loved Goofy since I was two.

"Yeah, of course," he says. "It was a great game, but it's the music that really got me."

I raise a suspicious eyebrow.

"What? I'm serious. The soundtrack has a lot of fun stuff but the main tracks, *Simple and Clean*, *Passion*, and especially *Dearly Beloved...*" He shrugs and shakes his head. "It's just, the embodiment of innocence lost. You know?" He swallows hard and then gives a soft laugh, but if I'm not mistaken, it looks like his eyes glisten.

"Can I listen? I haven't heard it since I played it."

He smiles at me and moves his chair next to mine. He hands me his earbud and we listen to the music. Innocence lost. He's not wrong about that. It was just a pretty melody at the time when I played the game, but listening now, it makes me think of how much older I've become in those few short years.

My eyes slide from my textbook to his hand, so strong and firm, just resting there next to me. As if he can see my eyes, his hand turns over and offers me a place to rest mine. When I look to him, a warm, hopeful smile spreads across his firm lips. Had it been his devious grin, I would have smacked his hand away, but that face, that soft smile with his eyes swirling like dark honey... I don't know if I'll ever be able to say no to that face.

I roll my eyes and sigh as if he's bothering me, as if I'm doing him the favor. "You're lucky I'm left-handed." I place my hand in his.

I'm used to guys with calloused hands from playing guitar or drumming, but his doesn't have that exactly. Callouses still mar his hand, but only in the grip. The image of him with his shirt off, chopping wood with an axe plays in my mind for a moment. These hands see work, but what work would earn him all the money the stories say he has stashed away? Strength pours through that hand. Power that lays dormant. Yet, as hard as his hand feels, it's so soft underneath. There's a tenderness to the way it folds around mine. Just like his eyes, there's an intensity to maintaining contact. Staying in that tender embrace should surely cost something. I almost recoil from it.

Almost.

When Aub starts to put her books away, our hands separate as we go to do the same. My hand feels like soggy bread with how much I'd sweat. When he wipes his hand on his pants, I nearly cry out in shame.

To my surprise, he offers his hand again on Friday and it goes on like that for a couple more weeks; with him moving his chair over to me to either ask for help with his Calculus or offering to listen to music together. Aub and I keep wondering how long this is going to go on for before he either reveals it has all been a cruel joke and he's played me for a fool, or he asks me out.

The first Wednesday of October rolls around and Aub and I are in the study lounge taking a break for the day, just reading novels. My favorite author B.R.T. Jackson released a new book only a couple weeks ago. I own every book he's ever written, which consists of nine fantasy novels that were finished in the unheard-of rate of only five years. He has three series going, one a horror, one pirate adventure and the other a paranormal romance. This one is part of his romance series about a guy who fell in love with a woman that turns out to be a vampire. It was light BDSM in the first book, but by book three, things have gotten way crazier. Aub reads the same book, we've always kept up with each other ever since we met. His fantasy novels had been one of the first things that we really bonded over. That and our love of black.

Late as usual, Jack styles a navy-blue suit without the jacket, a light blue shirt, and a navy-blue tie with an American flag pin.

"Are you running for president?" Aub asks when he sat down.

He laughs after placing the jacket on his chair and rolls up his sleeves. "Nothing so pedestrian. Is that *A Light in the Darkness?*"

"Yeah, so?" I fold the book into my lap, using my thumb to keep my place.

"You like that sort of stuff? I mean, I loved The Sun Maker's Chronicles, but after that..." He shrugs. "I feel like he kinda sold out."

"What the fuck would you know?" Aub snaps.

She's a bigger B.R.T. Jackson fan than me. I love his books, but she wants to have his babies. She, and a million other women on the internet, always joke about saying Be Right There, Jackson, when he will one day reveal himself and call them to his bed. She also jokes that he might be a fifty-year-old, three-hundred-pound recluse, but much less often.

"You ever publish a book?" I frown and wait for him to concede. Even on such a silly topic, it would feel so good to have Jack bow down for once.

He nods with a smile that told me he's not about to concede. "I see your point, but that doesn't mean I can't have an opinion. I was a fan and then he started writing stuff I feel is more geared towards women, but only for the purpose of selling more books as women are a larger demographic. I mean, he said he was going to write companion books to Sun Maker's but where's that at? If you go to his website, he has his list of books and *Zatrina's Lament* was scheduled for last year, then it got pushed back, but his two other books came out on schedule and then suddenly *Light in the Darkness* hits ahead of schedule? Seems like he's had his priorities readjusted if you ask me."

"Well, I didn't." Aub snarls.

"You sound like you really liked Sun Maker's and now you're butt hurt the other books didn't come out." I tease, pouting my bottom lip. "I happen to love Sun Maker's, but I like his newer books better."

"Of course, you would. All his books are for women."

"You don't like a little sex and scandal?"

Jack rolls his eyes. "He had sex and scandal in Sun Maker's, there was just more going on."

"You just want action," I say with a dismissive wave.

"No. I liked the other parts."

"But you don't like the other parts unless there's action. You need a bad guy to fight." I lean in. "You can't just have sexual tension."

A hungry grin spreads across his face as he leans in as well. "I can handle sexual tension," he whispers.

My heart rate spikes as if I'm looking over the edge of a roller coaster. I'm safe, but my mind screams danger for a moment. I try to swallow but I find the lump in my throat too stiff. Thankfully, Aub comes to my rescue.

"You didn't come to talk about this fucking amazing book," she says. "So, what's got you grinning like an idiot?"

"I'm going to do something today that I've been wanting to do for a while now," he answers softly, not freeing me from his enthralling eye contact. "Something special for my birthday."

A light tug on my corset strings from Aub allows me to sit

back in my chair, granting me life-saving distance. My brain finally has clean, non-spice infused, air to work with.

"Happy fucking birthday. Are you going to sign up for the Army?" I ask.

"Well, not far off. I could end up getting killed," he says as though he seriously agrees with my silly suggestion. "So, can I ask your advice on something?"

How can he ask something so casually while looking at me like a tiger near pouncing?

"I swear to god, if you ask me about math, I'm going to stab you." It isn't that I don't like tutoring him, but damn, after all this eye contact, he better be asking me how I like my back rubbed.

"It's something a bit more private than that."

He stands over me like he has all semester long, but this somehow makes me feel so much smaller than normal. He isn't just tall, he's insurmountable. He doesn't stand over me, he *towers* over me, his hulking mass threatening to crash down into me. If he does, I'm not sure if I'll run and hide, or if I'll spread my arms and welcome the collision.

"Can we talk in the hallway?" He holds his hand out to me like an eighteenth-century gentleman asking a lady to dance.

I just stare at his hand, unable to move, unable to breathe. The hushed voices and soft pencil scratches from the rest of the room fade till I could only hear my heart thudding.

That soft, yet strong hand just hovers there, as if it will never faulter. It will wait for my answer for all time if it has to. That hand, attached to that million-dollar body, attached to that confident and inviting smile all pull at me, tugging on my desires. His eyes are full of kind hope like when he first offered me his hand but this time, they also hold a strength that touches dominance and a heat that promises satisfaction.

Heat blossoms in the flower between my legs, a scintillating warmth that spreads slowly within me, taking it's time to thoroughly melt each fiber of my being.

"Look." Aub's words reach me in slow motion, but her voice snaps me out of my trance and her words pick up speed as she continues, "If she doesn't want—"

"I'll go," I interrupt. "I don't need your stupid hand though."

I stand up and he turns to lead the way out of the room. My eyes slide to Colin and all the other jocks at the table. Several eyes follow me with dumbass grins plastered underneath. Seeing them sparks that ferocious heat in my chest, spreading like wildfire through my body. It clashes briefly with the heat coming from my core after gazing upon Jack, but it's an overwhelming victory for Team Pissed. My lips curl into a smile as I delight in my choice to wear my boots and jeans. If I'm not able to steel toe him in his dick, I can at least get a knee in there.

As we walk out into the hallway, his muscles ripple under the fabric of his taut shirt, almost like he's physically preparing himself. This is supposed to be his big moment.

Too bad.

The maddening frustration that he has any effect on me dispels any notion of letting him take control. No man can make me his damsel, not even Jack Billard.

"Why are you suddenly hitting on me this year?"

He turns around, his mouth agape, but I keep walking down the hall. His eyes on me cause those warring heats to swirl into something new. I'm not sure what it is, but it reminds me of adrenaline, that rush of danger and joy, though this is far more…erotic.

"I was hoping to talk." He follows after me like a lost puppy, hopeful he's found his new home.

"Well, we're talking. I want to talk about why you have such a sudden interest. You didn't last year."

"That's not exactly true." Trepidation thick in his voice.

I turn around. "What's that supposed to mean?"

He came to stand in front of me in the hall, putting the walls to our backs. "Last semester, I was an English T.A., I graded a lot of papers. At the end of March, there was this one paper, this poem, about a girl and a flower."

What the... My hand lashes out and slaps him. The *crack* of my palm meeting his skin rings through the hall as I think about doing it again. The air in my lungs burn, and my hand stings. I would have done it a million times over, but fear of breaking my hand on his granite chin stops me. "That wasn't meant for you!"

No one was ever meant to see that poem except Mrs. Iggit. It was a metaphor for how I'd almost given my virginity to Les just a couple weeks before. I'd fucking cried over that paper! To think that Jack, of all fucking people, had read it.

"Okay." He nods and takes a deep breath. His eyes land on me but they aren't angry, or sad. If anything, they understand. "I know it wasn't *meant* for me, but I had to grade it."

"Why were you even grading my paper? You weren't the T.A. for my class!"

"That's not how it works. I sat in Ms. Iggit's classroom, but I graded for the whole English department, all grades." He takes another deep breath, his eyes pleading with me, holding a world's worth of compassion. "A poem made its way in front of me, and it took me by storm. I saw your name, and... Shit." He curses softly. "I mean no offence. Please, Abigale, believe me, I... Fuck." He hesitates for another moment before admitting, "I wasn't familiar with your name."

If I wasn't rooted to the ground by just how fucked up this is, my foot would shoot his balls into the roof. Luckily for Jack, my muscles won't respond to my mind's demands. "You—You weren't even aware of my existence?" Even I can hear the hurt in my voice. "Wow! Thanks. Great talk, Jack."

This is so fucked! I want to bury my head in the sand, I want to vanish. I want to shove my foot so far up his ass I'd give him brain damage! He didn't even know who I was. We'd been in the same school for four years. I'd fantasized about him! I was nothing to him.

"No! It's not like that! I knew you by your face. I'm not good with putting faces to names, but I'm good the other way around. Look, if someone handed me your picture, I would have been able to say, that's Abby. On your work, your name was written as Abigale and I didn't recognize the name. It just didn't click. I'm Dumb-dumb, remember? Listen, I am sorry for that. More than you know." He sighs. "After that first poem, I couldn't get enough." He sheepishly rubs the back of his neck as he looks at me, almost wincing. "So, I went looking for your work, and I ended up reading everything you did that semester. From the recap of your winter break to the short story about a boy and his lost grandpa."

"Those were not for you!"

He steps closer, holding a hand up to calm me, but doing very near the exact opposite. "Please, don't yell. I couldn't stop. You have to understand that. The woman that wrote them. I had to meet her! She was so brave to write the way she did. To expose herself so deeply. To write so passionately about life and beauty! I couldn't let that woman slip past me. I went home and tore my room apart for my year books, I still can't find what I did with them. I was too much of a coward to ask anyone to point you out. I didn't know what you looked like till year books came out. By then, it was too late. I had no time to make a connection with you when I finally put your magnificent name to this gorgeous face."

My rage for him suddenly extinguishes, as if a million gallons of water fall on the inferno, leaving me steaming, still angry with him for his invasion of privacy, but also feeling a dim glow of melting heat low in my belly. How do his words work so well on me?

"I didn't have the courage to walk up to you and ask to be part of your life. From what I knew of you, I'd have one chance, and I was so scared I'd mess it up. I was shaking, Abigale. I was sick to my stomach thinking about meeting you and failing. When I walked in here at the start of the year, I saw you sitting there with Aubrey, the two gothest girls sitting in the darkest part of the lounge."

"It's not dark," I weakly protest.

He smiles. "One of the lights right above the table has been off all year. God was pointing me straight to you. I was filled with a courage that wasn't my own, and I suddenly found myself sitting in front of you. The woman who wrote so majestically. My throat was so dry I thought I was going to shrivel up right there on the spot. When Colin called me away, I was so pissed because I didn't want to be anywhere else but next to you, but I was also so thankful inside because I knew it was only a matter of time before I screwed it all up. I thought I ruined my chance with you when you were upset about your birthday, but things ended well so I thought: push on. Then you rejected my birthday present but there was a last gasp of life at the very end of the day again. I managed to rebound in the past month, but I can't keep this up."

"Keep what up?" I ask, locked into those tender yet gripping eyes.

"This façade that I'm satisfied by being at arm's length. Holding hands for only an hour of the day. Talking, but only about schoolwork. It's not enough. Abigale, sweet and wonderful

Abigale." One of his strong hands brush my hair over my ear, to then slide down to my jaw. "I want more. I want more of you."

My heart slams in my chest, as my body prepares for fight or flight. I'm not in danger, but I want to do something dangerous. "Show me," I breathe.

He pushes me up against the wall in a rush that makes me squeal, one hand grips my corset at the waist while his other hand slips behind my head to protect it from the impact of his sudden attack. Those hands move to become pillars on the wall, trapping me. His massive shoulders loom over me as his head droops, putting his face inches from my collar and cleavage. The heat of his breath plays over my skin, coaxing a heat from inside me to the surface as he moves up from my chest to neck. He inhales deeply and gives a shuttered exhale once his lips are just millimeters from my ear. My skin pebbles, and my hair stands on end.

"Oh, God, Abigale. You smell so good."

Two fingers run down my chest to my cleavage, sending miniature shockwaves through my skin that seep through to my heart and lungs only to be met with a rising rush of adrenaline. My body shakes and a moan escapes my lips, but I don't care. All I'm interested in is riding that wave of pleasure.

His sizzling tongue glides up my neck to the back of my ear, melting the skin it touches.

That wave of pleasure surges into a tidal wave that I have no hope of riding. It takes over me and my only goal is to survive. When it surges passed my knees, they buckle but something catches me around the chest like the world's thickest seat belt so I don't fall on all fours. The tidal wave rips through me, finally splashing down between my legs and I moan again, this time with what sounds like a painful tilt at the end, even to my ears. Yet there's no pain, only a pleasure I've never known before. I've never come like that, such a powerful arrival at sensation and glorious satisfaction.

Air enters my lungs for what feels like the first time in years. That firm solid something turns out to be Jack's arm, still holding me up, my fingernails biting into his muscled bicep. Then I feel it, hot and wet, and running down my legs.

I peed? I mentally scream.

Chapter Eight

I press my back against the wall and look up at Jack. Shame burns my skin, but I hope our eye contact will distract him from what I've done. I barely manage to control my breath enough to huff, "Go tell Aub to meet me in the bathroom."

"Are you—"

"Don't talk. Just go."

He nods and walks off, looking over his shoulder only once before disappearing back into the study lounge.

Once he's out of sight, I run to the bathroom. *Why the hell did I pee?* I thought I was having the best orgasm of my life! It was even the first one I didn't give myself. *And all he did was fucking lick me!*

Once in the bathroom, I hurry into the big stall and rip my boots off. I practically jump out of my wet pants and sit on the toilet, the sensational feeling of my orgasm a long-forgotten memory as embarrassment floods through me. Tears well up in my eyes, so I take deep breaths to keep myself from crying. The last thing I need is to have eyeliner and mascara running down my face to add to my shitty day. I take each breath in and hold them for a few seconds.

As I wipe my legs and butt of all the wet, my eyes move to my pants. They're black denim so it's a little hard to see, but the wet spot covers the whole crotch and some of the butt, as well as a large portion of the inner thighs all the way down to the knees.

Why did I pee? It just doesn't make sense. I know what an orgasm feels like, even if that one was more intense than any other that came before. *But if it wasn't pee...* I pick the pants up and put the dark stain lightly to my nose.

It's not pee.

Holy shit, I squirted! I squirted? What-the-fuck-ever, thank god! I didn't pee myself in front of the hot boy! As relief flows through my veins, my eyes once again threaten to pour out tears, this time droplets of joy.

The door opens with a resounding *crack* and Aub calls out for me.

"I'm in here. I have a serious problem."

"Yeah, I guessed. Jack told me to bring our backpacks. I didn't want to get ahead of you in the book, so I started working on Physics. I had like, all my shit out on the desk so it took me a minute to put it away." Her gaze darts to the pants in my hands as soon as she comes in stall. "Oh, shit, bitch! You peed yourself?"

"No. I fucking squirted! Worse, better, I don't know, but I didn't pee. Oh, god." I sigh in relief. "Better, definitely better."

"You what?"

I tell her the whole story in as much detail as I can remember, taking two or three times longer to tell the story than it took to happen, saying it all out loud makes me shiver.

Aub's jaw hangs for a moment. "Wow! That's a big wow moment right there. He fucking licked you, in a school hall. That sounds so dirty thinking of it being Jack Perfect Billard." She looks at me with a warm smile and then wraps me in a tight hug. "I'm so happy for you!"

"Uh, yeah, thanks. I guess." I give her a couple pats on the back, not knowing what's happening exactly.

She pulls back and gives a bright smile. "Don't you get it, though? He really loves you."

"Love?" I shout. "That's a bit much. I mean—"

"Think about it, dummy! He didn't even know what you looked like. He fell in love with your poetry, your writing. He's clearly attracted to you with that boner a few weeks ago. In a way, he's been after you for months. He's really into you."

"I still think 'love' is a bit strong. Let's just stick to 'into me.'"

"Well, I'm really fucking happy for you. I think he's a bit over the top sometimes, but he's been a real great guy so far. We'll have to keep a look out for what his deep dark secret is. But not too much! Don't let it get in the way of having fun."

Having fun with a guy hadn't crossed my mind for a long while after what happened with Les. All this flirting with Jack, and I still haven't really considered where it's leading. It's as if I'm sure it's all a dream and I'll wake up before anything serious actually happens.

A knock comes to the outside door and then Jack calls out. "Abigale, are you in there?"

"Go away, Jack," I say.

"Yeah, go away," Aub echoes with a nod.

"I will, I promise. I have something for you. Aubrey, will you come get this please."

He has something for me? Now? What the hell is it?

"This is the girls' bathroom," Aub shouts.

"Yes. I am very aware. Look, classes are going to get out in like…three minutes."

I nod to Aub as he speaks and she slips out of the stall, making sure he won't be able to peek all the way from the door, even though that's impossible given the design of the room.

"I don't want to be standing next to the girls' restroom like a pervert when everyone comes out."

"You are a pervert," Aub tells him. "Now go away."

Aub returns to the stall with a Target bag and pulls out a black full-length skirt. "Looks like he got you options, there's another one in here."

He went down to the fucking Target to buy me skirts? Why would he—

"Oh, no! He had to have seen. He thinks I peed. Fuck! Oh, but I really like this." I slip into the long skirt. "It's so soft."

"Uh, I can see your ass through that."

While Aub laughs, I look over my shoulder at the slightly see-through fabric hanging over my ass. "Damn it, Jack! Why are men such idiots?"

"Well, if you put this one over it, you should be fine." She pulls out the other.

"Fine, I'll do both. They fit pretty nice."

"You think he stalked you to get your size?" Aub asks.

"An obsessive stalker! That's his dark secret. I mean, it's not super bad."

"What if he has a doll of you at home? With a lock of your hair and maybe some things you touched and threw in the trash, but he pulled them out?"

I wince. "Okay, that would be very bad."

"I can't wait to talk to Deanna about this. She's going to flip!"

"Yeah. Can't wait." I frown. Telling Aub the whole story is one thing, but telling Deanna is another. Sometimes she's best-friend-sister, but other times she's overprotective-ruins-everything-sister.

As we come out of the bathroom, Jack leans against the wall across the hall like GQ's man of the year. He shoves off with his shoulder and walks up to me. I'm not sure I'm ready to see him yet, so I decide to flee.

"Wait." He places a light, discreet hand on my stomach as I try to pass by him. "I need to ask you something."

My nerves shoot through the roof. It's like his hand impregnates my stomach with eagle-sized butterflies. *Why did I think of it as him impregnating me? What the fuck is wrong with me?*

He looks over to Aub. "We'll just be a minute."

When I nod to her, she walks a little further down the hall but not out of sight.

"Things got a little carried away," he says with an apologetic smile. "I was working my way up to asking if you'd be willing to go on a date with me. I'd like to take you out this, or next Friday. Will you go on a date with me?"

"We hold hands almost every fucking day," I snap as scalding heat pours into me. "You *licked* me." *And gave me a knee-buckling orgasm.* The thought brings the melting heat up to warm my skin. "And now you want to go on a date? I thought you were going to ask me to be your girlfriend, but you just want a date?"

"No, no." His eyes burn bright with excitement. "I didn't want to jump to any conclusions. I'm sorry. I'm bad at this. Yes! I would love to be your boyfriend; I would love to call you my girlfriend. Yes, please."

The two heats solidify in perfect harmony as I answer, "No. We'll see how the date goes. *This Friday.* Where are we going?"

His slack jaw slowly slides into a grin. "I have tickets to the theater. They're playing Phantom of the Opera. This Friday will actually be the opening show."

"You're going to take me to a musical?" I ask, not able to hide my laughter.

"Yeah. Why not? It's very dark and broody." He smiles. "I thought that would be perfect for you."

"Ass. Just because I'm goth doesn't mean I *only* like dark and brooding things."

His sly grin fades as the honey in his warm eyes swirls, pulling me into them. "That's what I hope to learn. I want to get to know you more than what you show here at school."

The eagles in my stomach flip and I focus on the heat to keep my composure. Its solid fire gives me the strength to keep from swooning. "Fine. When does the show start?"

"It starts at seven-thirty, so I should get you around six-thirty."

"Do you know where I fucking live?" My eyes narrow on him.

"I don't. Technically, I had access to your address because of English but I've never looked, I figured that would be a step too far."

"*That* would be a step too far?" *Reading my heart and soul wasn't?*

His demeanor turns from playful to sincere as his eyes soften. "I'm not going to apologize for reading your work. I'm not sorry. It was the best thing that ever happened to me."

I lower my head and gaze at our feet as enough heat runs into my face the sun could be jealous.

Students pour out of the classes and his playful smile returns. "We better get going. I'll see you in class."

"Yeah." I nod and then turn to get the hell out of here.

When I reach Aub, I grab her hand and squeeze as we walk. I have to get my energy out somehow or else I'll scream.

"You're breaking my hand, bitch," Aub whispers.

"He asked me to be his girlfriend. I told his bitch-ass no!"

"What?" She rips her hand away and massages her palm.

My hands grip my new skirt, balling the fabric in my tight fists. "I made him ask me out and then I turned him down! It was so good."

"Damn, you're fucking ruthless."

"We're going on a date Friday. He's taking me to a musical."

"Oh, swanky." She smiles as we enter Psych.

Aub spills the beans to our classmates who salivate over the news. Thankfully, she leaves out the part where I came so hard I had to get rid of my pants, but makes sure to tell them of how I'm wrapping the All-American legend around my pinky.

Jessie shook his head. "I'm serious, girl. You had better be careful. *Everyone's* got something wrong with them. Everything this guy touches either turns to gold or comes so be careful he's not actually wrapping you up."

"That's a good point," Lacy says. "He's the kind of guy that could suck you in, and then turn around and be a power-hungry ass behind closed doors. Then, when you try to tell people, he just shakes his head and says you're the crazy one and points to all the good shit he does out in the open. My uncle was like that. Made my aunt for real go crazy till my cousin found videos of him tying her up and shit! It was fucked up."

Aaron frowns. "I doubt that. Look, I've known Jack for a long time. I don't want to say too much, bro code and all but, dude volunteers at our church all the time, he was a fucking Cub's scout leader for a summer. Usually only like, adults get to do that, and he's been in martial arts classes all his life. He's like super disciplined."

"Disciplined enough to wait a whole summer before trying to get at his fantasy girl," Lacy says. "Just because you go to the same church doesn't mean you *know* him. He read her papers, like sniffing her panties."

"Oh, that's gross." I groan.

"I'd bet a million dollars he smelt one of your papers." Lacy leans into me on the couch and adds, "Just to get a taste of what would soon be his."

"Fuck no!" I laugh as I shove her off me.

We all laugh but my gut churns thinking about what's wrong with him. Friday would be a perfect opportunity to find out what it is he's hiding.

Romanticism goes by in a daze. Jack just grades papers. Though he does have a rather large smile on his face.

Forensics is fun, if slightly annoying. Cinthia can't stop

looking at *my man* with her little dreamy eyes. It's both sad and satisfying to watch her pine over him even though she's already lost.

When we make it home, Deanna sits on the couch while Zest reads one of my B.R.T. Jackson novels.

"Are you old enough to be reading that?" I ask, as Aub and I put our backpacks on the floor next to the coat rack.

"I can read," she snaps back with enough attitude to fill a city block. "I have a collage reading level."

"She found out today with some test they took." Deanna says. She finishes texting someone and lays the phone on her stomach. "I gave her one of your old books."

"You gave her book three of his series, you idiot." I snatch the book from her hands. "Go up to my room and get book one. Touch nothing else!"

Zest hops out of her chair and runs up the stairs.

"Did you pick this randomly? He's been writing more sexual stuff the past few years. What if she'd picked up one of those?"

Deanna scowls at me. "You think I don't know that? I have all three of the House on the Hill books and his first book for Ocean Breakers. I didn't care to read his Lord of the Rings shit, but his new books are right up my alley." She sticks her tongue out. "I knew his earlier books would be safe. If you had them in the right order, she would have the first one."

"I have them ordered by favorite," I say in my defense.

"Great, now are you going to tell me why you left today with pants and came back with a skirt?"

"No," Aub yells from the kitchen. "Wait till I'm done making sandwiches or come in here!"

"I'm not waiting!" Deanna stands and pushes me toward the kitchen. "Let's go, bitch. What did you do?"

"It's not what she did," Aub sings as she bobs around the kitchen in anticipation.

"So, Jack asked me to speak with him," I start, just as Zest comes back downstairs. "Go to your room, Zest. This is women's talk." I point back up the narrow staircase.

"*Women's* talk?" Deanna laughs. "What happened to big girl talk?"

"This is the next level." Aub nods with a massive grin. "That stuff you do with your boyfriend when your parents aren't home, and you think no one can hear you. It's like that."

"Go to your room, Zest," Deanna orders. "And if you hear anything we say, you don't tell Mom or Dad."

"Fine! Bitches," Zest pouts as she starts back up the stairs.

"Hey! You're not this tall. No cussing!" When we hear her door shut, Deanna sits on one of the bar stools. "Okay. Spill it!"

Over the next hour I proceed to tell her everything that happened. She's certain I'd pissed myself till I show her my pants and she gives them a not-so-tentative sniff. She twisted them like a wet towel and whips me with them as I run from her around the kitchen island, all the while she laughs and calls me every dirty name under the sun. She's so proud of me for setting him up just to shoot him down that she awes and gives me a hug.

"Oh, that's so good Abby! You're just like me and Mom. I can't wait till you get him into the really bad shit."

"What kind of bad shit do you make Curtis do?" Aub asks.

"I peg Curtis, bitch," Deanna laughs. "That little fucker does *whatever* I tell him to do."

"You do not." Aub looks over to me for confirmation, but I frown and shrug. "No!"

"I have an eight-inch strap-on, I put it in his ass and make him cry." Deanna says it as though she's describing the taste of a five-star dinner. "It's what we Augustia women do. We dominate men. We can't help it," she adds with a shrug.

"Oh my god! Are you going to peg Jack?" Aub ask.

"*Ew*, gross! No! I'm going to have normal sex. Nothing crazy like this twisted slut."

"Speaking of sex. If he's half as big as you say, you're going to need some practice before you take on the big meat."

"I'm not going to fuck small dick boys just so it's easier with Jack."

Deanna rolls her eyes. "Toys, hun. Aub, you're going to have to play babysitter on this one, I am not going to miss my sister's first foray into Heavenly Toys."

Chapter Nine

Heavenly Toys is a store, standing all on its own in a nearly, but never completely, deserted parking lot ever since I can remember. Deanna and I wanted to go there so badly as kids. What kid wouldn't want toys from heaven? But when Mom told us it was toys for adults that helped with adult's backpain and headaches, we lost interest.

"I can open your eyes," Deanna sings as we walk up to the shop. "Take you wonder by wonder!"

"So, I'm just getting like a vibrator or something?" I ask, not letting my trepidation reach my voice.

"No, silly. We're going to shop for *exactly* what you need. Best part, I have a wonderful rapport with the girl who runs the counter during the days."

Walking past the blacked-out windows sets my heart to racing. I'm about to be in an adult establishment for the first time! For some reason, I've always pictured a bar, but I guess I hadn't really considered the other options. Deanna opens the door and I step inside what at first reminds me of a shitty thrift store, temporary metal racks, buy two get one free signs, but then reality sit in. The racks are full of slutty lingerie, the buy two get ones are for pornos, now in Blue Ray.

"Deanna, what's up girl?" the woman at the counter says. "This your fucking twin or what?"

"Sarina, meet my younger sister, Abby. She's just turned nineteen and she has a boy who wants down her pants so bad he bought her a skirt."

"Damn, girl." Sarina walks around the counter. Denim jeans and knee-high combat boots cover her long legs. A leather vest covers her top but shows off the lithe muscles of her arms. Her afro sways hypnotically as she moves, and she reaches out her hand with a smile.

I shake her hand. "Nice to meet you."

"More manners than your sister, at least. Come on, let's see what we can get for you. You just a little kinky or are you into the crazy shit like your fucked-up sister?"

"No. Definitely not."

"She just doesn't know it yet." Deanna smirks as she gives me a hip bump.

"I am not into pegging!"

Sarina laughs. "Girl, you missing out." She brings us over to a wall of dildos. "You know how big your man is yet?"

"Well, not exactly." I admit, looking up at the wall. It's majestic in a way, all neatly arrayed by color and size, like a growing rainbow with rubber dicks so big at the top they look like a joke. There's no way any city needs so many fake dicks. "I've heard some rumors."

Sarina nods with a frown. "Other girls always exaggerate. If they broke up bad, it's small, if he was great, it's huge. The truth is somewhere in the middle. Why the fuck you wagging your finger at me?"

"This isn't like that," Deanna says with a wicked smile. "The dick informant? It's a guy."

"Oh, your man's bi?"

"What? No! I mean, well, probably not. He's a wrestler at the school and puts in a lot of hours so he showers there and one of my friends saw it. He said it was like seven or eight inches flaccid."

Sarina laughs before heading down the wall, bringing a tall step stool along with her. "You seem like a dark purple to me. How's that sound?" When I nod, she continues. "Most likely, he won't get all too much bigger. Most guys who are really big just stay big. So, we can safely assume he's eight inches when hard, at the least." She grabs one dildo the length of my hand as she positions the step stool. She takes a few steps up to reach another purple dildo that's as big as my forearm. When she hands it to me, the packaging reads, *8in.* "So, you gonna have to put this up your cooch before you let him in, because it's possible that he's even bigger. Start with the smaller one first, work your way till it's comfortable for about two weeks, then start trying out the monster. And we gonna get you lubed up real good. Don't ever put these in dry, you'll kill yourself."

"There's one other thing," Deanna says. "Apparently, this guy has Superman dick powers. He made her cum by running a finger down her chest and then got her to squirt by licking her neck."

I groan in embarrassment, but Deanna keeps going.

"She's had a crush for like three or four years now, so she wants it bad." She pouts her bottom lip. "But I'm worried she's an itty-bitty premie. Is there something that can help her not cum blast her pants whenever he rubs up against her?"

"Deanna! Fuck! It's not like that!" Shame scalds my cheeks.

Oh god! It's exactly like that. What if he touches my arm at the theater and I'm wet as a fucking broken fire hydrant the whole night? *How the hell did he get me to come like that?*

"I'd say…wear a pad?" Sarina shrugs. "Don't get many premie girls."

"No, damn it! I'm not a fucking premie."

Deanna chuckles. "Uh. A guy licked your neck, not your clit, and you came. If that's not the textbook definition of premie, I don't know what is."

They both laugh, so I storm off into a sea of panties and fur handcuffs.

Oh, those look fun.

After picking up a few skimpy things and a dice game, I find the pair in the Bondage section. Deanna's holding some plastic device when she sees me.

"You going to cage your man, sis? You'll have to get a bigger one than this, but it's the Augustia way."

"Cage? You put Curtis's dick in that?" It's so small, it doesn't seem like any dick could fit. The heat in my chest from Deanna's teasing had faded but what's left merges with the heat the little cages coax from between my legs. That erotic adrenaline feeling returns. It swirls inside me as I gaze upon the little plastic and metal cages. There certainly is an allure to them.

"It's a chastity belt for men," Sarina explains. "It clips onto the balls and their penis gets locked in while flaccid. They can't get hard with it on, and only you can take it off."

"I'm not caging Jack."

Deanna's lips tighten while her jaw clenches for a moment. "Cocks are either in their cages, where they're supposed to be, or they're free roam. You want him running around fucking other girls?"

"You might need that for Curtis, but I don't need it to keep Jack."

"This bitch made him ask her out and then told him no," Deanna brags to Sarina. "Maybe she does have him. But later," she says, turning her attention back to me, "you'll need more tools in your arsenal."

"Weapons go in an arsenal," I correct as I eye a light riding crop. I pick up the crop and tuck it into the bundle of goodies I've collected. "Like this. I can see this being useful."

Deanna smiles. "See? It's in her blood." She stands there for a moment assessing me. "Remember that thing I said I'd get someday soon?"

Realization sparks across Sarina's face. "The—"

"Don't say it. Put two on my bill today. I'll come back for them tomorrow. I want to surprise her."

"If it's some gross strap-on or some pop rocks for his asshole, I'm not interested."

The two of them turn to one another with eyes as wide as dinner plates.

"I could totally make it, but how do we manufacture?" Deanna asks.

"I don't know, but we have to figure it out. There has to be someone we can talk to. An angel investor, something," Sarina says.

"What are you two talking about?"

"Ass pop rocks," Deanna shouts. "That's a fucking genius idea! I can test different formulas on Curtis."

"Okay, I'm going to leave you to that." I grimace, abandoning them to scheme about ass candy.

I make my way through the sea of pornos. I'd never been into watching till Les turned me onto it last year. We watched a few, but it really irked me to see him drooling over another woman. I like watching the more sensual style. None of the cheesy forced set up with a plumber or pizza guy. Just two people in bed that love each other. They're probably still faking it, but at least they put on a convincing performance that they're in love. Walking through the aisles, I don't see a section dedicated to sensual porn. It's all alphabetized but it jumps from *Robots* to *Single*.

My eyes drift to the marker for Big Dick. *Maybe I should see what I'm in for. A little mental preparation goes a long way.* I roll my shoulders and put my game face on, but it lasts all of half a second when I see the movie covers. *God! I need preparation for the preparation. These guys are hung like fucking animals!* There's no way I could ever get something like that inside me. I pick one up to look at the back and fumble the case when I see she has two in her! A cold shiver runs down my spine as I put the case back and walk away. The BDSM section catches my eye, but I'm too freaked out to stop. I'll stick with the lovey-dovey sensual stuff, for now.

I forego any more shopping and head straight to the checkout island. Placing my stuff on the counter I assess my haul. Handcuffs and a blindfold, the dice game and the riding crop, the pair of dildos and two pairs of skimpy panties. *This is good enough for now, right?* The thought of a costume appeals to my adventurous side, but I'll wait, see what he's into first. There's no need to scare him off with an officer or better yet, a vampire roleplay. *Then again, I'm a goth queen. What* could *scare him off?*

As if in answer to my question, Deanna slams a red footlong down on the table. Ridges and bumps travel from top to bottom with the word 'Obey' molded into the side.

"So, Sarina thought you were a red?"

"*Blood* red," Deanna corrects.

I point at the lumpy amalgamation. "Is that supposed to simulate an STD dick or something?"

"Oh, sweet little thing," she says, gently brushing my hair from my face. "Just be thankful you came here with me and not Mom."

"Wait, did Mom actually bring you here?"

"Yeah, dumb ass." She smacks me on the side of the head. "What have I been saying this whole time?"

I rub my head and grimace from the sting. "I thought you were saying you learned from her, but like, when we snuck in her room and found shit. I didn't think she actually taught you stuff. She hasn't said anything to me."

Deanna's face hardens for a moment, almost to the point that her lip curls into a hint of a snarl. "Just wait," she says with a forced smile. "Especially when she hears you have a man taking you on a date. She'll probably be pissed I brought you here first, but you'll be glad I did."

"I don't even want to think about that shit. Let's just pay and go."

"Add the thing," Deanna says as she hands Sarina her card. She looks at me. "One red, the other white for the little dove."

Sarina smiles. "You got it, sis."

Chapter Ten

Today, black slacks grip Jack's cute ass as the waistcoat wraps his chest and abbs like a second skin. A black shirt and red tie complete the dark look. Part of me wishes he still had his mohawk, but I really liked the whole twenties vibe. He even has a gold chain hanging from the waistcoat.

I point to the chain with my pencil. "That thing have an actual pocket watch?"

Low and behold, an actual pocket watch appears when he pulls on it. "It works, too. It was my grandpa's. I have to wind it up every twelve hours or something, but it makes a really loud ticking noise, so I don't."

"Best not be late," I warn. "I'm only giving you this one chance. I don't like wasting my time on boys."

He leans forward, his deep-set eyes locking with mine. "You're done wasting your time on boys. I can promise you that."

It feels less like a promise and more like a threat, kicking my pulse into high gear.

I imagined those honeyed eyes last night when I brought myself to a decent climax using the smaller dildo. I didn't really like it in me, if I'm being honest with myself. My fingers and imagination did most of the work. I tried the big one with my mouth, considering that's likely going to happen sooner. I nearly threw up gagging. My confidence is shaky at best, but I can only hope that I'll improve over time.

Can I really handle this man? His eyes seem to swirl again, sucking me in like a maelstrom.

I'm released from his gaze when he pulls his book from his backpack. I look over to Aub who wears an expression of stunned shock that I'm sure is on my own face.

"I look forward to seeing how you look all dressed up," he says in a normal, cheery tone. "I don't remember seeing you at prom or homecoming."

"Get to work, Blockhead, or you might not get your chance. If you need help, you'll have to ask extra nice today."

He chuckles and holds his hands up. "*Rawr*. All right then."

He opens his book and starts working but it's less than two minutes before he scoots his chair over to my side of the table.

"Hey," he whispers.

"Yes?" I reply with a heavy dose of eye rolling.

"I'm dumb, can you help me?" he asks with a pouty face.

It takes the highest level of control over every nerve in my body not to laugh at how ridiculous he sounds. While I refrain from outright laughter, I can't help the wide smile on my face. "Okay, dumb-dumb. Let's see where you are today."

The rest of the hour goes by too quickly. I'm forced to split my time between actually explaining things and staring at the curve of his jaw or taut cords of muscle in his forearms, or the way his shirt strains to hold his biceps and shoulders.

When the hour ends, I stand by him in the hall as he holds the door for the other students. "So, my parents will be home for the first time in a while. I'm sure it won't be a problem, but I'll ask if we can take my mom's nicer car."

"Why take your mom's car? I'm picking you up."

"Uh, because yours is an embarrassment." I laugh.

"I think that's a bit unfair. How about this, a little deal. You take another look after class and if you still think my car is an embarrassment then we'll take your mom's car."

"I remember very vividly how shitty your car is. It's hard to forget seeing something so grotesque."

"I've made a few upgrades. New rims, new windshield, new

everything. Just take a look and tell me if it's not up to your high society standards."

"What's in it for me?" I can't give an inch. Men always try taking more than they're given.

"Well, that's a great question." He glances back in the now empty study lounge. He grabs my hand and pulls me back through the door. One of his long, strong arms wrap around my waist, spinning me till I gently land on the wall just next to the exit. He peeks out the small window in the closed door before retuning his gaze to me, eyes hungry like a lion staring at a meal. "What would you like?"

His little dance twirl sends a thrill up my spine and quickens my breath, but I regain control quickly while he glances out the window. I gaze at him with a raised eyebrow and a half smile, as if I'm not having the time of my life. "If your car still sucks, like I know it does, you have to give me a foot massage when we get back from the theater. I don't wear sharp heels often, so I'm sure my feet will hurt."

The hunger in his eyes spreads to the grin that forms on his face. "Deal. If you don't like the car, you get a foot massage. If you *do* like the car—"

"I'm not giving you a foot massage." I make sure my face looks as displeased as my voice sounds.

"You have to admit that you should've trusted me." His intense eyes burrow into mine.

Even glued to his eyes as I am, I still fight back. "Fine, but don't expect to always make deals like this with me." I place my hand on his chest and his heat permeates my skin. He's like touching a marble statue covered in a heat blanket. I walk forward and he walks back in sync with my steps, not letting the space between us change. "I get what I want, and I don't make bargains."

"Not very American of you. A little you scratch my back, I scratch yours. You'd like that wouldn't you?"

"Now you can add a shoulder rub. I have to go."

His long arm finds its way to my waist again and he pulls me close, pressing our bodies together. "But do you *want* to?"

His breath is like honey, and this close to his skin, the citrus makes its way through the spiced wood. My arms slide up his, my fingers taking in every bump till I'm holding his face. Being so much taller, I have to stand on my toes which presses my chest into his. His heart hammers into me, demanding my heart fall in step. I'm playing with fire but without risk there's no reward. I pull him close and let my lips move millimeters from his. "What I *want* is to smack you across your pretty little face."

I shove his head back.

His eyes are still closed as he stumbles back a step. "Can't wait to see you in class."

I turn back as I push the door open. "Yeah, sounds nice," I say as if I'm slightly bored despite my pulse shooting through the roof.

In Romanticism, I catch him looking at me several times. *Not getting very many papers graded, Mr. Billard.* His head clears by the time Forensics comes around, acting his normal, joking self. When class ends, he walks with Aub and me to the parking lot.

"Can't wait to see this upgraded shitter," Aub says. "Abby said it has new wheels? Or was it just the AC?"

The car right next to us chirps and Jack stops. "It's a new alarm."

Behind him sits a glossy black Cadillac.

"Oh my god!" Aub jumps and circles the car, freaking out as if he's bought it for her.

"Wow. That's quite the upgrade. Did Daddy buy this or did you?" I still haven't figured out how he has so much money. Maybe this could be my opening.

"It's mine." He shrugs.

"What do your payments look like? I bet they *reamed* you."

His cocky smile slides across his face. "Something tells me you'd like that. But no. I paid for half. Put the other half on credit just to help my credit score some."

Half a fucking Cadillac? "What? How much is this car? Like forty thousand?"

"No, just thirty-five, well, eight after taxes."

"And you paid for half? How do you just have nineteen grand laying around?"

"Well, it's not laying around. I keep it in this thing called a bank. You might have one shaped like a piggy in your room."

"Don't shit on Oinkers." I laugh. "He's holding my future in his belly, but don't dodge my question. How do you make so much money you can pay off half a Cadillac? Oh my god! It just hit me. You're a drug dealer. You sell drugs, don't you? What is it? Coke? Weed? Oh, no! I bet it's steroids."

"Busted," Aub says as she comes back from circling the car.

He laughs before shaking his head. "No. Nothing so simple. I think I'll keep that to myself for a little while longer. A man has to keep some mystery about him to still be intriguing. But now to the question: Is this good enough for you to be seen in? Or are we going in your mom's Mazda?"

"Her nicer car is a Benz," I correct. It takes me a moment to swallow my pride, but I finally cave. "I should've believed you. But be careful, Jack Billard. Money doesn't get you everything."

"Don't worry about that. I can handle it from here."

"Don't be late," I warn.

As Aub and I walk the rest of the way to my car, I try to

puzzle out how he afforded a car like that. He has a full school schedule and sports. What kind of part time job can afford that?

"I'm so freaking jealous," Aub shouts once we were in my car. "You have a rich-ass boyfriend! *Ugh!* How did you get so freaking lucky!"

"I might be paying for it with a sore pussy the rest of my life." It's the only defense I can think of. We still haven't found his dark secret yet. "And that's only if I go through with all this."

"Cry me a river. We both know you're going to love it." She groans. "Shit. I'm sorry, Abby. I don't mean to make you feel bad or anything. You didn't ask for this. I'm just being shitty about it."

"No, don't say that." I reach over the console and hug her. "You're entitled to your feelings, Aub. We'll find you a guy. We'll make sure he's hung so you can have your vag stretched out, too."

"*Ah!* Gross," she shouts as we both laugh.

Chapter Eleven

Mom turns into a whirlwind when she hears I have a man coming to pick me up. My sisters and I all get our looks from Mom, almost to the point that we look like her younger clones. It's like we got zero traits from Dad with how much we look like her. The only real difference is that she wears normal makeup as goth isn't exactly hailed in the executive scene.

I gave her a brief overview of everything that happened between Jack and I, skipping the parts where his dick could be huge, his bank account is definitely big and the part where he made me come with just his tongue on my neck.

"Why didn't you call? I could have flown back down days ago." She paces back and forth in my room, her big curly hair bouncing with each panic ridden step.

I stand in front of my cheval mirror putting on my face. I decided to go hard black to see how Jack would respond to me staying goth even at a musical, but Mom insisted I put color on my face somewhere. I relented and put red on the outside edge of my eyeshadow. She gave me a pair of her diamond earrings, along with a small diamond stud for my nose ring. My hair is already done up, pulled tight and tied with a black ribbon that blends into my hair most won't even see the little bow on the top of the curly ponytail.

"He asked me out Wednesday, Mom. He gave me today or next week as my options."

"Oh, so that's how this boy is? Giving you *options*? The illusion of control, that's all that is."

"She's got him, Mom," Deanna says from my bed, braiding Zest's hair. "Even without your 'guidance,' she has it in her."

"It's easy when the stakes are low. It gets harder and harder as time goes on. Oh, my sweet girl you should have come to me first. There's an art to trapping a man under your heel. One missed step and they slide away like the snakes they are."

Trapping? What the hell is she talking about?

"Whatever, Mom. I'm going on a date. It's not that big of a deal. We'll see where it goes."

The doorbell rings, and she dashes out of the room.

I turn to Deanna for some kind of help, but she waves off my concern. "She's just going to assess him. Don't worry. She believes outside forces are bad for the taming process."

"Taming? Oh my god! Why is Mom such a freak?"

"That freak is in all of us."

"No, the flowers are for you, Mrs. Charleston," Jack say downstairs. "Your daughter is getting a whole date."

"My name is Mrs. Augustia, young man," Mom corrects him. I can just imagine her imperious pose. Hands on hips, nose stuck into the air, eyes looking down on him even though he's a foot taller.

"That is an incredibly beautiful last name, Mrs. Augustia. My apologies for not knowing that about you. I should have asked."

"You should have," Mom says sternly but I can hear the smile in her words that must be on her lips.

"What about Dad? What do I get?" Dad asks, thankfully breaking the tension that Mom's putting on the situation.

"You get a firm handshake, Sir," Jack says before the *clap* of their hands rings out through the foyer. "It's a pleasure to meet both of you."

"I've heard you've been pursuing my daughter for quite some time," Mom says.

"I have. It took me a while to build up the courage to talk to her, but I'm very glad I did."

Deanna nods in approval. Hopefully that's what Mom's doing.

"Let's talk in the den," Dad says.

The doors to the den slide shut and I take one last look in the mirror to make sure everything is in place. I'd already picked out one of Mom's better dresses before she handed it to me. It's a black silk dress that Mom had tailor made for herself. It's only a touch tight around my chest, I guess I'm outgrowing her. I've worn my fair share of corsets, but not one that had a whole dress attached to it and I'm not looking for my first adult date to end in a nip slip. The back reaches the floor even in heels, but Mom always has it mended to look like new. The slit goes to my upper left thigh, almost to my hip. I move around in the dress to make sure I'm not going to expose myself.

Zest jumps to her feet once Deanna finished with her braid. She stands next to me, the top of her head almost reaching my shoulders. "You look so pretty. Do you think I'll be as pretty as the two of you when I'm older?"

"Of course, Zest." Deanna slides off my bed and stands behind her two younger sisters. "You're an Augustia, just like us, just like Mom. You're going to be even more beautiful than all of us once you're our age."

"You really think so?" Zest asks.

Mom comes back in holding a bouquet of dark red roses. "You most certainly will, Zest." Her eyes sparkle as she looks over me. "His jaw will hit the floor when he sees you. I'm glad he's taking this seriously as well. A very dashing three-piece suit with a chain and everything. Oh, let me go get the coat." She hurries off to her room.

"Lucky, bitch." Deanna says with a sarcastic frown. "Mom never let me use that dress."

"That's because your boyfriends suck and never took you anywhere you'd actually use it."

"I could have used it for prom." She shrugs as she stands behind me, fixing my hair even though it didn't need it.

"Just so Justin could come on it?" Mom scoffs as she came back. "Yeah, I don't think so."

"His name was Mark. Justin was the boy before," Deanna corrects.

"Whatever." Mom holds the coat over my shoulders just to see how it will look.

It's real fur made from a black bear. My deep love for all things dark is also inherited. I've held it a few times in the past and it's *heavy*. I just hope I won't start sweating once I have it on.

"Well, no surprise, it looks wonderful on you." She hands the coat to Deanna and then feels the dress on me. "Is it too tight anywhere? Too loose?"

"My boobs feel a bit squished."

Zest snickers.

Mom frowns at her while her hands come up under my breast line. "It's fine. It's supposed to squish a bit. Gives the girls a little umph."

"Well, I'm ready." I brush the skirt several times as I look at myself in the mirror one last time.

"Oh, come here sweetheart." Mom turns me around to hug. "You're going to do great."

Her warm embrace does wonders for my confidence. That's another inherited trait, but while being in her presence makes me feel like I can take on any challenge the world might throw at me, being in her arms reminds me that she has taken on those challenges and beaten them. Her strength is mine. *I miss this.* Hugs have become rare these past couple years. I could certainly use more of them. "Thanks, Mom."

"We're going to give your father a little more time with the young man." She looks over to Deanna, Zest and then back to me, her eyes welling up.

"Mom, why are you crying?" A ball of emotions rises in my chest, heading for my eyes.

"You girls are my pride and joy." She extends an arm over to Deanna and Zest, calling her oldest and youngest to her. When the two join us, Mom's head rests against mine and Deanna's while Zest looks up from in between us. "Everything I do, I do for my girls. I'm sorry I'm not home as much as I wish I could be, but believe me when I tell you, it's all for you."

"Mom," Deanna pleads. "Stop. You're going to make Abby cry."

"You're the one crying, bitch." I choke on the ball in my throat.

"Enough, enough." Mom releases us and fans my face. "No need to cry. You girls know I love you, nothing new to get emotional over." She lowers to her knees in front of Zest and kisses her cheeks. "I need to talk with your sisters. Something you're not quite ready for. Go to your room and I'll come see you when Abby and her date leaves." She places a finger on Zest's lips just as my little sister starts to argue. "Go on."

Zest nods and gives me a hug before leaving.

Mom sticks her head out my door till Zest's door closes down the hall. "Now, I want your word. Both of you. No sex in this house tonight."

"Only tonight?" Deanna asks as she carefully wipes her eyes.

"Yes. You're women now. I told you that when you turned eighteen. And I've been so busy, Abby, I'm so sorry I haven't been able to have this talk with you."

"You had the talk with me back when I had my first period."

"Oh, it's not that talk," Deanna says.

"It's the woman's talk, dear. We have a long history." She looks over her shoulder for a moment before turning back. "I don't really want to only have half of this conversation with you, but I think your father is nearly done. We'll have to have it in full when I get back next week. But please, do not have sex with that young man till I've talked to you. Can you do that?"

"Can I do that? As if I'm chomping at the bit to spread my legs or something." I roll my eyes at the ridiculous notion. "I'm not ready to have sex. Okay? Does that make you feel better?"

"No. It doesn't." Her words ring like hard steel. "We Augustia women have deep sexual needs, sweetheart, and those needs and desires can overwhelm us when we're young. So, I'm telling you; don't rest on just the thoughts you have now. Later tonight you might just say, fuck it! Let him do me! I know, hun, I've been there. Deanna knows, she's been there. But I'm telling you now; do not have sex till I've talked to you in full. I should have done this a while back but I…I got so wrapped up in work."

Deanna's eyes roll as her jaw clenches.

"Fine, Mom. I won't fuck him," I say to get her off my back.

Heat blooms in my chest. I don't need her crowding me like this.

She sighs with a smile. "Good."

"So why can't I have sex tonight?" Deanna asks.

I raise an eyebrow at her. "You expect Curtis over?"

"No, but things can be spontaneous." She shrugs.

"I want you to make sure she keeps her promise," Mom says. "Give her space, of course. But I want you to be the last line of defense."

"I'm a cockblocker!" She slaps me in the face with her over-eager smile. "Yeah, I can do that. Make sure my little sis doesn't get in over her head."

I groan. "Fuck you."

"Hey, no fucking," Deanna says sternly.

Mom frowns. "That's enough. Come on. I think your father should be done or wrapping up by now."

Does she have a fucking timer on Dad or something? Oh my god! Do they have some rehearsed dad talk? I hope it isn't too embarrassing.

We head down the stairs and I hold onto Mom's arm to keep my balance. Most of my heels are thick but these are like standing on pencils. Just as we reach the landing, the doors to the den slide open and there he is.

His black and red striped tie matches his black three piece and dark red shirt it's clipped to with a gold tie clip. He stands with his hands in his pockets which pull his jacket back, making his shirt and vest strain against his granite chest. He watches me with a growing smile and warm eyes that I can tell have shut out everything else in the world but me. When I reach the middle of the stairs, he puts a foot on the second step and reaches up to me, offering his hand.

Heat spreads out low in my core and quickly merges with the lingering irritation from Mom smothering me with her ridiculous promise. As that odd adrenaline-like sensation slides through me, I let go of Mom and take his hand as he guides me down the last few steps. For some reason, the image of a dark Disney princess and her handsome prince comes to mind.

"You look incredible." His eyes gaze into my own, the honey-brown melting into me. "I take it that's her coat?" He breaks eye contact to look at Deanna. His eyes widen when he sees her and then he looks back and forth between the two of us a few times. "You have very strong genes, Mrs. Augustia." He takes the coat and moves behind me.

I slide my arms into it, and he lets it down softly onto my shoulders. It's like the bear is hanging on my back! No wonder

Mom only uses it once or twice a year. Anymore and she'd have to see a chiropractor.

"I'll expect her home by midnight." Dad opens the door. "No later."

They'll be leaving just a few minutes after us, but Dad stood tall in his words, even though that still only put him at Jack's shoulders.

"Of course, Mr. Charleston." Jack puts his hand out for another handshake, which Dad gives with a smile.

He walks me to the car with my arm in his. After opening my door and he waits for me to give him a nod before shutting it. When he sits in the driver seat, he peers over at me as he cranks the engine.

"Hi there." He smiles that warm smile as his eyes swirl in the dim light.

I smile back. "Hi."

Music comes over the speakers, a driving beat with a woman's voice.

"You listen to trance, now? I thought it was all rock and video games."

"I like trance or synth when I'm driving. Makes me feel like I'm going fast even when I'm not."

He puts the car in first and we're on the move. The air conditioning is a cool breeze, even with the fur coat. I hope he isn't getting cold just for me. His large hands gripped the steering wheel except when he shifts gears. His head turns my way every chance he gets.

"You're making it impossible to drive."

"What's that supposed to mean?"

"I'm supposed to have both eyes on the road. I don't think I can do it with you sitting right next to me."

"You seem to be able to keep your eyes on your work at school just fine."

"No, I really don't," he replies with a sly smile.

Once we're on the freeway, he puts the car into sixth gear and his hand lingers on the stick for a moment before slipping to my partially exposed thigh.

The gentle brush of skin sends a rush of heat up through my chest to my cheeks. I turn to the window, so he won't see me smile, loving his touch so obviously. My heart falls in step with the thumping beat of the music as he moves up and down my leg. His hand stays there, gently massaging, till we exit the freeway. One of these days, we're going to have a date where he drives around the freeways endlessly.

We pull up to the theater and a valet opens my door, offers me his hand. I gladly take it, not trusting myself to stand up on my own. Jack offers his arm a second later and I grip it, feeling his muscles under the fine wool. I never thought I'd be so into muscles. It never really mattered much to me, but he has them, and I like it. Using his arm, I lean up and kiss his cheek.

He smiles down at me. "What was that for?"

"Good boys get rewards."

"Oh? Is that right?" He leans down till his eyes hover just an inch from mine. "Then I'll be the goodest good boy you've ever seen."

We walk into the building, and he takes my coat, handing it to a waiting attendant. He sticks the ticket they give him into his jacket pocket, and he leads me through the crowd till we come to the elevators. I'm slightly jealous of the adults getting to enjoy cocktails and talk about whatever while they wait for the show.

"Jack," a white-haired man calls as he walks over to us. "I thought that was you." He shakes hands with my date while his jovial smile reaches peak levels, pushing his apple cheeks up and showing off more teeth than anyone ever should. "Glad to see you somewhere other than a wrestling mat, son."

"It's good to see you, too, Mayor Laurence," Jack says with a smile.

Mayor! How does Jack know the fucking mayor?

"I'd like to introduce you to my date, Miss Abigale Charleston. Abigale, this is Mayor Scott Laurence. His youngest son graduated last year. He was on the wrestling team for another school."

This guy has a son my age? He looks like he could be my grandfather.

"It's a pleasure," I say with what I hope isn't too terrible of a smile.

Mayor Laurence's eyes dance over me. A look that I'd relish coming from Jack, from a man his age, my stomach sours. After a quick and horribly creepy flick of his tongue to wet his lips, his eyes light up with an eager disposition. "The pleasure is all mine, Miss Charleston. Were you going to your seats?"

I sigh in relief when his attention goes back to Jack.

"Too early for that, my boy." He places a hand on Jack's shoulder and motions to the room. "You have to mingle; I'll get you two a drink. You won't get me in trouble now, will you?"

"Of course, not, sir." Jack says with a winning smile.

"That's a good boy," he says as we reach the bar. "Two virgin martinis. But not virgin," he adds in a low mutter as he hands the man several bills.

My first public drink is going to be illegal, at the Arts Theater, and thanks to the fucking mayor! I can't have done better if I'd planned it.

He hands us our drinks with a wink and then nods for us to follow.

"Good boys get rewards," Jack whispers as he toasts his glass, nearly making me spit the sip I just took.

I slap his arm before taking it as we follow Mayor Laurence.

"Your mother would be very happy to see you at the theater," the Mayor says over his shoulder. "I can tell you'll carry on in her name."

Shit, dead mom talk right out the gate. I've never heard him talk about her. *Maybe that's his dark secret, just how much her death affected him.*

The Mayor leads us around the room, introducing us to different people. Some of them Jack already knows, but nearly all of them have heard of Jack or his family, and if they haven't, the Mayor is quick to talk him up.

I'm slightly annoyed by the number of eyes that follow me, but then again, I suppose the dress is meant to be a head turner. Part of me does enjoy the attention, but the part I love the most isn't how the women catch their men looking at me, though that is a sweet victory on its own. The best part is when a man notices me first, then his eyes move to Jack. Watching the hope die in their eyes is enough to make me laugh like the Wicked Witch.

When we pass another bar, the Mayor gets us another glass each. Eventually he leads us through a dense group of people. I trail behind Jack just so I don't have to bump people's shoulders. Walking behind him, my hand in his, is like having a shield with legs pushing forward. Looking over his shoulder from time to time to check on me, he barely touches anyone physically, but the people move all the same.

"I want you to meet Kevin Seltzer," the Mayor says, pulling up to a man in a fine suit and glasses.

His wavy blond hair is pushed back into a small ponytail, and he looks down at the two of us even though I'm eye level and Jack stands a head taller.

"Kevin, this is Jack Billard."

"Jack, it's good to see you again," Kevin says with a big smile, his haughty demeanor vanishing in an instant.

They shake hands and Jack smiles. "It's very good to see you as well. I was wondering if I'd see you here."

"You two already know each other?" Mayor Laurence asks.

"We met about ten years ago," Jack answers. "He'd just written his third book and I met him on his book tour."

"Has it been that long? I thought you were ten at the time," he says with a finger pointed to Jack's drink.

"Gives us something to do with our hands. Abigale, like the Mayor said, this is Kevin Seltzer. He's an author and director. He's the director here for the year. Kevin, this is Miss Abigale Charleston."

"Wow. I'm meeting all sorts of important people." I offer my hand to Kevin.

"Well, what did you expect with Jack?" Kevin asks before laying a kiss on my hand.

I was going for a light handshake or something, but okay.

"Coming with a wrestling jock, I didn't expect all this."

"Oh, come now." The mayor laughs with a dismissive wave. "Jack's family has been one of the Arts' largest donors over the years."

"Mom and Dad have a bench outside," Jack says as if he's slightly embarrassed.

"And your work," Kevin adds.

"I'm still private on my work." Jack jumps in. "I'd like to make it through college without my classmates knowing, or my coaches for that matter. If they thought I wasn't all-wrestling all the time, *phew*, I'm not sure how bad I'd get it."

The three men laugh, making me the odd woman out. I squeeze his arm, trying to make my nails bite through his jacket.

"So, what about you, Miss Charleston?" Kevin asks. "What's your focus?"

"I'm finishing up preliminaries this year, but I'll be pursuing a law degree with a heavy lean towards forensics."

"Wow!" The mayor gives a long whistle, looking at Jack. "You think you can keep up with that?"

"Well, we share a few classes. But I'd probably be failing if it wasn't for her help," he adds with a laugh. "It won't be too hard for people to figure out which of us is the brains."

The other men laugh, but this time I'm able to laugh as well. I squeeze his arm with a soothing massage.

"When you find yourself in Law School, let me know," Mayor Laurence says. "D.A. Gibbson and I are good friends. Even if you move out of state, knowing a district attorney can help."

The lights flicker before I can respond.

Kevin claps his hands. "That's the start of the show. I look forward to seeing you all after. I hope you enjoy." With that, he turns and walks through the milling crowd.

The mayor walks with us to the elevator and a woman in a sparkling white dress comes over to take his arm. She's taller than the mayor but only because of her heels. She has diamonds around her neck and wrist and a very large one on her engagement ring, though the wedding band sparkles just as much in the dim lighting. I'd guess she's about Mom's age, but she has a light greying at her temples that fades into her blonde hair.

"Jack, so good to see you. And who is this beauty?"

Jack introduces me to Mrs. Jane Laurence, the mayor's wife.

"I take it you'll be in your box?" she asks as we step into the elevator.

"Of course. I still buy the season tickets, even though I'm

not always able to make it." Jack shrugs. "Dad and Elaine come sometimes though."

"I saw them at the last show of the season," she says. "He seems to be doing very well. I was glad to see that."

Jack nods with a smile. "Yeah. He's doing much better ever since Elaine came into his life."

"Do come see us when the show is over." She smiles as we step out of the elevator.

"Will do," Jack replies as he leads me the opposite way.

I want to ask about his late mother, maybe it ties into his big secret, but instead, I focus on his work.

"Nice save back there." I keep my voice flat. I still take his arm, I'm upset about being left in the dark but not mad enough to give him the cold shoulder. Not yet anyway.

"When?"

"Director boy almost gave away how you make all your money, but you were fast to cut him off."

An attendant opens a door, and we walk into a small room. Two seats wait for us on the balcony, made of plush velvet cushioning with gold fucking trim on the polished wood. I've been to the Arts Theater before, but not in the upper box seats. I would have never imagined it's like this. A wet bar sits off to the corner, but no one stands behind it. It reminds me I still have my drink. I down what's left and place the glass on the counter.

"If you need anything, just let me know," the attendant says before shutting the door behind us.

"I didn't make all my money through my job," Jack explains. "My dad was one of the first people to buy dot com names and sold them for a hefty amount. He invested a lot in the stock market and bought me stocks as well. I've moved some of that money into tech start-ups. That's what the Mayor knows about. He has no idea what my profession is. The money from my work isn't that big of a deal, but I promise I will tell you about it." He gently grabs my shoulders as I go to turn away. "Once you know what it is, it will change things, and I need it to not change things. So please, just trust me for now."

"You're going to tell me at the end of the night," I whisper as I lean into him, my neck stretching.

He reads my signals and leans in as well, his eyes closing. Just as his lips begin to purse, I knock his hands away and walk to the chairs.

"Good boys get rewards, remember?" I let my hands glide over the wood balcony banister. "Keeping me in the dark isn't good."

I look out over the theater to find everyone shuffling into their seats. We're on the third floor in the balcony closest to stage left. I can see everyone, which means everyone can see me, and several heads have already turned my way in the short time I've stood here. Being so far above everyone causes that odd adrenaline to shoot into me, but I don't want an audience, not tonight.

"Would you like a bit more privacy?" Jack moves to the edge of the balcony.

"Yes. Who wants a crowd of people watching them?"

"The actors," Jack says with a smirk. He pulls on the curtain and walks it past the chairs. It leaves enough room for us to see the whole stage. No one except maybe the actors can see us, but they'll have to see past the stage lights. "That better?"

"It will do."

I take the seat on the right. I should have taken the seat on the left if I want to see better, but I hope that Jack's hand will find its way to my thigh again.

He sits next to me; his eyes lock onto mine.

"What?"

"You drive me wild," he says, and I jump in my seat as the music hits. His delicious lips curve deviously, making me wonder if he'd somehow planned it. He turns to the stage and lays a hand on my thigh.

Desire for his lips to touch my skin burn inside my chest, but I'm willing to settle for his fingers. He starts to massage my thigh like he had in the car, and for a while it's good enough, but it's not long before I'm too aroused for it to stop there.

I lean over, placing my hand on his shoulder, letting my lips rest right at his ear as he leans in, making it easier for me. "Be a good boy and go higher."

His hand slides up my thigh, sending a shiver down my spine but he still doesn't go where I want.

"Don't make me tell you again."

His hand freezes. He turns to me just as *The Mirror* comes to an end. He switches hands on the soft skin of my inner thigh. It slides higher till it disappears under my dress. His eyes hold mine, hovering only a meager inch away. His fingers move over my lace garments, batting them to the side with a gentle elegance. The theme music strikes as he grabs me with strong, yet delicate fingers.

My head tilts back and I gasp, but Jack wastes no time, striking my neck with his lips. I grip the back of his head and his jacket as he works me over. Two big fingers slide back and forth while his thumb softly rubs my clitoris. The actors' voices fade into the music, their words lost to my mind. His fingers are rods of heat, setting fire to my nerves, and I roll my hips with his hand. My heart hammers in concert with the music. I'm peaking faster than I thought I would, faster than I ever have on my own. Then again, he made me come last time with just a lick. *Maybe I should be grateful I've made it this far.*

The rush of pleasure surges through me again, a tidal wave

of heat and fire this time. Just as Christine reaches her vocal climax, I hit my own. I bite my lip so that I don't compete with the actress as my body shudders, and I felt the sweet release splash over my thighs. Good thing the dress is black. My chest heaves for air and I push Jack's head down into my eager breasts.

Good boys get rewards.

Chapter Twelve

There's more snuggling, neck kissing and earlobe nibbling before we leave. I'm surprised he even remembers to grab my coat on the way out. I'm certainly not thinking about it as we sneak out ten minutes early. The ride home is much faster and if it weren't for my seat belt, I'd be in his lap.

He opens my door and I give him big doe eyes. "My feet hurt." They do, sort of. I really just want to see if he'll carry me like he said he would.

He scoops me up as though I weigh nothing, and I point to the den once we're inside. I kiss his neck and repeatedly whisper into his ear. "My big strong man."

He places me on my feet and takes my coat, laying it on the chair next to the fireplace.

I settle onto the couch, putting my feet up on the coffee table. I hold a hand up before he can sit next to me, stopping him dead in his tracks. "Jacket, off."

He pulls the jacket off, shrugging it from his shoulders before he lets it slide down his thick arms. He tosses it on the same chair as my coat before he quickly takes his seat, crashing into me, one arm curling around my shoulders, the other gliding up my legs.

My hands spread over him, one hand feeling his rippling back, the other moving across his chest. I tilt my head to give him my neck, and he inhales deeply before lightly kissing my yearning skin. I still haven't let him touch my lips. He's tried several times, but I've forced him away with a soft no, or a single finger on his lips. Something tells me I can't let him have my lips, yet. At least not those lips.

"Be a good boy and take my heels off."

He kisses my chest just above my breasts before he turns to my heels. "You know, I'd rather you wear something that didn't hurt your feet." Since they're straps with a heel, when he unfastens the tiny buckle, it's like he's removed a straitjacket from my foot.

"*Oh*, that feels so much better." I cross my legs to place my other foot in his waiting hands. "A girl has to look good, and heels look good. You like them, don't you?"

He answers with a salacious grin as he removes the other shoe. "Would you like your foot massage now?"

A thrill plumes in my chest. "What do you mean? You won that bet."

He chuckles. "You really think you'd have to win a bet to get a foot rub?" He pulls me around so my feet rest in his lap.

"You have a fetish? Is that your dark side? You just *love* feet?" As I teasingly mock him, I hold my feet to his face, but he just gently lowers them to his lap and starts working the ball of one. "*Oh*, shit! Okay, you can have a foot fetish for all I care. *Ugh*, that's so good."

"I don't have a fetish, but I find your feet to be very attractive." His smile stays but a hunger consumes his eyes, the wolf returns.

"How attractive?" I close my eyes to soak up the entrancing sensations of this man's foot rub.

"I already said, very."

"Very is a *very* shitty adverb. You grade English papers; I think you can do better."

"You're *very* right. I can. I find the elegant shape of your delicate feet, and delectable toes, to be world-shatteringly attractive."

"Oh? World-shattering, huh?" I half laugh, half moan the

question as I bite my lip to stop myself from gasping from his firm hands kneading my soles.

"My world, at least." He pinches my heel, somehow squeezing out all the pain in one precise and powerful movement.

A full moan escapes my throat, and my eyes snap to him. His smile hasn't changed, and that hunger in his eyes looks dangerously on edge of taking over.

"Elegant, delicate, *delectable*. You wouldn't put my feet in your mouth."

"I'd put every inch of you in my mouth," he says with that deadly seriousness I've only seen him reach when he talks about things he's convicted about; wrestling, church, and now me.

My heart picks up speed right as he lifts my feet and scoots closer on the couch. His thumbs push the ache out of my arch like magic and I nearly let another moan escape, but I force myself to hold his eyes.

"Prove it."

He stares at me with a small curve to his lips as he continues to massage the pain away. He lifts my foot while lowering his head and Jack Billard, the man every girl at school would kill to have, kisses my foot. A long, tender kiss just above my toes.

That erotic adrenalin shoots through me like a rocket, knocking my head back as I gasp. It rips me apart and threatens to give me my second orgasm of the night. *Jesus! What the fuck is going on with me? A single kiss…to my foot?*

His lips come off, and I'm sure he's going to say something like, 'I told you so,' or 'nice taste,' or some other smartass comment. Instead, he slides his tongue from the bottom of my heel to top of my toe before setting it back in his lap and continues to massage. His eyes are closed for another moment till his chest expands with a deep breath and exhales as though it took a toll to do it. Not the act of kissing my foot or licking my heel, but the holding himself back from doing something more.

"Good boys get rewards." I push my free foot into his crotch. His mass is there, long and…soft?

I yank my legs back and shoot to my feet. "You're not even hard?" I hiss. I want to shout. I want to beat the piss out of him! I want to fucking smack him through the fucking window and out to his precious little ego boosting car, but I don't want to wake Zest and I don't want Deanna to hear any of this. She'll never let me hear the end of it. "After all that? What the fuck is wrong with you?"

"It's not like that." He slides forward to the edge of the couch, giving the impression he's kneeling in front of me. "Please, believe me. I am so hot for you right now. I'm holding on by a fingernail, I promise."

"That's bullshit! Your mouth moves but your dick just lays there. *Ugh*, Jack! Fuck! I wanted to believe you," I turn away. I can't even look at him! "You had me. God, you *had* me! I was so convinced. But your body doesn't lie." I growl as I round on him. "What is this? Just some game to see if you can get the goth girl into the super jock? That you could get the most unlikely girl—"

"Stop." He stands, towering over me, his shoulders rising like mountains, ready to crash down on me at any moment. "I'm not going to let anyone, *especially* you, misconstrue my feelings for you."

For the briefest of moments, I feel like a mouse trembling before a lion, but when he turns around, shaking his head, I can finally breathe.

"This is embarrassing, but you're going to know sooner or later, and at the rate things are happening, I guess now is the time." He turns back around to face me. "I…have a choker on."

He hangs his head in shame as his hands move to his hips. "It makes it so blood can't get through and I can't get a full erection."

Oh my god, he has a cock cage on? "Why would you do that? What would possess you to do that to yourself?"

"So that I don't have a massive erection!" he whispers. "What would have happened when we were here earlier, and I had a bulge in my pants in front of your parents? Look, I've tried to keep this under wraps because it throws girls off, and the last thing I want is for you to get scared or uncomfortable but... Fuck, here we go. I have a larger than average dick." Embarrassment splashes his face but an annoyed frown holds firm. He lets out a sigh and cradles the back of his head with both hands as he looks to the ceiling. "So, a few weeks ago, you inadvertently stretched... Well, I mean, you purposefully stretched, but you inadvertently showed off your breasts and I didn't have the choker yet. So, I had an erection that I had to go home to take care of. It wouldn't go away, and I had a spot seeping through my damn pants by the time I got to my house."

"So my boobs gave you an unstoppable hard on but fingering me and sucking my neck like a vampire for the past three hours is just nullified by your little choker? That's a load of shit."

"It's just science and you know it. Look, I couldn't find anything to help stop an erection besides cages, and I wasn't about to do that."

My eyes shift to the fireplace to stop the image of locking him up. *It's probably for the best that he doesn't want to do that. It means he's normal and not some fetish hound.*

"The best I could find were these things called cock rings. They're actually made to help circulation, but I got one that's really small for me. Small enough that when an erection starts, I don't have any room to grow, and then the erection fades."

"Bullshit." I shrug. "I don't believe you. If you have problems

getting it up, just say so. I don't need shitty excuses."
"Hey! This thing fucking hurts! Just looking at you now; the
firelight playing over the most tantalizing curves I've ever laid
eyes on." He surges forward, his hands cup my jawline on both
sides, tilting my head to look up at him. "Your dark glossy lips,
so full and ready, and those flames in your eyes that have
absolutely nothing to do with the fireplace!" His jaw clenches,
and he looks poised to strike, but his eyes close and he lets out a
small groan. "I want you in the best and worst ways possible."

Part of me wants to believe him. He hasn't lied to me before,
and he's proven me wrong on a couple occasions already. The
erotic adrenaline floods my veins. If what he says is true, if he
really is willing to deny himself like this, then this is my chance
to make it mine.

I slowly lower his hands from my face. "Show me then. I
won't believe you till I see it. It's too ridiculous. No man would
stop his erection."

"*That's* the bet you lost." His eyes open, looking at me with
something bordering resentment. "You said you would trust me."

"Jack, that was way different! You proved me wrong about
your car, which you were misleading about to begin with. You
said you made an upgrade as if you added to your existing shit
box, not bought a whole new one. I felt your dick, it was soft.
And you tell me this story about choking it. I'm sorry, but I have
to believe the facts."

He sighs in frustration as his hands cover his face. He paces
back and forth once before his hands slide over his hair, making
it look ridiculously perfect. "If I show you, and it turns out I
wasn't lying, will this be enough? Will this be the moment where
you'll trust me?" He moves to me once again, but this time I'm
able to put a hand on his chest to stop him somewhat, but his
hands still engulf my shoulders. They're like soft, firm pillows

caressing my skin, but under the surface, I can feel the iron vice I'm truly in. "We won't survive unless you trust me. If I have to show you proof whenever you have a small doubt, eventually, all the proof in the world won't be enough, and I'll lose you. I can't lose you." His pleading eyes turn so soft the fire in my chest dims. "So, please, promise me that this will be the last time. If I give you this, will you give me your trust?"

Part of me doesn't mind him asking for something. It's normal. Quid quo pro and all that, right? But another part of me twitches with anger, reigniting the fire. Despite the strange desire to shout him down for daring to bargain, I compromise. "I don't like making deals, but fine. I promise. If you're telling the truth, I won't question you ever again, till I catch you in a lie."

He slowly nods as he backs up a couple steps. He looked to the doors leading to the foyer and starts for them.

"No," I snap, stopping him in his tracks. "If you close them, Deanna will think we're having sex and she'll come downstairs. Even if she lays down in the hallway, the most she can see is the back of the couch. Trust me, this is where we always have our Christmas tree, so I know exactly how much she can and can't see."

His hands move to his belt, and he unfastens the clasp. The zipper goes down and he opens his pants. After pulling his boxer briefs down, a thick, luscious bush is exposed first, and I wonder if he uses shampoo and conditioner on it. It looks like the hair on his head it's so thick, and in the light of the fire, a sheen glistens along it. His pants go just low enough to show the minimal amount to prove his story. At the base of his cock, a gold ring glints in the firelight.

I gasp and clasp my hands over my mouth. "Jack!" I rush to him, my hands reaching too late to stop him from closing his pants. "No, no, no! You can't do this. Jack, that can seriously hurt you." A lump grows in my throat as I grip his pants, fighting him to open them. "Take it off, now!" I look up to him, his face becoming wavy behind the tears building in my eyes.

"I don't want it on either, but it's the best I could come up with," he says, grabbing my hands away.

"No, Jack. This is unacceptable. I will not have you wearing that thing. I mean it," I add with a heat that evaporates my tears. "You will do as I say, or we end here. I can't have you doing this to yourself."

He sighs and looks down. He closes his eyes for a moment as his jaw slides to the side before tightening up. "Well, I guess you're not giving me much of an option. There's something else," he adds with a disheartened sigh. "Please don't laugh, it was literally the only color it came in."

"Color? What?"

He opens his pants and reaches into his underwear to pull out an enormous cock. It's probably eight or nine inches with a little pink condom, puffed up like a tiny balloon, hanging off the tip.

"What the hell is that?"

"The ring made it so I couldn't get an erection, but I'm still aroused, and therefore… I'm still… leaking." He sounds humiliated, and it looks so ridiculous that he has every right to be.

I lift the pink bulb in my palm and feel liquid slosh inside. "That's precum inside the itty-bitty pink condom?" I chuckle.

"Please, don't laugh," he groans, covering his face with his massive arm. "I feel bad enough."

I drop the bulb and lean down to get the ring off him. "How do I take it off?" I fumble the ring in between my fingers, trying to not let myself fall into his musky scent. I lick my lips instinctively and taste a hint of the spiced wood with citrus. I have to work quickly, if I'm in this heady scent much longer, I'll keep him here overnight just so I can sleep in it. After turning the ring over for a few seconds, I realize there's no locking mechanism. It's kept in place simply by the weight of his cock laying over his balls. I lifted his mass up and I sling the wicked metal away, never to touch my man's skin again. "Good boys get rewards," I say as I straighten up and pull him in for a kiss.

My lips crash into his like waves crashing over unmovable boulders. His hands wrap around me faster than a python, pulling me into him as if he wants our bodies to merge into one; I sure as hell do. One of his hands slide up to the back of my head and holds me in place as a fierce passion takes hold of him. His tongue slashes through my lips to find its way into my joyous mouth.

His cock jumps in my hand. What was plump and soft a heartbeat ago, turns harder than a baseball bat, and nearly just as big since my fingers don't even touch when wrapped around it. I have him in my hand with my thumb pointed to his base at first, but once he comes to stand at attention, I switch my grip in order to stroke him.

His other hand runs from my back down my hip and under the slit of my dress. *God, his arms are long!* He grabs my bare ass and lifts me off the floor. A thrilled squeal is stifled in my throat since I'm not about to let go of our lip lock. My legs instinctively wrap around his massive waist, pressing his cock between us. A low moan rumbles in his throat like a distant thunderstorm as I continue to stroke him mid-kiss. A moment later and I'm on my back, the soft cushions of the couch supporting me. His fingers grip my hair and thigh, desperate and needy. His thick cock spreads over my mound and I open for him.

This is it. I'm going to fuck his brains out, or, more likely, he's going to fuck mine out. I never thought I'd lose my virginity on the couch in the den. I've always pictured it in my bed or some fantasy bed somewhere out there in the world.

Something my mother said crawls around in the back of my mind; some promise I made her. I can't recall what it was exactly. All I can think of is how my body opens for this man, so desperate for his sex. *Oh, wait, that was it. Wasn't it?* I'm *not* supposed to have sex. Some important reason that she couldn't explain. *But this man on top of me,* I moan in my mind. *I need him inside me!* My body screams for him, but she'd been more serious about that promise than I've ever seen from her. *But Jack's cock is so hard for me. He's like a wild animal.* His need for me pours over my skin. My hands grip his exposed chest. *When did I unbutton his shirt?* His body scares me for a moment. Even with his tight-fitting suits and vests, seeing how beefy he is without his shirt on is a surprise. He looks like a fucking brick wall, wide and impossibly heavy. His heart slams against my hands through his body behind what feels like ten-thousand pounds of muscle. *God, why am I so turned on by his muscles?* Just last year, I would have laughed at the idea of wanting a muscled meathead plowing me. Have the weeks sitting next to him day after day conditioned me? Will I ever want that slim skater or rock star body ever again? Running my hands along his densely muscled frame, I'm certain nothing less will do. Not after I let this man completely wreck me.

'Please, do not have sex,' my mother's words echo in my head. *Fuck!*

It feels like ripping my heart out, but I pull my lips from his and breath, "Down boy."

In a flash, he's on his feet pacing back and forth, gasping for air, clapping his cheeks and grunting. He starts to button his shirt and pull his pants up, but I'm not quite done with him for the night.

"No. Come here." I sit up and fix my hair. I point to the

floor in front of me and he stands there, his cock towering over me. I'd fucking kill for a tape measure, but just eyeballing it, I put him at a foot. Part of me scream in abject horror, but a deeper part of me feels like cackling like a Disney villain. I grip him, causing him to groan like a bear. It's as hard as bone and thicker than my fucking forearm. I kiss the underside of his manhood and lick my lips, savoring the spice and citrus. *Does he spray his dick with his cologne? This can't be his natural taste.* I stand and pull the little condom off.

"Do you have any more of these?"

"Not on me," he answers in a low rumble, his head tilts back, his eyes still closed and his breath still ragged.

"Good boys get rewards."

His head snaps down to look at me.

I pour the precum into my mouth, relishing in its sweet flavor as it rolls over my tongue. *How does it taste so fucking good?* Les's cum tasted like salty trash water. How is it that Jack's cum is like squeezing a damn orange?

Liquid streams over my hand as I stroke his cockhead. He spills a large amount of precum, and my chest burns with a need for more. I stretch to kiss the tip and use my tongue to lap up his tasty pre. On my last kiss I suck, pulling more into my mouth. He jerks and covers his face with his hands.

"*Ohh*, fuck," he breathes.

"You've been a very good boy." I gently caress him, letting my fingernails scrape just a touch. This is it, my moment of triumph. A rush of the erotic adrenaline lances through my spine with a pulse that makes me want more. "Now, I need you to go soft."

"What?" he shouts. He covers his mouth in shock, and then whispers, "What?"

"I want you to get soft now," I repeat, as if I'm telling him the most obvious of facts.

He glares at me like I've asked him to eat his dog. "I...can't. It doesn't *work* like that for me. I won't get soft till I come. Maybe not even then. Abigale, you—" A low growl escapes his throat as my hand slides to his hefty balls, giving him a light squeeze.

"You can, and you will, for me," I say as I stand. I wrap one arm around his densely muscled back as my other hand rubs his expansive chest. Seeing him torn between doing the impossible and telling me no sends another rush through me.

He stutters for a moment and then says, "I can't just... Especially with you next to me. Just the smell of you makes me so hard." He ends in a groaning growl. His hand grips my butt in a tight squeeze that nearly lifts me off my feet. His manhood bounces in its rigidity, a mean-looking vein throbs at me to help make his point.

"No touching," I say calmly. His hand comes off me in the blink of an eye. "You're going to get soft. I say when you get hard from now on." He starts to protest but I *shush* him. "You're going to do as I say. It's new and different, and I'll understand if you slip up a time or two in the beginning, but from now on, you get hard when I say and you'll be soft when I say." I pull his chin with a single finger to look at me. "I want you soft."

His hands go to his head and pushes his hair back over and over. His breathing becomes large deep, full-lunged breaths and hard, fast exhales.

I continue to rub his chest and whisper, "That's good. Get soft for me."

After a couple of minutes, his mass begins to lower. As it goes down, I step in front of him and lightly hold his falling head. When the soft skin of his head taps my palm, blood surges through large veins but I admonish him.

"No. I want it soft. Do as I say, Jack."

His cock stalls, which makes the strange adrenaline in me grow, this time spreading out over me rather than a shot through my spine. A few seconds later and his cock starts its descent. When it's fully limp, it feels like my stuffed animal snake, Jasper. Maybe a couple extra pounds though. I reach up to my hair and pull out the black ribbon, letting my hair fall around my shoulders. His cock begins to climb but he squeezes his eyes closed and continues to breathe deeply.

"Oh? Does that excite you?" I lean against him and the skin of our chests touch. "When I let my hair down?" I whisper into his neck as I stand on my toes to reach. I place my hands on the sides of his abs to steady myself, but also to feel the strength of his tank of a body. "Does that get you *hard*, Jack?"

"Soft," he whispers so low I almost don't hear him even though my lips are only an inch away from his. "I'm soft. I'm soft."

"That's right," I say in a much sterner tone than intended.

My lips curl in a light snarl as I struggle with the urge to bite him. That erotic adrenaline wells up inside of me, filling me to the brim with confidence and supremacy, and I'm suddenly able to put a name to that euphoric feeling.

Power.

All this time, it's grown in me when I've exerted my dominance over him or made him work for my touch. It pulses through me till it forms words on my tongue. "You're soft, unless I say so. Your cock belongs to me now."

"Fuck," he whimpers as his muscles tense.

I back off to find that his cock has jumped to near full mast, but he's quickly getting it under control. I take advantage of the raising to slip my ribbon around his mass. As he continues to lower, I wrap it in a crisscross starting just under the head and tying a bow at the base of his shaft.

"Now, if you get hard, you'll break my *favorite* ribbon, Jack. So, you will not get hard, and you will not untie this."

His eyes open and his brow knit, as if he's looking at a venomous snake, but his breathing exercise continues. "I take showers at school; guys see my junk sometimes."

"Then they'll know your big, fat cock belongs to me." I lean in and brush the skin of his neck with my lips.

His jaw clenches, and he closes his eyes. He murmurs something I imagine is 'soft,' but it's too low for me to hear.

"Good boy." I smile and caress his jaw. "You can still use your little pink condoms," I giggle while reapplying the one I'd removed. It just looks so silly on his meaty cock. "But do not take the bow off. Am I understood?"

"Yes." He growls.

"Swear it," I command, knowing full well he will anyway. I'm just having fun making a near three-hundred-pound bull bend to my will.

He looks down at me with those serious eyes that play no games. "I promise, I'll keep it on."

"Good. I trust your promises, Jack. I trust you to do what you say, and I trust you to tell me the truth. You've earned that. My trust is not something I give lightly." I pull him in hard and kiss him deeply. Three rough flicks of my tongue in his mouth and I push him back. "Get dressed, except your jacket. We're going back to what we were doing before we were thrown off track. I want my foot rubs."

He chuckles a bit before he pulls his pants up.

I'm a touch sad to see his cock go but it's for the best, and seeing it go with my ribbon wrapped around it nearly has me squealing in delight.

He buttons his shirt and tucks it in, then put his vest on before sitting down. He draws one more deep breath and pushes his hair back before grabbing my legs and putting my feet on his lap. He looks at me for a moment but then closes his eyes again as he takes a few deep breaths. "How do you do this?" His honey-brown eyes open, alight with a deep hunger. "You just look at me and I want to give you the world. Do I make you feel like that at all?"

I bite my bottom lip as I stare into those delicious eyes. "Not exactly," I admit as he rubs my foot. My other foot sneaks under his waistcoat and rubs his wide abs. "I want you to be my big strong man. I want you to stand tall and walk with purpose. But I want to give you that purpose. I want you to think of me and accomplish everything you set out to do. But I want to be the one to tell you what to do, and I want you to do exactly what I tell you to do."

"*Mmmm*, so you're a control freak." He nods with a smile.

"But you like it, don't you?" It's less of a question and more of a statement, I know he likes it. God, he might even love it.

"Yeah." His eyes softens as he gazes at me. "I can't get enough of you."

"Too much of a good thing can be bad. After this foot massage our night ends, okay?"

His devious smile returns. "Well, I'd better slow down then." He rubs my foot with godlike precision, my back arching in immaculate pleasure at times. "This might be absolutely redundant, but you turned me down yesterday saying that you would have to see how things went. Did I pass your test?"

"With flying colors," I say, nearly moaning. "How are you so good at massages?"

"It takes too strong of hands." He grips my foot hard enough it begins to hurt. "That way you can dial it back to where it doesn't hurt. That's the magic spot." His grip softens and he presses his thumb into my arch.

This time I do moan, *loudly*.

"Yeah, give it to her, Jack," Deanna calls from upstairs.

"It's a fucking foot massage, bitch!" *God, where the fuck were you when I really needed you?*

After a moment, Jack smiles and kisses the top of my foot. "I think I should be going."

"Not yet." I pull my other foot out from under his waistcoat. "I told you, the night ends after I get my foot rubs, plural. I also said that you would tell me what your job is before the night was over."

"Right." He nods slowly; trepidation written on the hard lines of his face. He picks up my foot and rubs. "So, what I said before is true. Most of my net worth comes from stocks. Though, that money is mostly tied up. My play money comes from writing books. I started when I was young, so I had to use a pen name. My agent thought it would help my books be taken more seriously."

An author? That would explain how he could be a T.A. for college.

"What kinds of books?" My mind swims in the relaxing massage.

"A little bit of everything."

"Have I read your books?"

"Oh, yeah." He smiles and his hands continue to rub ecstasy into my foot. "I have two middle names. Thomas Remy. Jack Thomas Remy Billard."

My heart stops when I realize what he's saying.

"B.R.T. Jackson," he says putting my thoughts into words.

Chapter Thirteen

"Okay, that's some next-level shit," Deanna admits while laughing.

I've just gone over my night with Jack, including the ribbon wrapping. We sit at the top of my bed, leaning against the thick wood headboard eating popcorn that Deanna insisted on. Wrapped in towels, I haven't even been able to change into PJs yet since Deanna wasn't keen on waiting to hear of my exploits.

"What? You or Mom never bound a multi-millionaire, foot-long cock on your first date without even a full blowjob?"

"Wow! Okay, bitch. I hope his dick breaks you in half." She throws some of her popcorn at me as she laughs. "I can't wait to see Mom's reaction. She'll probably cry from pure pride."

"Speaking of Mom, she told you to watch out for me. Where the fuck were you? I was this close to fucking him." I hold my fingers a millimeter apart.

"Up in my room, hoping you'd get laid."

"I thought you wanted to be my cockblocker."

"Nah. I said that shit for Mom. You need to get some dick, and you were about to get a lot of it before you let Mom get in your head."

"It just, she seemed so crazy serious about it. What does it matter? She wants to have some talk, but what? We're all into kinky domination shit or something?"

"As much as I'd like to, I can't give you the talk. Letting you fuck is one thing, giving you the talk…Mom would flay my ass, but I can give you some kinky domination shit." Her eyes light with excitement before she hops off the bed and goes to her room down the hall.

I take the opportunity to change from my practically dry towels. I slip into my pajama shirt as she comes back holding spiked heel, thigh-high boots and a corset with coattails that looks like something one of Dracula's whores might wear. The black pleather with a white inlay coaxes that feeling of power awake.

"And you have the same in red."

"Yeah, but maybe you should have the red. You make me look like an innocent little dove by comparison."

"You peg Curtis," I remind her. "And you trap his cock in a tiny little cage."

"You wrapped yours in a bow, it's the same thing. Give it a few years and you'll have him bent over the railing, plowing his ass with a dildo." She punctuates her words with several lewd thrusts.

"*Ew!* Can you not be gross? I would never do that."

"Never say never." She hesitates for a moment and then curses under her breath. "Listen, I *am* going to give you some of the talk now because you need to hear it. Who fucking knows when Mom's going to come back to actually tell you? It's power, Abby. You said you felt it when you were controlling him, and that's what it's all about. You have a powerful man, physically, financially, and I bet you a million dollars, he's willing to lay on a wire for you. That power is what moves us. It's our perfect drug, and the more powerful the man, the better the high."

She stands behind me and raises the corset in my hands to my chest. Looking into my mirror, I can imagine myself in it and power blooms inside me. *Oh, Jack. I can't wait to show you this.*

"Maybe you do deserve the white. I look forward to seeing Jack kneeling at your feet while you're in it."

She gives me a hug and says good night as I stare into the

mirror. I can practically see Jack kissing my feet while wearing it. She's right. It's a drug, and I want more.

I run through the dark halls of Mercyhurst, only the emergency exit lights with their dim red glow light my way. I stop in front of the study lounge, not sure of what I'm going to find. When I open the door, Aub sits at our table with Jack leaning over her, the two laughing about something. When Jack's eyes turn to me, he walks over.

"I was wondering when you'd get here." He smiles and takes my hand to lead me back into the brightly lit hallway.

Wasn't it just dark?

The thought is quickly dismissed as Jack grabs me, one hand on my ass, the other on one of my exposed breasts. His lips clamp down around my nipple and the moan that escapes my throat rings through the hallway.

The seductive tendrils of power seep through me, pushing aside my pleasure of being manhandled by him. Those whispers of dominance tell me to be displeased and that Jack needs to be punished.

"Jack." I moan. The power wants me to tell him to stop, to get on his knees and worship me, but the whirlwind of pleasure he pumps into me won't let me say another word.

His lips slide from my breast, down my naked body till he's on his knees, kissing my hips and then my belly, just above where I really want him. Those lips move down till they find their home on my clit. His tongue flicks my little nub that has never been so energized before in my life. His powerful hands grab my cheeks as my hands play in his hair, stroking him for encouragement.

He throws one of my legs over his shoulder as he takes his oral gift to the next level. I moan loud enough that the entire campus must have heard. A moment later and the doors to the classrooms all open in unison as students and teachers pour out into the hall. They move like robots, in a perfectly organized fashion to surround us.

For a moment, panic tries to take hold of me. My mind screams to run but my body isn't about to follow that idiotic command. *Let them watch. Let them see the real me, and the real Jack.*

Jack continues to serve, as my eyes dart from one face to the next. The Power coils in my chest, like a hot snake laying in the den of my heart, ready to lash out and take over me. Each face I recognize adds to the serpent, growing it from something as small as a garden snake to the point it threatens to burst out of my chest as a python. When my eyes land on Aub, my legs start to shake with the impending orgasm.

I jolt up in my bed. My breath hard and ragged, and my legs are slick with more than just the sweat that covers my body. I slap the mattress, more than a little pissed I missed the climax.

The next morning, I pick up Aubrey for a little shopping before we study the rest of the day. Texting her the details of last night was too much work so I left her in suspense till she hops into my car.

"Okay, bitch, then what?" she asks as she drops into the passenger seat.

"You mean what happened after I told him to show me the cock ring?" I tease. I put the car into drive and we're on our way.

"I swear to god, Abby. I will yank that wheel and kill us both." She laughs. She pulls out her phone and clicks away on her dial pad.

"Who are you texting?"

"Abby! Do not fucking change the subject," she shouts. "I'm texting Derrick to see if he's at work. Now spill!"

I go over the rest of the night in *great* detail.

"I knew he was fucking perverted! I just knew it." Lust coats her words thicker than molasses, but sure, *Jack* is the pervert. "He likes getting dommed. That's his dark secret."

"You think that's it?" I keep a straight face since there's one last thing I haven't hit her with just yet. Jack emailed me a picture of his contract last night to prove he really is B.R.T Jackson. With all the shit he's written, being a bottom might be the least of his fetishes. "Being submissive isn't that big of a deal."

"You said it yourself, he's a good little Christian boy. That would be super dark in their circle."

I shrugged. "I guess, but it might be worse. Remember how I told him he would tell me how he makes all his money?"

"Oh, shit! I totally forgot! What was it? Is it drugs? Guns? Is he a fucking pimp?" She leans over the center console at me as we pull into the mall.

I laugh at the thought of him being a pimp. He kind of fits the bill with his twenty's mobster look. "Help me find a place to park first. If I tell you while we're moving, we're going to get in a wreck." When we park, I meet her eyes, not wanting to miss the moment realization hits her. "You are going to shit yourself. He told me that he is a fucking published writer."

"What?" Aub shouts. She thinks for a moment and then shrugs. "I guess he could do it. He's an English T.A. That's not that big of a deal. I mean, you know, good for him and all, but like, I'm not shitting myself."

"Think about this. He could have bought the Cadillac outright, he only put it on credit to help his score. If he has that much play money, then the books he's written must have done well. Number-One-Best-Seller well. Since he was underage, his publisher told him to use a pen name so that his work would be taken more seriously."

Aub's eyes widen, and she asks the same thing I did. "Have I read him?"

I nod and give her the same clue Jack gave me. "His middle names are Thomas Remy. Jack Thomas Remy Billard."

It's delicious watching the gears turn in her mind as her jaw drops. "No," she whispers.

"B.R.T. Jackson." I pull out my phone and open the picture Jack sent me. "You can't see it very well, but that's his contract with his publisher. It's him."

She sits there looking at my phone for a minute as her breathing becomes heavier and heavier. She hands the phone back. "Can you step out of the car for a minute?" She keeps her face down but I can hear the tears in her voice.

Shit. Aside from being shocked, I hadn't thought about how she would take it. I completely blanked on the fact she's in love with B.R.T Jackson.

"Aub, I didn't—"

"Please?" She raises her voice just shy of shouting at me. "Just give me a second alone, please, Abby."

"Yeah, o-okay." I pull my purse from the back seat in a rush and step out into the parking garage.

I shut my door just as an older couple walks by. They both smile as the man nods and the woman gives a little wave that I mirror.

Aubrey lets out a throat ripper of a scream.

The couple nearly falls over as I jump back, hitting the truck behind me.

"Is she all right?" the old man asks.

"Boys." I try to smile through the panic that courses in my veins. "College drama, you know."

The older woman, her brown knit in shocked worry, nods and pulls her husband along.

Aub steps out of the car, her red face with tears streaming down her cheeks.

I freeze as she stomps over to me. Something inside me says I deserve whatever she's going to do.

Jack is a dream catch that we've both crushed on a little, but B.R.T. Jackson posters make up half of her fucking bedroom. Everything from book covers to character art, she even has someone's rendition of what they think B.R.T. Jackson looks like by smashing all his lead male characters together. It looks nothing like Jack, but still, she's in love with the man's writing. *Just like he was in love with mine.* The sad thought crosses my mind and I calmly exhale, ready to take the punch, kick or slap heading straight for me. *Let her get her frustrations out now so the healing can start; hopefully.*

She wraps her arms around me in a crushing hug. "I love you, Abby."

"You—You aren't mad?" I let my arms slowly drift to her.

"Of course, I'm mad." She chokes out a laugh. "If he's really B.R.T., then I can't fantasize about finding him one day and marrying him. My fucking dream is dead." She pulls back and looks at me as she wipes her face. "But I'm glad it's you. If I didn't get the golden ticket, I'd want it to be you."

I snatch her back into a hug that I pour all the love I can into it. I can't say if I would be that good of a friend. I hope that I would if the situation was reversed.

"I love you, Aub. I don't deserve you," I say, holding back tears.

"If you don't fuck him, can I?" she pouts.

We both laugh through the lumps in our throats before we take a few minutes to let the emotions die down.

Once we're on our way to the front doors, Aub gasps, "Do you think you're Zarinna?"

"If I'm Zarinna, that would make you Tasha."

"No, Tasha fucking sucks! Do you really think he's using us as characters?"

"I don't think so," I admit. Thinking of myself as Zarinna from the Darkness Falls series is kind of hot, having a guy write his sexual fantasies about you and then publishing them to the world, but it's ultimately flawed. "He started the series two years ago. He wasn't into me yet."

"Maybe he saw you in the halls one day and was like, 'It would be sweet if she were a fucking vampire!'" We both laugh as we go through the front door. "Oh, could we stop by Zweets?"

"So, Derrick *is* working today?" I tease.

"Yes." She smiles. "He said he would give me a deal on earrings if I came to see him. I don't know if they have anything I'll like but it's worth checking if I get to flirt the whole time."

We make a quick stop at the bathroom to make sure we don't look like we've just been crying. A few touch-ups and we're back on track to Zweets.

Zweets is a skater shop with an edgier vibe than Wheelz and their lazy California theme. Panic! at the Disco blares over the speakers as if they're trying to supply the whole mall with music. The dimmed lights make the dark clothes look even darker, and the back wall is covered in skateboards with dark designs: demons, skulls, blood, and of course, a few naked women. Can't call yourself edgy if you aren't showing tits.

Derrick's blond hair frosted with light blue tips drifts over the tall clothing racks. It's good he's tall, otherwise we'd be running through a maze trying to find him. He sports a full chin strap beard, but I doubt he could grow much more than that. While he's cute in his baggy shirt and tight skater jeans, his attractiveness never fully relied on his looks. If it wasn't for his dad being in jail, he'd be in med school rather than working a job to help his mom. Aub could do much worse.

When we come around one of the clothes racks, Derrick smiles, pulling his lip ring up. His blue eyes aren't overly special, not that super light ice blue and not Aub's dark blue of the deep ocean, but they still light up seeing her. He pushes his thick mohawk to the side, so it's out of his face. "Hey, Aubrey! Good to see you. You two come to make my day a little less boring?"

Aub gives an enticing smile. "I thought you could use some intelligent conversation after your last text."

Derrick scoffs and looks over his shoulder. "New guy is like, super depressing," he says in a hushed tone. "His girlfriend dumped him and she's with someone else now. It's like, that sucks and all, but bro, I don't know you, I don't know your girl, sounds like it was for the best, let's move on."

"*Ugh*, that sucks," Aub says as she turns to sift through a shirt rack, pushing her ass out for Derrick. Years of practice let her do it without being obvious. Unfortunately for Derrick, he hasn't perfected hiding his gaze. "Eyes are up here," Aub playfully admonishes, even though, she bounces on her toes, giving her butt a jaw dropping jiggle.

Derrick rolls his eyes and sighs. "That was a dirty trick."

"What can I say? I play dirty."

I decide to quietly slink away to let her work her ass magic on him. She'd worked Derrick over pretty good last year, so she doesn't need backup anymore. I can shop a little in this store. I've found a few hidden gems in the past, but I'm not holding out any hope. After several minutes and only finding a few shirts that I would rather see stretched across Jack's body than my own, Les walks out from one of the racks and stops like a deer in the headlights when he sees me.

His dyed black hair droops to his shoulders, but it's not the vibrant bouncing hair he had last time I saw him. It's slick with grease as if he hasn't showered in days. His light blue eyes that I'd found so pretty against his black hair appears sunken and sickly. His gaunt face is riddled with acne, and unless he's decided to wear bigger clothes, he's lost weight over the summer break.

"Abby." He drops the bundle of clothes in his arms. "You're here. I-I was just talking about you and now you're here."

The name tag clipped to the sleeve of his arm catches my eye. *Holy shit. He's the boring new guy. What the fuck happened to him?*

He steps forward but when his foot hits the clothes he dropped, he stops and picks them up. "Shit, I'm sorry. I don't know what that was about." His brow knits in confusion as if he just woke from a dream. "Hey, um, could we talk?"

If there's a god, she has a morbid, if not direct, sense of humor as the new Fall Out Boy hit *Thnks fr th Mmrs* blares directly overhead. *How fucking poetic.* Yet, it's so loud, I'm not sure if I heard him right. *Did he really ask to talk? Did this fucker ask me to talk to him?* Fire explodes through my chest, and I desperately wish Jack was here so I could sic him on this little shit.

"Yeah, I don't think that's a good idea." I take a step back, stopping myself from jumping him and choking him to death. "Last time we talked, you said I was a slutty tease, and I quote, 'I wish you were dead.' So, that's pretty much a no."

"That's what I want to talk about. I'm really sorry for all that." He sighs in frustration. "I'd like to sit down if you're willing. I have lunch in an hour if you're still here. I just, losing you made me see just how wrong I was. I'm better for it now, and I'm not going to ask to get back together. I know you're with that…guy." His jaw twists as his upper lip curls into a snarl. "I just want to properly apologize."

He doesn't deserve the satisfaction. He doesn't even deserve my verbal lashing. He deserves nothing from me. "No." I take another step back. "I'm leaving." Let it eat him alive.

I turn and he calls out to me, but it doesn't sound like he's following me. I zig-zag through the clothing racks just in case he decides to catch up with me. I need out. I can't be in the same room as him, even if I can't see him.

I find Aub and Derrick at the front, looking at earrings.

"Yeah, sorry," Derrick says. "I really wanted you to come."

"Most of their earrings are for guys," Aub explains when I join them. "You find anything?"

Nothing I'm going to take home. Les' sickly image flashes through my mind. I smile so I won't dampen their mood even though I'm about to end it. "No. I'm hoping Kastle has something for me," I say, signaling to Aub that I want to leave.

"Yeah." Aub puts the pack of earrings down on the counter. "Thanks for the talk." She gives another sultry smile. "Be sure to text."

Derrick smiles and nods. "For sure. Look forward to it."

I glance over my shoulder for Les as we walk out, but I don't see him.

"Fucking Les was there!" I hiss while we put more distance between us and the skate shop. "*He's* the new guy." I tell her about the encounter and add, "He's got to be on heroin."

"Fuck! You think so?" Aub looks over her shoulder for the fifth time, even though we've reached the third floor. "That's fucked up."

"No, it's worse," I correct as we make it to the assumed safety of Kastle Boutique.

The shop used to be called Hot Topic, but it was bought out

by Kastle two years ago. Kastle caters a bit more toward women, making the store about eighty-percent women's clothes. *Love You to Death* by Type O Negative plays overhead, and maybe it's because Kastle has higher ceilings, the music isn't as oppressive as Zweets's. T-shirts fill the back wall with every death metal, heavy metal, goth, hard rock, and grunge band that existed since the mid-80s, but the side walls are a stark contrast with fun, fluffy gamer and anime merchandise.

"The fucked-up thing is that he knows I'm with Jack." My eyes quickly graze over the body piercing case as we make our way past the checkout counter.

"Oh, shit, yeah. What the fuck is up with that? He's not in college, right? Who would have told him?"

"That's what I was going to ask you." We move past the anime stuff on our way over to the shoe section. I like the height the heels gave me last night, but I want something that doesn't feel like a spear in my foot. My current boots are basically glammed-up combat boots. I want something with a little more sex in them.

"I mean, you hold hands almost every day in the lounge. Maybe someone told him since he's your ex."

I pick up a pair of boots I like. They have a thick four-inch heel to them and plenty of spikes for decoration. "Yeah, maybe," I sigh, unconvinced. As I roll the shoe over in my hands, my eyes lose focus on the dark leather. Something just doesn't seem right about all this.

After breaking up with Les he'd withdrawn from his friends. A couple of the guys I'm still friends with tried to get me to take him back just because he'd turned into an ass who stays home all the time. They don't know why I broke up with him, so I don't blame them for hoping we'll get back together. If he isn't talking to any of our former classmates, how the fuck does he know about

Jack? The cold, unsettling feeling whispers that not only am I not done with Les, but he's somehow connected to Jack. The thought of them being connected in any way makes my jaw clench and my fingers tighten on my new boots.

Chapter Fourteen

On Monday, Jack walks into study hall looking…rather upset. His brow furrows in a deep knot, the hand at his side balls into a fist and the other holds onto his backpack strap as if he's about to rip it in half.

"Hey, babe." I give him a kissy face and a wink.

He smiles at that, but his demeanor doesn't change. An energy comes off him and it takes me a moment to realize what it is. It's so thick that it lands on my tastebuds like electric bubbles. When I realize it's sexual frustration that radiates from every pore on his body, it tastes even better.

"Can we speak in the hall for a moment, please?" he asks.

"No." I smile as I look down at my textbook. "I'm a little behind on my work. Going on our date set me back. I'm sure you'll understand."

He nods and chuckles. "Can I talk to you here?"

I look over at Aub who's already looking at me with wide, eager eyes. Can she taste his frustration as well?

"Sure. Be as loud as you want."

Jack laughs. "That's good. So, um, I am in desperate need of your help."

"With what?" I let my chin rest on my hand as I lean over toward him, giving him big, innocent green eyes.

He scoffs and grins while his jaw clenches. "Well, see, now that's the part that I wanted to talk about in private, but…" He takes a deep breath. "Here it goes. You've both dropped some subtle and not-so-subtle hints that you think I might have some deep dark secret." His playful grin brakes through the strained surface as his eyes take hold of mine with that winner's confidence. "Something that would explain the money, the novels, the undefeated wrestling record, the taste."

I give my upper lip a long, purposeful lick.

Jack ducks his head as he laughs. "Fuck." It was incredible to see what depriving a man of coming would do. "Well, I'm just going to outright tell you my big flaw. And actually, let me just say, I never claimed to be perfect."

"You're a fucking boy scout," Aub said. "All boy scouts are perfect little angels."

"Well, boys grow into men, and there's no such thing as a perfect man. Jesus did it and no one is ever doing it again!" He drops his head again and growls another curse.

I bite my bottom lip, partially reveling in how hot I am and partially intrigued by how turned on I am seeing him like this. I lean into his ear to whisper, "What's wrong, baby?"

"These past two days, not seeing you, only speaking through texts… Staying soft has been nearly impossible. And now, being so close I can taste you in the air." His head raises till we're eye to eye, but the swirling honey fixates on my lips. "It's like breathing again."

Woah! Can't say I don't like hearing that. A little intense, but Jack is a bit over the top sometimes. I pull back to allow a fraction of extra space. "Don't get distracted. What's this big flaw, Jack?"

Jack blinks and his eyes raise to meet mine. "My flaw is that, and you might have noticed this the other night, I can get extremely worked up."

"Your big secret is you get horny?" A smile spreads across my face even as I try holding it in place.

"No, no." He laughs. "That would be ridiculous." Those serious eyes take over and I almost feel shackles clamp around me, holding me in place. "I get *very* worked up and I have to handle it. Every time." He looks around for a moment but then comes back to me. "I usually use pictures, sometimes books. I haven't gone more than a couple days in nearly two years. After how riled up I got at your house, the need is… Let's call it, extreme."

Power blossoms in my chest as another opportunity for control presents itself.

"Aww, my poor baby." I place my hand on his. "You know. If I was barefoot right now, I'd give you a foot job right under the table."

His eyes roll to the back of his head as his breathing becomes heavy. He quickly gains control, mumbling to himself.

"Unfortunately, I'm in brand new boots today." The succulent energy run through me, thumping along in my blood. "Aww, that's too bad. By the way, what did you expect in the hall? Were you thinking I might put it back in my mouth? Did you imagine my black lipstick running the length of your cock?" I lean forward and run my tongue along my lips. I point to the floor next to me and gently command. "Sit next to me with your book out."

He pulls his book out and throws it on the table, moves his chair over to me and opens his book to a random page. It isn't even right side up.

"Are you soft?"

"Yes."

My eyes slide to his crotch, but I resist the temptation to reach my hand out to check. "I trust you're not lying to me. I did tell you this would be difficult."

He speaks slowly, as if choosing the best words he can to plead with me. "Yes, but I don't think you were aware of the severity of the repercussions your rules were going to have. *I* didn't even realize."

"You're going to thank me for this. What you're feeling, this is withdrawal from your addiction. A sin of the flesh," I add while pouting my bottom lip. "It's probably going to get worse before it gets better, hun. But I promise you." I lean into him again, placing my hand on his soft cock. "I will break you of it. Remember, I say when you get hard. Not you, not your addiction." I back away, letting my hand slide his generous length. "Did you have any missteps this weekend?"

He closes his eyes and whispers 'soft' to himself for nearly a minute before he sighs. "No. I had to take an ice pack to my crotch to keep it that way. What's weird is that I had a dream about us." He focuses on his breathing again before continuing. "But when I woke up, I wasn't hard. It was only when I was thinking of the dream that I started to—" He lifts his head and looks around. "Well, I was able to get to that ice pack pretty quick, so, I saved it."

I smile at his admirable performance. "Good boys get rewards. But now that I know you have a problem; it will have to wait. We'll need to get you through this first."

He leans forward so that his lips hover next to my ear. "Why do I like this so much, Abigale? How do you make something so painful feel so good?"

My heart nearly jumps through my chest from the shot of pure power his words fire into me. I turn my head to face him. "It's your natural state, sweetgums." I tap my lips, inviting him to a taste.

He's fast to oblige. His kiss lasts a little longer than a peck, which is exactly what I want. He's good at reading my signals it seems. I push him away, and he reclines in his chair with an exasperated sigh

"You know, if he really is B.R.T.," Aub says with a wicked grin, "I bet he'd *love* to call you Mistress."

"You're *so* right." I smile. "You have your characters do it so often. Is that a little kink? You want to have a mistress?"

He smiles that confident smile he does so well. "I wouldn't mind, really. I mean, you are, aren't you?"

My toes and fingertips tingle hearing those words. It's like licking a battery.

"But if you'll recall," he continues, "in all three books there's been a reason. It was cultural for the vampires and positional for the pirates and Mistress O'Duella. The situations turn the title sexual, but it is just a title."

"Call me Mistress," I whisper as I lean over to him. "Just once. Use it in a sentence for me."

Jack smiles and then leans in as well. "I'd do anything for Mistress."

That glowing sensation of power lances through me, coursing through my glistening bud. "Oh, that's good. Maybe I'll have you do more of that later."

"What gets me," Aub says, as she eyes her copy of *Light in the Darkness*. "This series started two years ago, Ocean Breakers started four years ago. Making you seventeen, but you would have started writing them even earlier. How did you know about half of this shit? Like, most guys don't even know about a clitoris let alone how it works?"

"I was seventeen when I started them," he says with a shrug. "Once you've been writing for a while and you've done the process a few times, it gets faster. The internet has a great deal of information. It's important to do research on topics that are real. I just made shit up for my fantasy series because the rules were whatever I said they were, but a clitoris has some established rules."

Established rules, eh? It seems that he knows them very well. I hate the thought of any other woman having him first, but it's clear that's just a fact I'm going to have to live with. "How many girls have you been with?"

His smile drops and his jaw churns in consideration. "The answer to that question is attached to a much larger conversation that I would like to have alone. If you'll allow me that." The honey in his eyes swirl, begging me to give him this one thing. "It would be better after classes when we don't have any time constraints. It might spiral into a very long conversation, where the number of women I've been with would be a relatively small part."

I can't do much more than blink at that. That's not an answer I would have ever anticipated, most certainly not the answer I wanted to hear. "How could saying a number possibly spiral into multiple hours?"

"Because the number is misleading." He places his hand on mine. "This is one of those times I'm asking you to trust me. I can come over today if you'd like."

"All right." I agree with a tightness in my chest. I don't like that he's not answering me, but he has that damn sincere look on his face I just can't bring myself to say no to. "Come over right after class." I order, regaining some semblance of control.

The day moves in a blur.

Jessie heard from a friend of a friend that someone saw Jack showering with a black bow on his dick. I'm not one to brag but when he suggests Jack might have another girl, I tell the Psych group a little about our date and how I wrapped his dick with a ribbon. I leave out the parts about bending him to my will and the order to stay soft. To them, the ribbon is a token of our newfound love, which is all they or anyone else needs to know.

Jack keeps busy in Romanticism, grading papers, but he walks me and Aub to our Physics class. I rather enjoy the heads turning to see the dark brooding goth with the school's star athlete. It just feels like winning somehow.

In Forensics, Cinthia's missing, but Jack says she's having an episode of some sort.

Part of me doesn't like that she has his phone number to text him not to worry, but another part of me finds it very sweet that he looks out for her the way he does. I suppose that means I need to settle our little grudge when the opportunity presents itself.

Soon enough, we head home. Jack has to stop by his dad's house to feed his dogs, so that gives me a little time to prepare.

When Aub and I come in, Zest lays on the couch in the living room, watching a cartoon with the interest of a heavily medicated mental patient.

"Where's our sister?" I ask.

"She's in the kitchen," Zest says in a monotone voice.

In the kitchen, Deanna stands at the stove making an actual meal that requires cooking. Someone's in a good mood.

"What's wrong with Zest?" I ask as I put my backpack in one of the chairs.

"She's hitting that point where she realizes that life is pointless, that everyone and everything that has to live is suffering and that we'd all be better off dead."

I think back to my first dark thought. "I feel like I was ten when that happened."

"Nope, you were nine. I remember because it happened right before school photos and your fourth-grade picture is the first one you aren't smiling in. Same for me, same for Zest. She'll be full goth in fifth grade, right on schedule."

"Your family is so fucked up," Aub says. "It's like a mental illness."

Deanna smiles. "It spread to you, too. I remember you coming to our house for the first time, cute little jeans and pink

No Doubt t-shirt. One shopping trip later and you were all black with your very own eyeliner. Mental illness spreads, you know. We like to think of it as a superpower." She winks at Aub who rolls her eyes.

It's sad to see Zest lose her innocent smile, but it's inevitable. "I guess Zest won't be so zesty anymore. Look, I'm having Jack over in a few minutes. He has something he wants to tell me, it sounds important, so I'm going to do it with the door closed. I just wanted to give you a heads up, so you know we're not fucking."

"Oh, I'll know when you're fucking," she laughs. "When I hear you scream like you're getting ripped in half."

"Wow. Okay, jealous bitch. I'll see you later."

"I'll make him a plate," she says as Aub and I climb the kitchen stairs, but just as I reach for my room's doorknob, the doorbell rings and I'm down the front stairs in a flash.

I just barely manage to beat Zest to the door, and I shoo her off. I fix my hair with a couple strokes and fling the door wide open. My jaw nearly drops when I find Les standing there in his favorite shirt that's too big on him now.

What the fuck? "This is not okay, Les. I told you—"

"I know what you said, but I had to speak with you. I need to apologize." He falls to his knees and places his hands together as if he's praying up to God. "I'm sorry, Abby! I—"

I shut the door in his face and place my back against the hard wood. *What in the actual* fuck *is going on?*

Aub stands on the landing with her jaw hanging loose, while Deanna leans against the archway to the living room with a knowing smile on her face.

"Let him in," she says. "I'd like to see this."

"No! What? Are you kidding?" I shout.

I look for Zest but don't see her anywhere. Hopefully she's in the kitchen.

"Abby," my sister says as if I'm being ridiculous. "He's not going anywhere. You should let him in before the neighbors see him."

I look back through the thin window to the side of the double doors. He's still on his knees with his hands reaching out to the door.

"I'm not letting him in! I don't want Zest to see this. He's a fucking mess."

"I sent her to the kitchen. She's making sure the pasta doesn't stick." Deanna pushes off the wall. "Open the door and let the little puppy in."

She walks over to me, but I hold my ground. "I'm not letting this fucker in! He's a drug addict," I whisper.

She laughs. "Oh, he's an addict all right. Abby, move." She orders with finality.

I've never beaten Deanna in a fight, though we haven't tested that for a couple years. *Can I take her, now? Shit. Is this hill even worth dying on?* I decide it's not as I reluctantly move from the door.

She opens the door and points to the floor just on the inside. "Stay on your knees, Les. If you're as sorry as you say, you'll crawl."

Power surges as he crawls on all fours. It's not as strong a sensation as what forcing Jack to go soft provided, but now that I know what it was, even a touch is recognizable.

"Come on, Abby." Deanna steps behind me and pushes me forward by the shoulders. "Stand here and let him apologize." Once I'm in place, she steps to the side. "Well? Start apologizing, bitch! We don't have all day!"

"Yes," Les yelps as he ducks his head. "I'm sorry, Abby!"

"Don't call her Abby, you piece of shit," Deanna shouts. "You're not her friend!"

"I'm sorry, Abigale. I'm sorry!" His face smushes against the marble tile as he bows at my feet.

Power flutters in me, but it's offset by the disgust that's flooding my stomach. Seeing Les on his knees at my feet is hot. As much as I wish I could say it's not, I can't deny it, but the fact that he probably weighs less than me, his boney frame shaking in fear of Deanna, and his pathetic cries of apology, it's all too sad to enjoy what little power it gives me. Hearing him call me by my proper name is also a major turn-off. Jack has turned my name into something sexual. Everyone calls me Abby except Jack. Hearing Les call me Abigale taints that, and that's something I can't allow.

"Keep my name out of your mouth. You haven't even said what you're sorry for. You just sit there saying you're sorry, but that doesn't mean shit. You said you wished I was dead." Heat rushes through my chest, burning up my heart as I live through his tirade all over again. The worst day of my life, the deepest scar on my heart. "You degraded me. You took my trust and fucking tossed it in the trash! All because I wouldn't spread my legs? Because I wasn't ready? That made me a fucking slutty tease? Or, what was it you said?" I ask, knowing full well what he said. I've never forgotten his words, and I sure as hell won't forgive him for them. "Oh, yeah, a 'cock whore.' That's what you called me, Les. You called me a *fucking* cock whore!"

My fists shake at my side as I consider putting my boot through the back of his head while he cries on the floor in front of me.

How fucking dare he cry?

"I'm so fucking sorry, Ab—" He cuts himself off before saying my name.

His weak mewling makes me sick. My lips curl, and my teeth ground together as I restrain myself, my foot so close to lifting off the floor.

"Show us!" Deanna orders. "Lick her boot, you fucking shit!"

Before I can even ask what Deanna's thinking, Les pushes forward to lick my boots like a fucking viper lying in wait.

I jump back and shout at my sister. "I don't want him touching me, bitch! Get the fuck out of my house, you fucking prick!" I march to the door and pull it wide, more so to keep a couple feet between us so he can't try lunging at my boots again.

He gets one foot under himself, but Deanna shouts, "Crawl, worm!" She kicks him in his side. Not her hardest kick, but her years of soccer have made her kicks nasty no matter what.

Les grunted as he falls over, but he recovers and crawls.

"Do not come back, fucker! I mean it." Just as he's out the door, power flares in my chest, and I kick his ass with the heel of my boot. *Hope I fucking clipped his balls.*

I slam the door and look over at my sister. Half of me wants to beat the shit out of her, but the other half wants to hug the fuck out of her. "That felt really good."

"Let me guess. He got a taste, wanted more, and you said no."

"Wait, what?" Aub asks as she comes all the way down the stairs.

"You didn't mention it to either of us," Deanna says with a scandalous tone.

I grit my teeth as I tell them the whole story. "Everything I told you is true. I just didn't mention that..." I hesitate for a minute, not wanting to admit the worst mistake of my life. "Before I denied him, I let him put his hands down my pants. He was going for a few minutes, then stopped and tried to take my pants all the way off, and that's when I stopped it and he blew up, saying all that shit I told you about."

Aub lunges for the door, but I block her. "I'm going to rip his ass apart," she shouts.

I restrain her. "No. He's not worth it! That's why I didn't want anything to do with him. He's not fucking worth it."

Deanna looks out the window, her arms crossed under her breasts as her cool eyes follow Les outside. "Men. They don't deserve us." She sighs, letting her eyes slide closed before she turns and glares at Aub and me, freezing us in place. "Let that be a lesson to both of you. Men are dogs that need taming, and without us, they're nothing."

She stalks off in a power march, her hips swishing back and forth enough to make any man drool. I feel a bit like taking a good march around the house as well, subjugating a man like that has certainly given me a little power rush. Though, I imagine it would've been better if Les wasn't such a shit.

"What was that?" Aub asks, bringing me out of my thoughts.

"I don't know. He's out of his mind."

"Not with him." Her lips curling in disgust. "Fuck him. Never talking about that fucker again. I'm talking about you and Deanna," she says, concern thick in her words.

"What about us?"

"Your sister was, like—" She cranes her neck to look after Deanna, but my sister's nowhere in sight. "She was salivating. She was watching you like a fucking mad scientist watching her creation come to life."

I'd been so focused on Les, I didn't get much of a chance to see her reactions except when she gave him orders.

"It was like she knew what she was doing," Aub says. "But what was worse, is that she looked like she expected you to know, too."

"Fuck it." I give up for the moment as I head for the stairs. "Jack is going to be here any minute and I need to make sure my room looks good. We can worry about Deanna and her weird power trip shit later."

Chapter Fifteen

It doesn't take Jack long to show up. This time, Zest makes it to the door as I'm coming down the stairs.

"Are you Abby's boyfriend?" she asks.

"I am. I don't think I've had the pleasure of meeting you yet. You must be Zest." He crouches down, swapping who had the height advantage, though not by much.

"Yeah," she says in her new melancholic tone that still sounds strange coming from her.

"Yeah. Well, your sister told me about you. She talks about you all the time."

"Really?" Her voice perks.

"Really." Jack nods. "I can tell she loves you a great deal."

"You think so?"

"I do." His eyes find me on the stairs. "I think you should ask one of your sisters to come to the door. It's best to leave talking to strangers to an adult. We'll get to know each other better soon, but for now, one of your sisters should invite me in. That would be a good way to honor your mother and father."

"Deanna, Abby," she shouts.

"I'm here." I pretend that I've just reached the halfway landing when Zest turns around to see me. "Come inside, hun."

When I reach the door, I tousle Zest's hair as Jack comes inside.

Once Zest walks off, I ask, "Where would you like to talk?"

"Ideally?" He shrugs his shoulders and looks around from the den to the family room. "Anywhere is fine as long as you're sitting in my lap."

"Really? You want to tell me how many girls you've slept with while I'm sitting in your lap?"

He chuckles softly. "Well, not exactly, but it will make more sense once I start talking."

I take his hand and press myself against him. My boots do their job, giving me some extra height so the stretch to reach him isn't as severe. Our lips meet in a slick heat. My heart ticks a couple notches higher and I want to melt into the man. I reluctantly pull back but leave our lips brushing. "If I sit in your lap, you have to stay soft."

He nods in reply.

"Okay. My bedroom then."

We walk up the stairs hand in hand. When we get to my freshly cleaned room, I close the door behind us.

I look at my bed, my desk chair, and my vanity stool. Between the two seats, it should be the desk chair. It's sturdier, but then again, I'll be able to see myself in the vanity. I can watch as I toy with him, dominate him. That sends a thrill up my spine.

Before I can tell him, he sits on the edge of my bed and offers me his hand.

A wholly different type of thrill goes up, down, and spiraling around my spine. A man on my bed? *Yes, please.*

I take his hand and sit on one of his bulging thighs. I choose the right side to let me see the lump of his cock going down the left pant leg.

"When your tailor saw your bulge, what did he say?"

He laughs, his head tilting back. "He said…" He starts laughing again but regains control over himself. "He said, 'Son, you've got a mean growth.'"

We both laugh till I put my hand on it. My ear-to-ear smile stays but his turns into gritted teeth.

"So, you wanted to tell me something while I was in your lap?"

He nods and his hands wrap around me like a machine. The

hand that goes around my back pulls on my hip while his other hand slips over and around my knees, lifting my legs to lay over his.

I smack his chest to show him my displeasure at having my fun interrupted.

"I'm going to hold you here," he says softly, almost as if he's letting me know this is my last chance to back out. "Potentially against your will at one point or another, but I think by the end, you'll be glad I did. I know you and Aub tell each other everything, but what I'm about to tell you can easily be misunderstood. So, maybe hold off on telling her till you're sure you can explain it right, and I'd be happy to help if you want." His eyes hold a certain severity, and his voice is firm but an unease hides underneath. "I'd originally planned on only telling my *wife* this, but I think we both know there's not going to be another woman after you."

That's right, there won't! I smile and give him a little kiss to show him I'm playing along.

"The reason I have so much money, the reason I'm an excellent student, athlete, author, all of it, the reason I am who I am..." he breathes deep as his jaw quivers then sighs, "...is because I'm from the future."

His hands brace as if I'm about to run away.

I'm not about to leave my new favorite seat, but the words that came from his mouth make absolutely no sense. *Is he serious? What is he playing at?*

"I was originally born in 1990 and I lived till 2018. One night I went to sleep, and I woke up when I was three. My sister was there, still four years older than me like she was before. My parents were there, again, same age difference, but we weren't in the same house, and it was 1991. For some reason, that I don't have an answer for, while our age differences didn't change, the years we were born in all shifted two years earlier. As you might imagine, my parents freaked out when their three-year-old started telling them in perfect English that I was from the future. It took them a couple weeks to come around." He sighs again. "So, after I convinced my parents that I wasn't possessed or anything, I realized that I had loose knowledge of the future, so I took advantage of it. I told my dad to get on the dot com explosion that was a couple years out. I told him to invest in Apple and Amazon as well as a few others. Apple came out with the iPhone a little late. Amazon will likely take off a little late as well with smart phones being delayed."

"I don't even know what Amazon is." This is getting weird and part of me shouts to stop him, but his eyes are so serious, and my hand on his chest bounces as his heart hammers against it.

"It's an online shopping center. It's going to kill malls." He starts to explain but shakes his head. "That's not super relevant. So, I started writing my fantasy series when I was about seventeen, and by write, I mean daydream and jot notes. I always liked medieval fantasy, but it started as daydreams from playing games like World of Warcraft. I didn't fully finish my first book till I was twenty-four. I wrote five of the *Sun Maker's* before I woke up as a three-year-old, but I had deep outlines of the last three, so I knew where I was going. I started writing them again as soon as I was handed a paper and pencil. That's how I managed to write eight books by the time I was twelve, because I'd already written them." His hand rubs my leg for a moment before he asks with a wince, "Still with me?"

"I mean, you sound like a lunatic but, sure, you're from the future." I shrug. I don't really believe him, of course. Yet, a small fraction of me does. It's that underlying trepidation that convinces me. Something that say he knows what he's doing is dangerous and that he might actually lose me by telling me this, but he has to do it.

"Okay." His smile warms my heart, but it doesn't reach his eyes. Those soft eyes hold so much fear. "My parents were financially in a better place than before, and their parents were as well, so all that was putting me in a better starting point. I started martial arts as soon as we found a good place. As I grew, I was eating better and training better. Right when I hit puberty, I started taking supplements, that's why I'm so big."

"Like steroids?"

"No, no. Looking back on it, this was actually a bad idea on my part, I'll admit. I took estrogen blockers and testosterone boosters. Different amounts for different lengths of time. I knew it was a little risky, but I didn't expect the exact results I got."

"Testosterone?" I wonder aloud. "And that made you bigger? As in all over? That's why your dick is huge?"

He scoffs. "That was not my intention. I wanted to bulk up. It's very easy to grow muscle when you're young, when your body is in its natural growth period. So, I was not looking to make my dick any bigger. I was just under eight inches before. I was very happy with that, but of course, all guys really want just one more inch. Grass is always greener, type of thing. I ended up getting an extra five."

Five? "What are your exact measurements?"

He bites his bottom lip, but not like I do when I'm hot and bothered. His is closer to a grimace. "Twelve and a half by eight and a half."

"Good," I say with a sharp nod. *Good? What the fuck am I saying? Twelve literal fucking inches? Eight around? That will destroy—* Best not to dwell on it.

"Yeah," he says with a smirk. "Again, not what I was trying to do. It's just, there's a lot of hormones in our food that can mess with that, so I kind of overcompensated on that one." He shrugs with a grimace. "But besides the physical, I decided that rather than just getting a GED when I was five, I could actually take harder classes and learn new things. I was always a bad speller, and my handwriting was atrocious, so going back through school did help. I also wanted to learn survival skills, so I joined the Scouts. It was easy to do some of the things that others had trouble with, just because I wasn't shy about it. In my past life, before I became a full-time author, I sold credit card processors, the things you swipe your card through when you're checking out. So, when we had to talk to people or sell things, that wasn't hard for me, but my point is, each decision I made helped make my life so much better. I mean, just think about how radically different your life would be if you woke up at three and you could choose your path. You actually know what's available, you can plan better, you have more mental discipline. That's why I'm unnaturally successful, because I'm *not* natural."

"So, in your past life you weren't a wrestler? You didn't go to college?"

He frowns and shakes his head. "I was only five-nine, a hundred-forty pounds or so. I didn't do any sports throughout high school. I joined the Army at twenty, went up to one-seventy, one-eighty. I'm already two-eighty-five now, and I know a great deal more than I did before. I've taken some…let's say extremely advanced classes since I have the money for it. But I've also taken some gentler classes, massage being one of them." His arms pull me closer to him and his deep, honey-brown eyes soften to the point of desperation. "So, we're at the point where I answer your original question. How many women have I been with?"

I ready my hand to slap him across his gorgeous little face.

"And now you know why the number is misleading because we're talking about two different lives. In this life, I've only ever kissed one other girl, Vanessa Chavez. *Everything* else, you've been the first, and you'll be the last. In my previous life, I was with four women, and a few girls in high school as far as playing around goes, but real, serious relationships, with intercourse, I was with four."

Four. That seems like a lot. Though, it would explain how he's so good at kissing the right spots, so good at touching me oh so perfectly. Even if he's telling the truth and he'd been with them in a past life, four still feels like too many. Even with my hand at the ready, I decide not to smack him, at least not yet. I sit there for a moment thinking about his story. *Why is he telling me this lie? What point could it possibly serve?*

"You don't believe me," he says with a soft voice and sad eyes. "I don't blame you. It's crazy. There are crazy things in the world. Crazier than what I'm telling you, I'm sure. A girl once told me she was merged with an alien entity from another galaxy." He laughs. "I thought she was out of her fucking mind. I'm not going to ask you to trust me on this. I don't think that would be fair. What I am asking, is that you believe that *I* believe what I've said."

That's a bit easier to do. As I think about it more, the part about him writing his books actually start to make sense to me. How on earth could a kid write The Sun Maker's Chronicles? Those books are so complex and so deep. It's such an adult voice. Then there are his other books! There's an intimate knowledge of a woman in those books. Not just physically, but mentally and emotionally as well. And all of his books display the complex dynamics of serious relationships. He can't have written them so young.

"It's a big lie to tell me," I say with a warning edge to my words.

"I will never lie to you, Abigale."

His words feel like they can carve themselves into stone, but it's just all so hard to believe. Yet, things actually make more sense this way.

"So, what else?" I ask, trying to delay when my brain will have to truly process his words. "Your life is different. Is everyone else's?"

He nods. "Some things have been different. That's why I wanted this to be between us. I can't predict the future accurately. 9/11 still happened, but in my time, the follow up attack in Paris was just a train attack. The Eiffel Tower was still standing in 2018. Hurricane Evie was early. In my first life it was Hurricane Katrina. Movies, games, music; things as small as an album release date being late or early. Some movies never being made, some bands never forming, things like that. So, there are major world events that are different and there are smaller events. When I woke up as a child, I accepted that things were different, and that I wasn't going to have the same life I had before. I had to grieve everyone that I knew in my old life, but now I have a new life, and I want to share it with you."

He reaches up for a kiss, but I hold my chin up to deny him. He steals a kiss from my neck, and I admonish him with hard eyes. "Disobedience is punished," I warn. "We aren't done talking, yet. I have a few questions." A fucking million really. "Were you married?"

"I was." He nods solemnly. "Her name was Rebecca, she died in a car crash. She was hit by a drunk driver."

Holy shit! A dead wife? Would he really make something like that up?

"Did you have kids?"

"Thankfully, no. I would have felt much worse leaving kids behind. I've wondered sometimes what happened to me in that timeline. Did I die? Did I become comatose? Did a three-year-old version of me take my place?" His eyes start to well with tears, but he shakes his head. He gives a deep sigh before he continues. "I try not to dwell on it too much. There's nothing I can do about it."

"What about our age gap?"

"What age gap?"

"Jack, if you're being honest with me, you've lived an extra thirty years. That's pretty fucking sizable."

"So, you think I'm fifty? Should I pursue a fifty-year-old woman? Even if I went after a thirty-year-old, I'm not going to have much in common with them. Age is mostly what you grew up with that ties you to the others who grew up at the same time. It's weird, I get that. Twenty-eight plus twenty is forty-eight, sounds simple enough, but I'm not a fifty-year-old man in my head. I didn't experience my forties when I turned ten."

"Not many ten-year-olds are writing bestselling novels. That's something middle-aged men and women do."

"Touché. Yeah, I guess my career path is a bit advanced. Abigale, I don't have a perfect answer for everything. This shit is weird to me, too. All I know is, I don't feel like I'm that old." As if he senses my trepidation, his hands pour out a reassuring warmth, gently massaging my thigh. "Look. Everything I've said, to a certain point, it's meaningless and I don't mean that to belittle anything I said. What I mean is, our lives, they are what they are. What I experienced in my other life doesn't count in this one. The only reason you needed to know any of that was so that you can know me better. If you want to drop it and never talk about it again, that's fine. It's in the past. If you have questions, I'll answer them. Just, please, don't feel like it needs to define us."

That's good to hear, I guess. This is fucking crazy, and I probably shouldn't entertain any of this. Putting it behind us is probably best. This has to be his dark secret, right? Mental

illness? Some sort of delusion? But what kind of delusion? *Okay.*
One more question.

"So, how did you go back in time?"

"I have no idea. I put my head down on my pillow one night,
and then I woke up in my toddler body."

"And you've just left it at that? You haven't theorized or
investigated how it might be possible?"

"All things are possible for YHWH." He answers with a
shrug.

Yahovah?

"If something in our universe could produce the
transportation of consciousness from one time to another, I have
never heard of a theory that would explain that, and there are
some far out ideas that get more and more mainstream in the
coming years."

"I thought you just said Yahovah could do it." I smirk.

"He's not a part of the universe." He corrects with a smirk
of his own. "He resides outside of it. YHWH is the only answer
I have as to how, but I still don't know why, apart from you."

"Apart from me?"

"All the money and success in the world doesn't go with you
when you die, but those we love can."

"You think you were brought to an alternate dimension to
convert me to Christianity?" The suggestion is overtly ridiculous,
but he nods with a smile. "You think God would really send you
to another— Do you really think that?" Somehow that seems
crazier than him thinking he's from another timeline.

"Look. There is nothing that YHWH would stop at to get
His creations back. Yeshua's death on the cross proves that. But
really, I don't know why I was sent back. I started off thinking I
would correct past mistakes, and in some ways, I have, focusing
more on my education and my body, but I'm not reliving my old

life while avoiding all the errors I made the first time around. I'm living a new life, with new people." His gleeful smile turns sly. "Getting to know you has been the highlight of this life. Believe me when I say, nothing will get in my way, Abigale. I'm madly in love with you." His fingers dig into my body as he squeezes me against him. "And I couldn't be happier than when I'm with you."

"You don't love me." I smile as I caress his chin. He's being silly to say something like that so soon. I'll have him saying it honestly soon enough, but I don't like him using that word so flippantly.

His eyes become fierce, the honey turning to fire and defiance. His back straightens while he slides me down till he towers over me. His grip tightens again, but it's not the grip of need or lust, it's of control and dominance. His elbow at my legs pins my ankles against his side and the arm around my back curls behind my shoulder, pressing my upper body against him. "I told you I won't lie to you, and I told you the other night, I won't let you misconstrue my feelings. I was married before and engaged to another. I know what love is, Abigale," he says sternly. "I know the difference between infatuation and a lasting love. Do you really think I would give myself over to you so easily? Do you think I would throw everything I've made myself at your feet if I was just *hot* for you? Do you think that little of me?"

I push on his chest, but no new space emerges, a stark reminder that everything I do to him is only because he allows it. Being so easily dominated makes me feel small, and while that would have caused a fire in my chest to explode with righteous indignation, that fire in his eyes sucks all of mine out of me, leaving me at his mercy.

"I'm scared."

"You should be." The timber of his voice rumbles through me. "Love isn't a game. Love isn't something where you win or lose; love lives or dies, and when it dies, a part of you dies with it. I do love you, Abigale. If you're not ready to say it back, I understand. Everything is happening so fast, but I know what I'm about." His grip loosens slightly, enough that I'm not pinned to him, but not enough that I can escape. "You promised me that you would trust me, and you didn't trust me just then. How much more than all-of-me do I have to give before you believe me?"

He's right; I broke my promise. *Damn it.* Losing fucking sucks. *God! I don't fucking like this!* The need to control rattles around inside me like a caged animal, railing against its bonds. *What is going on with me?* Why do I have such a deep need to be in control? Men are always the ones in control, but I have the strength to be different, I have the power to dominate! *I wrapped his cock up like a birthday present. I made him deny his urges and be soft. He has no right to hold me! He belongs to me, not the other way around.*

I glare up at him with wild fury slamming through my veins, only to be crushed by the hope in his big brown eyes.

He wants nothing more from me than my trust. He's not trying to dominate me like I am him. He's trying to stop me from running from him, from us. I'm the one who's letting my lust get in the way. I've been turning him into a piece of meat.

What the fuck is wrong with me?

Tears well in my eyes. "I want to hug you," I whimper.

His vice like arms soften but at the same time pull me tighter into the most secure hug that's ever graced my body. His hands wrap so far around me that they touch my sides as he holds me firmly against his vast chest.

I lay my head on his shoulder and cry. I've been so bad to him. *'It's all about power,'* Deanna's words echo. Well, fuck that! I don't want to ruin my man just for my pleasure. I want a husband, a man that can stand up to the world on my behalf, not just some fuck toy. Jack is a fucking unicorn and I have been treating him like a damn mutt.

"I'm sorry," I eke out. "I believe you. I do."

As he gently rubs my back, my breathing eases, and it feels as though nothing can get past these massive arms to hurt me. I can't remember a time when I've felt safer, a time when I was more protected. Dad's never been one to make me feel safe, he's too nice and far too quiet. And Mom… Well, Mom makes me feel safe in the way hiding behind a steel wall makes me feel safe. This, what Jack gives, it's so much more complete.

"I'm so sorry for all this fucked up shit I've done to you. I don't know why you didn't run screaming. It's my mom and my sister, and now it's me. I just, I want to take it all back."

"No," Jack whispers. "I don't want you to take any of it back."

I push back, this time he allows the separation. I hold his face in my hand to search his eyes. "You really mean that?" I swallow the lump in my throat and wipe the tears from my face. "All this stuff I've done? I wrapped you up and made you stay soft. I got you so worked up and then told you no."

He smiles deviously. "I told you, you drive me wild. I never said I wasn't into it. Abigale, I want all of you. Don't hold any part of yourself back from me. I might change you over time and you'll change me, too, but that won't happen unless we give ourselves over to the other completely. I've been with strong women before, but you…" His lips grace my skin as he speaks, sliding across my neck and chest like a sizzling skillet, melting me like butter. "You take me to places I never could have imagined. I never knew I wanted this."

"Tell me what you want." I moan.

He lifts me up from his lap and lays me on the bed. A soft kiss just under my jaw curls my toes as my fingers dig into my sheets. His hand in my hair controls my head to expose my neck more and his other hand slides under my shirt to grab my corset. "I want to rip this from your body." A low growl from his throat ripples through me, making me squirm and squeal.

"Are you Azmir or Oliver?" I breathe, wondering if he's the vampire villain of his books or the alpha werewolf.

"Both," he answers before he bites my neck.

I jump and my hands grab his head. His teeth sink in, pressing my skin with a firm and powerful bite, but just like his powerful massage, he edges the line of pain and pleasure perfectly.

The hand on my corset moves down to my skirt and pulls it up so he can escalate the situation even further. His fingers brush by my thighs that open, eager to let him in. If he can repeat what he did the other night, I'll let him in whenever he wants.

"Dinner's ready," Deanna calls out from the kitchen, crushing my dreams in the process.

My hand snaps to his brick of a forearm just in case he doesn't know to stop, but he's already pulling back.

He breathes deep and measured for a moment. "I'm very horny, hungry. *Ha*! I meant…well, both, but I meant hungry."

He leans forward and I catch his lips with my own. His kiss is like drinking water after a run on a hot day, my body just can't get enough of him. My arms wrap around his neck, and he picks me up as he stands. I can't keep the smile from spreading.

"Good boys get rewards," I say, as he carries me out of the room.

Zest's green eyes snap to us as he's carrying me down the stairs. "Did you get hurt?"

"No," Jack answers. "I just like carrying her around."

"How can you even lift her? She's so big." She sticks her tongue out like a brat.

"You little shit," I shout, almost jumping out of Jack's arms.

He struggles for a second to keep me in his arms but then pulls me in. "I love your weight." He looks back to Zest as he continues down the steps and explains, "An adult woman, not some little child, but a real woman, has some weight to her. Real men only want real women." He jerks me to his chest again and I let out a yelp against my will.

Once we're off the stairs, he puts me on my feet, and I let my hand slip down his back to grab his ass.

Mine, I greedily think as I stare up at him.

I'm still not sure what to make of everything he told me. Maybe he just had some crazy-ass dream as a kid or something and it really changed him. The books are the missing piece; they make his story make sense. Time travel just isn't real. I'll have to get to the bottom of this. I'm not going to let him live in a delusion, not just for my sake, but more-so for his own. It isn't good for him. I'll straighten him out eventually, but there's no need to rush, there's plenty of time.

Chapter Sixteen

The next few days are hard on Jack. His obedience training is going very well, and I congratulate him multiple times for staying soft, though that doesn't make it any easier on him. He slips on a couple more occasions than I was originally going to allow, but I can see just how hard he's trying. I decide not to berate him too much for getting hard, but I'm still committed to breaking him of his addiction. I have to rewire his brain so that I am his outlet, not pornography, and by dictating when he can and can't get hard, his mind will soon come to the natural conclusion that if I'm in control of erections, I must also be in control of the subsequent release.

On Wednesday, he has a hard time keeping his hands off me, I let him get a taste between classes, which is where most of his slip up occurred, but otherwise I made sure he behaved himself. This morning he sent me a text.

Jack: I'm staying home today. I'm just going to write to keep my mind off you. I'm literally sitting in a tub of ice right now.

The week wasn't overly easy for me either. I've been using what I'd bought from Heavenly Toys at a frantic pace. Deanna said that I'll get used to size much quicker than what Sarina suggested. Apparently, Sarina gave time frames for normal women, but we aren't normal women. Whatever the fuck that means. But while Deanna encourages me to explore with my toys, she also told me point blank that I should just get it over with and fuck him. As much as I scoff and roll my eyes at her consistent taunting, a growing fear whispers I might not have a choice.

Jack reassures me on several occasions that our first time is completely in my hands, but that did little to assuage my fears since I can't get him out of my head. Wednesday night brought another scandalous dream where I had him on his knees, licking between my legs. I sadly woke far too soon, but I used that image of him while using the toys. But just like the first time, the toys bring me to mediocre climaxes. Had Jack not fallen into my lap, they'd actually be good or even great climaxes compared to what I'd known before, but after what Jack did to me, my body is determined to have the real thing.

When I came home on Thursday, Mom and Dad's luggage waits in the foyer.

"Your mother wants to speak with you," Dad says from the den, sitting on the couch that I nearly lost my virginity on.

Seeing him on it now feels wrong somehow, like he shouldn't be touching something that has such a personal connection to me. *God, what the fuck is wrong with me? It's his fucking couch, Mom doesn't even claim it, she hates it so much.*

He's turned toward me with is arm hanging over the back of the couch, looking at me with dark brown eyes behind his stylish glasses. His short, thin blond hair is light enough that the wind from the ceiling fan moves it. He smiles at me and nods. "She's in her office."

"Okay. Good to see you, Dad." I give him a wave and then head up the stairs.

Roaring laughter booms from Mom's office down the hallway, and when I reach the room, Mom sits behind her heavy oak desk with Deanna sitting on its edge.

"There's my girl." Mom squeals, jumping out of her chair. She hurries over to me, her heals clacking on the hardwood, and gives me a big hug. "Thank you for keeping your promise, hun. Now, it's time we have that talk." She shuts the double doors and locks them, then points to the couch. She dips behind her minibar to prepare drinks.

Mom's office is big enough to be a decent bedroom, though it has no closet. A large window makes up most of the wall that faces the cul-de-sac. She often joked about staring out over her domain since we live in the center house, giving her a perfectly even view of everyone else. The wall across from the doors is covered with cherrywood bookshelves and cabinets. Most of the books are self-help or inspirational, but there's a large set that's dedicated to her profession of fund management.

I glance at Deanna as I walk to the plush black couch on the wall across from the window. My sister has a knowing smile on her face, but apparently, she isn't willing to give me anything more than that.

Mom brings over three glasses of vodka and hands one to me and another to Deanna. "Don't drink this till you need it. I'm not pouring you another glass."

"Your first official drink," Deanna says with a salute of her glass before knocking it back.

"Actually, I had a couple martinis courtesy of the mayor at the Arts Theater."

Deanna sprays her drink and chokes. "Oh, damn it!"

"Well, well. Your sister didn't tell me that part." Mom hands Deanna a napkin. "You met the mayor?"

"Jack knows him because his son was a wrestler last year. Which, as an aside, I will be going to the first meet of the season tomorrow, so I'll be late coming home."

"A bunch of guys grabbing each other's buttholes?" Deanna laughs. "You're way kinkier than me."

Ignoring my sister, I ask, "So, what's up Mom? Locking the door, a glass of vodka. What's so important to warrant all this?"

"I understand your sister has let some things slip." Her eyes narrow on Deanna before she turns back to me with a bright smile I've rarely seen her wear. "So, let me clarify all of this. You come from an exceptional line of women, and any daughters you have will be the same. If you have sons and they have daughters the traits won't pass on, only *direct* female descendants. What I'm about to tell you will sound like the craziest thing you've ever heard, but hang in there with me and take a drink when you need it."

Crazier than my boyfriend being from the future? Yeah right!

"There was a man, our ancestor, named Ventonious Xurellious. He was a wealthy Roman Senator, but every wife he had died, so people began to think the gods had cursed him. Ventonious went to the temple and prayed to Venus because he wanted a beautiful wife. That night, a beautiful woman came to him. Her name was Augustia, and she demanded the payment he had offered up to Venus."

"Augustia? As in your last name?" I ask.

I've asked Mom in the past why she never took Dad's last name, but she never gave me a straight answer.

Mom's gaze flashes with heat for a moment but she rolls her eyes and frowns. "Yes. When I learned all of this, I had it legally changed. Now don't interrupt. So, she demanded payment. Ventonious had offered *anything* and so Augustia, being as clever as she was beautiful, chose *everything*. He willingly agreed, given how enticing she was. Any man in his right mind would be a fool to say no to her. So, he invited her into his home, and she broke him that very night."

'I will break you of this.' My own words crash through me like a bolt of lightning.

"Pouring out everything that made him who he was and filling him up with a deep need to please her every demand."

'You just look at me and I want to give you the world.' My heart crumples hearing Jack's echo in my mind.

"After she popped out a couple sons and daughters, she

moved to their country estate as to not attract so much attention. She started taking in more men, and she built a *Collection*. To passersby, she was the wife of a wealthy Roman with a collection of slaves who tended her lands and her needs. Ventonious' career soared with her controlling him. He was well known, and having so much land and so many slaves, no one questioned any of it, but if someone looked closer, they would have seen gladiators, centurions, senate members. She had them kissing the ground her shadow fell on."

The image of Deanna standing over Les flashes in my mind. *'Lick her boot, you fucking shit!'*

"She was always satisfied, and at the same time, it was never enough. Her gift, her curse. Her daughters had the same gifts and the same needs." Mom's deep green eyes burn a hole into me, as if branding me one of these women. "To take men and break them. To make them lick our heel and do as *we* command. We are her daughters, and we have the same abilities to wrap men up and make them beg for our orders."

"Any of that sound familiar?" Deanna asks.

I lift the glass to my lips but only rocks clatter. *When did I drink that?*

This is crazy, but my gut says it's true. This is how I'm able to control Jack. This is why he loves doing what I tell him to do.

"He said he loved me," I whimper.

"Oh, hun, he does." Mom places a hand on my shoulder, but it feels so distant I hardly register the gentle squeeze. "He does love you."

"Not if it's some bullshit spell or whatever this is!" A well of tears chokes my words. I put my glass on the table, worried I'm going to drop it. It *clanks* on the glass tabletop so loud I'm shocked they don't both shatter.

"Don't think of it that way, sweetheart." Mom scoots closer

and wraps her arm around me. "He does love you. He loves *everything* about you. There's nothing he wouldn't do for you. He'd jump right in front of a bus for you. Not to save your life, either. Just because you told him to. We *own* men, sweetheart."

'I own him.' My words to Cinthia punch me in the guts.

"You've found yourself quite the catch. I'll be honest, I, your mother, am quite jealous of you." She smiles and raises her eyebrows as though that should somehow make things better. "He's strong, smart enough to be in some of your classes, already has a career, and apparently has some connections. That's all very good, all *very* impressive for your first. Don't let your emotions get in the way of that. Every man after him will be the exact same. They'll love you because of what you are. I've told you from birth that you're special, and unlike all the other mothers in the world, I wasn't lying. Look at us." She laughs. "We are the ideal. Brains, beauty, drive, and we fuck like tigers. No man would say no even if we didn't have the Power in us, but the Power ensures it. You can own the world if you're smart enough."

"I don't want any man after him. I don't want the world. You don't own the world. I mean, you and Dad, you're executives or whatever," I say, trying to wrap my head around all of this.

"That's not at all what your father and I do." Her smile suggests I should have known that. "I don't manage wealthy executives' money. I manage the executives. Your father and I travel around the world so that I can keep my influence over them all. I don't have a field for my slaves to tend, so I have to make house calls."

"What do you mean, keep your influence over them?" I ask in horror. She called them her slaves. Who the fuck is this woman?

"This is part of the reason I didn't want you to have sex with this boy. Sex reduces your Power over *other* men. It increases your

Power over the one, but you'll lose your ability to have others, and many men don't need sex to control. A little kiss on the cheek, a foot job, hell, a kick in the balls will work for some."

"You keep talking about men, like you have more than just Dad. You mean these executives are…" I can't find the words. I don't *want* to find the words to finish that sentence.

"I do. I have twelve others. Once Zest is eighteen, I intend to bring them all together. I didn't want you to grow up confused."

Deanna pushes my hanging chin back up with a finger and I turn to her for help. "I never lost Micha." She admits. "I go see him once a month."

I stand up and walk past the coffee table, putting space between me and the two women I thought I knew. The deep breaths I take don't reach my lungs.

"Hun, sit down, you don't look well," Mom says.

"Maybe you should get her a refill, Mom," Deanna suggests.

Panic shoots through my body. My hand trembles as it weakly covers my gaping mouth. My life is a lie. What part of me doesn't this touch? "Do not fuck with me! Are we even full sisters? Is Dad my real dad?"

They both pause and then Mom heads for the minibar. "I think a refill might be a good idea."

Deanna reached out her arms, following me around the table. "Abby, you need to sit down. I went through the same thing. I'm your big sis. Zest is our little sis. We have to watch out for her, just like we always have."

I lurch toward Mom, my feet dragging, though I manage to keep out of Deanna's grasp. "Are there others? Do you have other kids?" I stumble into Mom's desk and grab onto the edges with weak fingers that fail to hold. Deanna's face blurs. "Please be my sister." The room spins and the floor rises to meet me.

When I open my eyes, I'm back on the couch. Mom fans me with one of her work folders and Deanna holds my hand, checking my pulse.

"There she is," Mom says. "It's going to be all right, sweetheart. We'll get you through this."

"Good thing I wasn't like this." Deanna scoffs.

Is this really my fucking life? Jack's from the future, and my mother's some kind of Roman domination goddess?

"Mom." I groan. "Are there others?"

"No." She shakes her head as she lets the folder fall to the coffee table. "They'd be here if there were. I wouldn't let any of my children grow up without me."

"And…Daddy?"

She bites her lip and then shakes her head. "He's not your biological father. He didn't give me any of you. But he *is* your father, and you *will* treat him like it. He put years of his life and his love into raising you. Don't diminish that just because you don't have the same DNA. Here." She hands me another glass of vodka.

I slosh it back as tears of rage and anguish burn my eyes. "And we're all half-sisters then?"

"No. The two of you have the same biological father, Zest is from another one of my men. Listen very carefully to this, Abigale. This is the most important part of this talk, and you need to know this above all else. You can only have sex with three men. After that, your Power over *new* men is gone completely and your Power over the existing men falters without constant check-ins. My first was a boy from high school right as I was learning about our Power, my second was your father, and my last was Zest's father."

"So, you've never had sex with Dad?"

"We have sex. We just don't use *his* penis," she says with a smile. "The curse is that we can only have sex with three, but the gift is that we gain sexual gratification from our Power over them."

Oh, fuck! That's why I'm so torn between dominating Jack and letting him have his way with me. The Power is just as good as sex, maybe even better.

I look over to Deanna. "That's why you peg Curtis? You don't want to have sex with him."

She nods. "I've used one so far. So, I'm going to build my harem before I choose another."

"Stop calling it that," Mom snaps. "We don't have harems, we have Collections."

I shake my head. This is the second bonkers-as-fuck story I've heard this week and I'm not sure which is worse. How am I going to make sense of all this?

Mom cuts my thoughts short. "Here's my advice. Don't dwell on all this. When you first had your period, I told you that you'd have to deal with it for the rest of your life till menopause, and you've done that so far. When you told me you wanted to pursue a career in law, I told you it was going to be a long and hard road, but you're doing it. I'm telling you that you have this wonderful gift, and you'll thrive with it. I'm not telling you what you have to do with it, I'm just telling you it's there. I love you so much, sweetheart." She gives me another hug. "You too, hun," she adds, and Deanna embraces me from the other side.

I let my head rest on my mother's shoulder and clutch my sister's hand to my heart as I wrestle with the fact that Jack doesn't love me. He only thinks he does.

Chapter Seventeen

Jack walks into the study lounge, and I'm glad to see him looking more himself. When his eyes land on me, his smile grows and so does mine...for a moment. Having Aub and Jack next to me makes me feel so damn good, so fucking normal! I can take on the world with the two at my side. Then I remember, *It's all bullshit.*

At least Aub is real. I haven't talked to her about what Mom told me. I'm not sure how just yet. At some point I'll need to figure it out. Aub and I don't keep secrets. I'll have to play the part till I can tell her. Jack and I are blissfully in true love, no weird-ass Roman goddess magic forcing this man to love me. No bullshit.

"Hello, ladies." Jack sits down across from us. "Do you know what today is?"

"Friday," Aub shrugs.

"True, but it's also the first meet of the year." Jack grins.

Aub rolls her eyes and frowns. "Oh. Whatever."

"Can I count on your support? It's being held here," he adds, as if that sweetens the deal.

"I suppose I don't want to miss your first loss." I flip through several pages in my notebook, acting as though I couldn't care less. Teasing him still feels good. Normal even. But that damn voice in the back of my mind reminds me that it's *all* a lie.

His lips spread grin. "You'll have to come to every meet if you want a chance at seeing my first loss."

"Can't wait to see you get pinned." I meet his eyes. "Or whatever it is you boys like doing to each other."

"I heard you can get kinda scary when you wrestle," Aub says. "Why is that? 'Roid rage or something?"

He laughs. "Or something. I'm told I'm very intense."

"You don't know?" Aub leans forward on the table with a bright smile. "Do you black out and wake up when it's all over?"

Jack laughs again and my heart breaks thinking that this would have to come to an end at some point. Laughing with Jack, Aub teasing him right along with me. The phrase, 'Too good to be true,' comes to mind and dampens my heart.

"I'm just kidding," I whisper. "I don't want to see you lose."

"As long as I do my best, you won't ever have to." He smiles that slick grin I love so much.

I gaze at that wonderful smile, wondering what the fuck I'm going to do about all this. Does love have to be a two-way street? If he doesn't love me, could I love him? Will that be enough? No. I want a man, not a slave. Well, not a *mindless* slave.

The rest of the day I go through the motions. Forensics is easier than the others with Jack being so silly. And that *is* him. He was like that before he knew me. Can parts of him remain after I take over the rest? Will I end up pouring him out like Augustia had that Roman?

When we get to the basketball arena for Jack's meet, I'm pleasantly surprised to find that Jack already bought us tickets. They aren't expensive anyway, but it's a nice little gesture that makes me think of his smile.

Far out of our element, Aub and I turn heads. Even more so since the tickets Jack left at the box let us sit in the front row. The matches are mostly set to go up in weight class with just a few exceptions, leaving Jack to come out nearly dead last. I watch with an interest I didn't think I had in me as the men get bigger and bigger. Seeing them ragdoll each other certainly does have an appeal. Their lightning fast moves, and their powerful explosions of muscle have me imagining wrestling Jack on my bed. Power seeps from my heart like a sleepy giant, looking for its first meal. Luckily, it's Jack's turn on the mat.

He comes out of the locker room in a forest-green and navy-blue singlet with 'Mercyhurst' emblazoned across the chest in white. Seeing him in nothing more than a second skin, I can appreciate just how massive he is. For a brief moment, fear strikes as my brain, a whole week later, finally processes just how big of a man I had pressing me into the couch. I lick my lips as my eyes glide up and down his body. I like how he doesn't look like most of the other guys with their bulky shoulders and narrow waists. While he has large shoulders, what really makes him pop compared to the others is how thick he is around the middle. He's like a bear.

I almost feel sorry for the others. Almost.

"Come here." I lean on the railing and crook my finger at him. I'm in the good skirt he bought me, so I wasn't in danger of exposing myself from behind. My shirt has a low cut to it, but my corset underneath has a firm hold of the girls, though it gives the impression that I might spill out at any second.

He jogs over to me but speaks first. "We can't touch. It's against regulation." He bounces on his feet as he looks up at me with a smile on his face. "I'm glad you're here."

"Me too. Listen." I lower my voice which brings him in closer. "I want you to show me just how strong you are. I want to see you get mean. Just this once, okay?"

His eyes go dark and serious, the smooth honey hardening in an instant. "Are you sure? Do you know what you're asking for?"

Honestly, no. I have no idea how mean he can get, but I answer, "Yes. I just want to know what you're capable of." I blow him a kiss, but he only nods in reply.

Jack walks to the edge of the court and paces back and forth like a caged lion till his name blares over the speakers. He moves to the center of the mat as other man in red and white does the same. The size difference doesn't look fair.

Fear and regret shoot through me, corralling the Power. *They are in the same weight class, right?* I snatch the flyer they gave us when we entered from my seat to find that Jack's two-eight-five is the top of the heavyweight division. *He probably cuts weight just to be able to wrestle at all.* His first opponent, James Kellik only weighs in at one-eighty-three. *Holy shit! Did I just kill this guy? Wait! I thought...* My eyes dash back up to the weight bracket to see there's a one-eighty-four and a one-ninety-seven bracket before heavyweight, but heavyweight goes all the way down to one-eighty-three. *Why the fuck does it do that? What kind of fucking idiot would let two men with a hundred-pound weight difference wrestle each other?* The flyer slides out of my trembling fingers as I turn my attention back to the mat.

Jack shakes Kellik's hand, a quick and sharp motion. When the ref calls the match to start, they both lunge at each other, Jack bending the other man over backward. He lifts him up with both arms wrapped around the Kellik's body and slammed him down. While Jack lands on his belly on top of Kellik, the smaller man lands high and tight on his shoulders. He goes rigid as Jack pops to his feet and walks from the mat. The ref kneels over the young man and pulls Kellik's mouth guard out. Kellik goes limp and then starts to moan as he comes to consciousness. Medics see to him until he's taken away on a stretcher to the back.

Seeing that the guy lived, allows the fear to dissipate to the point that the Power spreads back out. *God, he's an absolute monster.*

I crook my finger again and he comes as close as he can. "Good boy. I want to see some finesse this time." Hopefully finesse won't end in serious injury, but the Power wants a show, and thinking of Jack wrestling for me, rather than for his school or for his title, makes my pulse skyrocket.

He continues to bounce on his feet as he nods again, his eyes hard as diamonds and his jaw clenched tight. There's something fascinating about the way he bites his mouthpiece. I can't wait for those teeth to be around my throat again.

It's several minutes later when his next match comes. It's a bigger man this time, a bit wider around the middle, though he has love handles pushing his singlet out while Jack's sticks oh so perfectly.

I check the flyer again to see the guy is named Kirk Svoboda who weighed in at two-seventy-three. *Okay, we're good. He should live.*

They shake hands and when they lunge at each other, Jack tosses Svoboda's arm over his head and grabs him from the back. He lifts the guy by the waist off the floor and throws him over head as he falls backward. Jack doesn't release him, so it looks like Svoboda lands on my man's gorgeous face, but a second later, Jack rolls over the man. The ref holds his hand up twice through the action, I'm not sure what for, but I guess it isn't bad as he doesn't stop the two from wrestling. The crowd cheers for the throw and the roll over but then quiets again as Jack holds onto his opponent, the husky man on his hands and knees with Jack at his side. Jack has him with one arm cradling his neck and pulling the back of a knee up while his other arm is pulling on Svoboda's opposite arm between his legs. All in all, Svoboda's tied up like a confined pretzel and I don't see any way out for him.

The arena gasps in unison as Jack dead lifts Svoboda. He walks across the mat before flipping the helpless guy to his back and landing on top of him.

The ref rushes to the floor and slaps the rubber. Jack stands and takes his little headgear off while simultaneously making his hair look perfect in one fluid hand motion. He shakes hands with the opponent's coach and then comes back to the mat and shakes hands with his opponent. The ref raises his hand and his name blares over the speakers. He walks from the mat, hops up on the railing and grabs me by the waist to pull me in for a kiss.

It's short but there's an energy in it that hasn't been there before. The thrill of victory maybe? He hops back down and winks at me before heading off to the exit.

My phone vibrates a few minutes later.

Jack: I'll be out in a few minutes. You want to grab a bite?

Me: You're my meal.

Jack: Going to let Aubrey starve?

Me: I thought I'd give her a taste.

I want to see how he'll react to such a wild suggestion, but I hope he'll turn it down. It dawns on me that he might just do it if I ask. *How much power do I have over you?*

Jack: I know you and Aubrey are best friends, but I also know you would never share me with anyone. So, I'm gonna call bs on that one.

His response puts a smile on my face. It's a relief to see a normal reply.

Me: Where are you taking us?

Jack: Feel like anything in particular? I usually go to Outback but I'll take you somewhere else if you'd prefer.

"Hey, you want to go to Outback?" I ask.

Aub's face lights up for a moment but then she turns sheepish. "Uh, sure. You sure you want me there?"

"Yeah. Of course. It will be good for you to see him outside of school, you know? And vice versa. He needs to get used to you being there, because you aren't going anywhere."

I give her a hug that means more to me than it does to her. To her, it's just another hug, but to me it's real. Her love I can trust. My heart trembles near bursting thinking about lying to her. We've talked about keeping secrets in the past, and we promised not to keep things from one another. Yet here I am, holding onto two *big* secrets. I need her so badly and she doesn't even know it.

As we walk out of the gym, I text Jack to meet us in the parking lot and a few minutes later he shows up in a navy-blue suit with a white shirt.

"You two want to meet me there? Or I can drive there and come back for your car?"

"I'd love to ride in your car," Aub says with a smile.

I frown. "Traitor." I smile to let her know I'm kidding. "Why don't you take her to Outback, I'll meet you there. I don't like the idea of leaving my car here."

"Well, shouldn't I ride with you?" Aub asks.

"No, it's okay. Give the two of you, what, ten or fifteen minutes to bond a little?"

"Sounds good," Jack says. "Come on, Aubrey. Your chariot awaits."

"Okay," she says meekly.

"You can test out all the cool features," Jack says as they walk off. "If you're lucky, I'll show you how the airbags work."

"Jack," she shouts as she slaps his arm.

Their banter comes awful close to flirting, but I let it slide. I trust Aub. No man will ever come between us. When I get to my car, I already have three texts.

Aubrey: Your boyfriend is an idiot.

Aubrey: This car is really nice though.

Aubrey: I'm going to ask him what he likes most about you.

What are friends for if not to ask all the embarrassing questions for you? I wait a minute for her to respond before I realize I need to get going. I'm still sitting in the parking lot, waiting for a text that might not come.

On the drive I wonder what his response might be. 'I love how she controls me.' 'What's really nice is how she forces me to stay soft.' 'I can't get enough of her feet.' Hopefully, he'll say something halfway normal.

When I get to Outback, they're in the parking lot, standing in the spot next to his car to save it for me. I check my phone to see if she's texted me his response, but she hasn't. Jack offers me his arm which I take and squeeze. It only lasts till he opens the doors and holds them for Aub and me. Once inside, the hostess greets us with a smile, but her eyes shoot wide when she sees Jack come in behind us.

"Hey, Jack. Good to see you again. Your usual table is ready to go."

She leads us down through a crowded dining room to a corner booth where she puts menus in front of us.

"I'll let Mary know you're here," she says with a peppy smile before walking off.

A surge of jealous rage boils up in my stomach. "Who's Mary?"

"She's my waitress," Jack says. "When I told you I 'usually' go here, what I meant was I *always* come here after wrestling. I tip well, so I'm taken care of. Mary's customer service is the best, so they always sit me in her section."

"Oh, so because you're rich, they give you special treatment," Aub says as she looks over the menu.

"No. If I didn't tip well, I'd still be rich, but they wouldn't take such good care of me."

"And you just sit in a big ass booth by yourself?" I scoff.

"I normally bring the team, but I haven't started that tradition yet with Mercyhurst."

A redhead comes to the table with a bright smile and a notepad. "Well, hello there, Jack," she says with a slight southern accent. She's probably in her mid-twenties, and she has all the looks of a former cheerleader.

My jaw clenches as her eyes flick to me then back to Jack.

"I was wondering when I was going to see you again. And who are these two beautiful girls with you?"

"Hey, Mary. This is Aubrey and this is my wonderful girlfriend, Abigale." He gives my hand a squeeze.

"Well, it's a pleasure to meet you both. Can I get an appetizer started for you? Drinks? Or are you ready to order? I know what you want, Jack. No worries there."

We order our drinks and a blooming onion to start and Mary leaves with a smile.

"I need to go to the restroom," Jack says, giving me a kiss on the cheek. "I wanted to see you so bad, I forgot to go in the lockers. Be right back." He slides from the booth and walks off.

With the restrooms not far, I turn to Aub and ask, "So, what did he say when you asked him about me?"

Her lips spread into a devious smile. "He said he can't get enough of you. I asked if you were the inspiration for any characters, but he said he didn't know you when he wrote the books. Although, he did say you give him a lot of ideas for stuff in the future." She giggles and then rolls her eyes. "He said he loves that you're you, that you don't back down from that, and that you're honest about yourself. Then the freak said you have nice toes. I was like, gross! And he was like, you can't deny it. Fucking pervert." She laughs.

"He loves that I'm me," I wonder aloud. *That's kind of vague. But what does he mean that I don't back down from that?*

"I think he means he loves that you make him your bitch. Honestly, if he has a dark secret, this has got to be it. He's a bottom bitch."

I frown. "That's not really a *dark* secret."

"Maybe it's the redhead bitch," she says, just before Mary and Jack walk up to the table.

She's carrying our drinks and blooming onion, but they're talking and laughing, and I absolutely hate it.

"Well, thanks, Mary," Jack says as he sits down. "I'm trying to keep my record, but we'll see how the season goes. Do you know what you want?" he asks, looking over at us.

"You can order for me." I smile, sweet as honey, though I'm sure my eyes hold the fire that's burning in my chest from seeing him with the waitress.

"Oh, gosh! You're going to do me like that, huh? Okay. Aubrey, would you like to go first?"

"Can he order for me, too?" she asks low and behind her menu.

I put every ounce of fire in my eyes, hoping he'll melt under my gaze. "Yeah. Order for both of us."

"*Ooh!* Okay. Mary, help me out here."

Mistake number one.

"I have to get this right; my future depends on it," he adds.

Okay, I'll forgive the first slip up. The thought brings a smile to my face as I watch him struggle more than he did on the mat.

"I'm getting what I always get, so that's easy. Let's get them the same, but the six ounces. I'm thinking double fries for Aubrey. Abigale... I want to say steamed veggies and then a loaded baked potato. That seems like an Abigale thing to do."

"Fries and veggies for me," Aub corrects.

"I think that will work." Mary jots our orders and then takes our menus.

Once she's gone, Aub grins at me but her eyes slide over to Jack with feigned anger. "So, I'm just a double fry girl?"

"My sister is a double fry girl," he explains. "You remind me of her. A great many sisterly vibes coming off you."

"I've never felt insulted being called a sister, till now."

Jack laughs and picks a piece off the deep-fried onion. "It's a good thing. I assure you. Being a sister is a good thing, right?" He gives me a light bump with his elbow.

"Yeah. Sisters are great," I say.

Aub frowns hard at me. "You call your sisters bitches."

"But she loves those bitches." Jack smiles.

That gets both of us laughing.

"How'd you know I liked loaded baked potatoes?"

He gives me that delectable grin. "The supernatural connection between us."

Supernatural? Does he somehow know me better because of this weird magic power I have over him? Is that even a thing?

"Hey, I was just kidding." He scooches closer to me in the booth, pulling me against him with his arm around my shoulders. "I didn't mean anything by it. I know because of your winter recap paper."

"What?" I ask, my mind still reeling from my thoughts.

"In your paper. You talked about a family reunion you had for New Year's. You said the only part you actually liked was the food and you spent, like, half a page on a baked potato and how each part of it was so good."

"Why do you remember that?"

His smile is so warm and the honey in his eyes swirl, pulling me into the dream that his love is real. "Because I loved it. I remember I got jealous of how good it was, how detailed and how I could just see this steaming hot baked potato rise off the page."

I wrap my arms around his waist and let my head rest on his chest. His arm pulls me in even closer and safety washes over me here in the dimly lit booth. He knew me before he ever met me. He was in love before any kind of magic bullshit could ever touch him.

Unless it could work through written words.

No! It's not like that. Right? It has to be face to face. It just *has* to be.

I hold onto him till our food comes. The meats are filet mignon, cooked to perfection at medium rare, as all steaks should be.

When we finish, he pays with his card but leaves a hundred-dollar bill on the table. Aub pretends to steal it, but she puts it back. I kiss him goodbye in the parking lot and tell him to come see me tomorrow.

"Good boys get rewards," I say before letting him go.

When we get in my car, Aub looks at me with concern etched on her face. "What was that?"

"I told you already. It's just something I say to get him worked up." I shrug.

"No, I mean the part where you almost started crying."

"What? I wasn't almost crying," I say as I pull out of the parking lot.

"When you were asking about the potato. He said it was like magic or something and you— Holy shit!" she screams as I narrowly dodge a breaking car. "Jesus! What the fuck was that?"

The car I cut off blares their horn and I would give them the finger, but my hands are gripping the steering wheel tight enough to choke a grizzly bear. My vision blurs from new tears, so I turn at a neighborhood entrance and pull over. My hands shake as they finally release the poor wheel. We sit there, our heavy breathing and the air conditioning the only things breaking the silence.

"I have to tell you something. I'm not supposed to, but I need you to know." I turn to her and stifle my tears. "Please don't leave me."

"Leave you? What the fuck?" She sighs.

We both reach out to hug one another but came up short as the seatbelts lock on both of us.

"Piece of shit," I yell at my seatbelt.

"Are you freaking kidding?" Aub shouts at hers.

We unbuckle our seatbelts, and our bodies crash in a deep embrace over the center console. I grab onto Aub like a life raft as her hands grip through my shirt to the back of the corset.

"I love you, Abby. I'm not leaving you. Not unless you fucking crash and kill us!"

We both laugh and choke on our tears.

When I finally have enough of my voice back, I tell her everything. I don't have the story of the Roman down as well as my mom does, but I got the main points. I tell her that Dad isn't my dad. That Mom has more men, God only knows where, and that Jack doesn't love me like he says, because it's all magic and that the stupid potato set me off because I thought it might be part of it, too.

"He said supernatural and all I could think of was this stupid shit with my mom. Then when he said it was from my paper, I was thinking; Okay, great! This means that he was falling for me before he met me. The powers don't work that way, or do they? I don't know! So, I started freaking out that maybe the powers work through written words as well, and if they do, then he's never *really* loved me. It's all been some sick twisted corruption bullshit!"

Aub sits there for a long time looking at me when I finish. Just as I'm about to tell her to say something, she says, "That's what that shit was with Les." She breathes deep before continuing. "Your Mom is like super serious all the time and she scared the shit out of me when we were little, she still scares me. As cool as your sister is, Deanna scares me, too. And I love you, but sometimes you scare me."

"No. Don't say that!" I plead.

She tightens her grip on my hand. "Not like in a scary movie kind of way. It's like; I can tell that you could fuck shit up if you wanted to. If I was your enemy I would want to run away and hide but I'm your best friend and I know I'm safe with you."

"You really think I could fuck shit up?" I ask as if it's the sweetest complement I've ever heard.

"What? Of course, I think that! We're double majoring in law and criminal justice, bitch. We're going to fuck criminals up for the rest of our lives. Deanna is a chemist who could probably make a bomb with a toothpick and her hair tie, and Lilly runs executive accounts for billionaires, she probably has so many connections she could get away with killing the Queen of England! So, yes. You all scare me. As you rightfully should. But I'm here for you and the fact that you told me all of that just...I don't know." She shrugs and gulps as tears well in her eyes. "It shows how much you trust me, and I want to live up to that trust. I love that we're so open and honest with each other. This is what best friends are all about. I promise that when my mom tells me that I'm from a long line of women who do nothing but eat Doritos, I'll tell you all about it."

We laugh and hug again but when we separate, I say, "Okay, so that was the first thing I had to tell you. There's something else though. Jack told me something on Monday that I never talked to you about. It's weird as fuck, too."

Chapter Eighteen

When we get home, Mom and Dad's luggage is back in the foyer, which means they're leaving within the hour.

I tell Aub to wait in my room and continue down the hall to Mom's office. I step in and close the doors behind me.

"What's wrong?" Mom asks as I turn to face her. She sits at her desk, shuffling papers around. She's wearing a tight red dress that hugs her like a second skin. That means they were either going to New York or LA. "You have to make it quick, hun. Your father and I are leaving right now."

"The thing you told me about, can it work through something like a letter, text or email? Can it work before they meet you?"

She looks away for a moment and then answers to my dismay. "Yes. A letter, most certainly. Email I know works to some degree, but you make a very interesting point about if they've meet us before or not. I've always met them first. Obviously, I was hitting my stride before internet and texting became a thing. You think that because he was infatuated with you before he met you that might make a difference? Because it won't, sweetheart. They could hate you to death and it will still work."

"It matters to me, Mom! If he..." I take a breath to calm myself. Mom is the queen of shouting matches. I need to keep things on an even keel. "If it works like you say it does, but it only works after meeting, then that means, at least up till he met me, his interest was real."

"It *was* real, hun. Listen." She ushers me over to the couch and sits down with me. Taking my hands into hers, she gives them a squeeze. "With you being so dramatic yesterday, I didn't get the chance to tell you how the Power works and how it comes about. I'll need to make this real quick, so listen and don't interrupt. As you can imagine, being that it's of a sexual nature the Power starts its work when we hit puberty, but we Augustia women have longer puberty cycles than others. It starts a couple years early and it ends a couple years late. When your cycle ends, the Power blooms. I wanted to make sure you were feeling it's effects before I told you about it, otherwise it would have sounded ludicrous."

I can't deny that. If I hadn't already felt it, I would have thought her certifiable.

"I got a little nervous last year when you started dating that Les boy, but you didn't seem to be showing any of the signs. When I heard that Jack had walked up to you out of nowhere, I knew. I wish I had more time before your date so you could have made it a night to remember, but I wanted you to know the consequences. I didn't want you to end up like me and not know before it was too late."

I want to slam my head against a wall for how fucking stupid I am. Mom was fucking abandoned! She never knew her real mother. Grandma Sherry's the near opposite of Mom. She wouldn't have anything to do with this dominatrix shit. I take a deep breath so I don't explode with questions about how Mom figured any of this shit out and let her speak. I need to let her give me as much as she's willing, then I'll start pulling teeth.

She looks at her watch curses. "I have to go."

Damn it.

"You said that it didn't start last year, because you didn't see the signs." I grip her hands to keep her on the couch. I have to get everything I can from her. If she's off to LA or New York, I won't see her for at least another week if not more since she might go international from those cities. "So that means, last semester, when Jack was reading my work, he wouldn't have been influenced then, right?"

"What does that matter? Would he have been interested in you enough to let you piss on his face?"

"What? Mom, that's disgusting!"

She scoffs and heads to her desk to grab a few folders. "Would he have been interested enough to have sex with another man? Kill another man? Kill himself?" When I come over to her, she frowns at me. She places the folders down and gently rubs my shoulders. "It's a harsh truth, dear. Listen, I never wanted to lie to you. From the bottom of my heart, Abby, I'm sorry for that. I'm finally free to tell you everything, so I never have to lie to you again. You can text or email any questions. Just call it 'our gift;' no telling who might be watching and who knows what anyone might do if they found out. Look at me."

I restrain myself from crossing my arms at her authoritative tone. Mom can be a brick wall when she's pissed, but she gives abundantly when she was happy. I bite my tongue to keep her pleased.

"No one can know. Not even Aubrey. I love the girl but you can only trust *you* with this. I have to trust my daughters with it, but that's it. No one else."

"Wait. Are you saying Dad doesn't know?"

"Your father?" She laughs as she turns to leave. "Why would I ever tell any of the men? They're too dense to understand. We don't want to confuse them, hun. They live in bliss, best to leave them there."

They don't know? Can that be my way out?

"Would it break the spell, or magic, or whatever the fuck it is?"

She rounds on me and grabs me by my shoulders again, only this time it isn't her gentle mother's touch. The strength in her hands is second only to Jack's and her nails bite into my arms as she bends me backward over her desk, jarring the monstrous block of cherrywood to the point her lamp and stacks of folders clatter to the floor. Her eyes blaze with an inferno I've never seen before as her lips peel into a terrifying snarl.

"You will *not* tell that boy or any other! You will tell no one! Am I understood?"

"Yes!"

"I want your word!"

"I-I promise!"

"Good." She lets go of me. She slides her hands down her tight dress, pressing out non-existent wrinkles. "I'm sorry I was so stern." She sighs and massages the spot between her eyes. "Look, Abigale. This is exactly what I meant when I said to not think about this too much. You're trying to go against forces that make up who you are. There is no getting rid of it. I've tried. I've pushed men to see if they would ever deny me, and they never did. I'd have over twenty men right now if I had all the men I've turned over the years." She moves closer to me again, her hands delicate at her side. "They've jumped *whenever* I told them to, no matter what was beneath them. It is a great and terrible power we wield. I may not be here much, but I'm here for you more than my birth mother was for me. It took years to piece it all together and when I found my bitch mother, I pulled every drop of information from her. There is no cure and you needn't see it as something that needs to be cured."

She found her birth mother? That's certainly new info, but the bigger takeaway is she found out about the Power and what it is before she found her mother. I'm done talking to her about it, at least for now. She needs to cool down before I'll be able to get much else out of her.

"I'm sorry, Mom. I'm just scared. It's all so new. I won't tell anyone," *else*.

"Good." She wraps loving arms around me. "You're my sweet little angel, about to embark on her first conquest. I couldn't be prouder of you, hun. And don't tell your sister I said this but you are putting her to shame. Micha and Curtis together don't make half a Jack."

After kissing on my cheek, she leaves the office, calling for Dad halfway down the stairs.

I hurry to my room to tell Aub everything and we start to search for answers. If Mom figured a lot of it out back in the eighties with libraries and the card catalogue system, surely Google can tell me more in the span of a single night.

When eight a.m. rolls around, I'm grateful it's a weekend.

"Shit, bitch. We can't find fucking shit." Aub groans, flopping back on my bed.

The bed looks really good right now, but laying down would be giving up. Halfway through the night, we changed into pajamas to get a little comfier, but I'm not ready to give up.

"We've found…some things." My eyelids try to shut for the tenth time in the past two minutes.

It's really nothing. The most we can come up with are articles about succubae and demon porn. There's a lot more demon porn out there than I think is needed, but whatever.

"Like, can't you call on your powers and summon a sex ghost or something to tell us?"

"I have no fucking clue! I don't know what I can or can't do. According to Mom, I can tell guys to kill themselves and they'll do it but I don't know if I can just make a ring and summon Satan."

"Well, let's not bother him with this." Aub laughs.

I check my phone and find a litany of texts from Jack. They

start out flirty and cute but after I didn't answer since five last night, they become concerned, then worried that I'm mad at him, then back to worried that I'm not responding at all. The last one is just a few minutes ago.

Jack: I'm coming over.

My doorbell rings and I feel like I'm waking up from a deep sleep.

Another text silently appears.

Jack: Please just tell me you're all right. If you're mad at me, I'll take that. Just say you're mad. But don't make me imagine the worst.

I run down the stairs, missing a step here and there, but staying on my feet. "I'm alive," I shout.

"You want to be dead?" Deanna calls from her room.

"Fuck off, bitch."

I open the door and throw myself into his arms. "I'm so, so, so, sorry, baby. I've been working on stuff all night. I wasn't even checking my phone. I'm so sorry."

"Oh, thank God," he shouts toward the sky. He exhales and squeezes me against his chest, my feet dangling in the air. "Oh, God, Abigale. I'm so glad you're safe. I forgive you for scaring the absolute shit out of me, but if you've been up all last night, what about our date tonight? You won't be able to stand, let alone sing."

"Did you say sing?"

He's been keeping this date a secret all week, but he's just let the cat out of the bag. "I... Did I say sing?" He scratches his head as he lets me down. "I meant, *not* sing. See that. I missed that crucial word. I've been up all night, worried that someone was dead. I'm not thinking right."

I smile up at him, how can I not when he's being such a goof. "I'd love to hear you sing."

He smiles back as his hands slide up my neck, his fingers

cradle the base of my skull and his thumbs on my jaw tilt my head up to meet him. His kiss is soft but electric, sending a jolt through my tired body.

"Well, what are you working on? Maybe I could help."

My eyes shoot wide. "No! I mean, no, that's okay. It's not a big deal."

"It was a big enough deal to forget about me."

God, I'm not awake enough to have a battle of wits with him right now.

"I mean, it's not important *now*. I was just…engrossed last night. Aub and I were up all night."

"I should really get her number," Jack says almost as if more to himself that to me.

A tinge of jealousy spikes but nothing compared to what seeing him with the redhead had caused. "Why do you want her number?"

"Well, if I can't get ahold of you, it would be good to have your best friend's number." He shrugs.

"Shit! Abby! I found something," Aub calls. She rushes out of my room, nearly bolting through the hallway banister. "I found— Shit! Hi, Jack. I fucking forgot she was going to see you. I was just…ah…fucking around. I didn't find anything. We haven't found anything really all night and…I thought it would be funny if I acted like I had found something now. At this moment. Ha." Her laughter turns into sleep deprived hysterics as her hands press her forehead.

"You really don't want me to know?" he asks.

"I—" *Fuck it. He didn't lie to me. I'm not going to lie to him.* "I do want you to know. My mom made me promise not to tell anyone. Aub shouldn't know but technically I told her before the promise, so it doesn't count."

He nods as his jaw slides to the side. "Well, you can't break a promise to your mother. You've bound yourself to a rule. But do you know what I love most about rules?" He leans down to my height. "Bending them," he whispers, just before stealing a kiss. "You going to invite me in or what?"

"What, are you a fucking vampire? Get in here." I grab him by his soft package and led him through the door. "Oh, you're still soft for me, baby?" I pull on his neck to bring him in for another kiss. Our tongues press against each other's, battling for supremacy.

"Okay, maybe I should go home," Aub says.

I love how Jack's silky tongue feels on the inside of my mouth, but as much as I enjoy it, I *need* Aub right now. I shove Jack off me and wipe my lip. "No, no. Don't go. We aren't going to be doing *anything* right now. Isn't that right, Jack?"

"Actually, that's not true." Jack's cocky grin stretches his lips, but his eyes don't have the same sparkle as his smile, they still glow with hunger. "I'm pretty sure we're up for a day of rule bending."

"And just what do you mean by rule bending?"

"Well, this is a classic game of Who Can Say. It's super easy."

Aub leans on the banister. "Who Can Say? What's that?"

"Well, it works like most games," he answers, looking up at her and then back to me. "We go in a circle. It works like this. Can I say? Of course, not. I have no idea what we're even talking about. Now it's your turn." He points to me. "Can you say? No. You promised your mom you wouldn't tell anyone." His smile widens as he looks up to Aub. "Can you say?"

"That seems like cheating." Aub grimaces with a tilt of her head.

"Cheating is when you break a rule. It *feels* like cheating only because you expected it to be harder." His playful smile fades quicker than a fuzzy dream. "Now, what's going on?"

Deanna's door swings open and she looks just like Mom did yesterday with that blazing heat in her eyes. "Shut the fuck up now and promise me you won't utter a word of what my stupid bitch sister told you!"

From the foyer, I can't hear the whisper of terrified acquiescence, but I see her lips move in the right pattern.

Jack sighs. "Well, she can't say. Hey, Deanna, can you say?"

Deanna leans over the banister, her knuckles turn so white I'm surprised the wood doesn't shatter under her grip. "Fuck you," she spits, punctuating each word. She directs her rage at me as she shouts, "If he finds out, Mom will kill him. Fuck, I might kill him."

"You might kill me," Jack echo, his jaw sliding again. "That's a serious threat."

"Make him forget," she orders franticly. "Tell him to forget everything about this morning."

"Does that work?" Aub asks.

"Yes," Deanna snaps. "They do *whatever* we tell them. Tell him to forget, Abby!"

"Jedis. Or well, clearly Sith in this case." Jack paces back and forth, his arms crosses over his chest, one hand coming up to his chin to let a finger rest on his lips. "Jedi would never make people forget. Eh, well, maybe a grey Jedi would. Is that what this is? You're researching the Force?" He looks at me for an answer.

I have no fucking clue what he's talking about. "No."

"No? *Hmm.* Mental powers. Some kind of mental powers. Not clairvoyance, otherwise you wouldn't have been surprised when I told you of my past. You're telepaths."

"This isn't twenty-fucking-questions," Deanna roars from

the hallway. She hurries down the stairs and reaches for my arm, but Jack is suddenly between us.

"Why don't you do it?" he asks, though his words hold little question and a whole lot of threat. "You said 'we' a moment ago, but you want her to do it. Why is that?"

She places her hands on her hips and smirks at him. "I bet you'd like that. Upgrade to the older sister."

"Fucking bitch!" I go to claw her eyes out, but Jack's iron beam of an arm blocks me from committing sororicide.

"It doesn't work like that." She looks past him at me. "Do it. Tell him to forget. If you do, I won't tell Mom and she won't have one of her guys kill him."

The muscles in Jack's back ripple under my fingers before he turns to me and holds out his hand. "Look. Neither of us wants me dead. Where's the fun in that?" He smirks just like he would in class, as if nothing's weird, as if he isn't being threatened with death. "Just tell me to forget everything we've talked about. Tell me that I have a concussion. I'll probably ask questions, but I've had concussions before. I lost an entire day once. Tell me I slipped on an ice cube and hit my head on the stairs on the way down."

My vision blurs behind a sheet of tears. *I don't want you to forget, Jack. I want you to remember every minute we've had.*

He wipes a tear from my cheek. "It's okay. You aren't losing me. You're just going back in time." He leans in and kisses my cheek with the lightest of touches. "It's not so bad, I promise." He lowers to the floor and positions himself just off the stairs. "Remember, I slipped on ice, hit the stairs and you were all scared. You pulled me by my arm over to where I am now. And then I wake up. Simple as that."

I lower myself next to him slowly and take his hand into mine. "Do I just tell him, or do I have to do anything?"

"Yeah, you have to have his cock in your fucking ass," Deanna says with a roll of her eyes.

"I'm doing it, okay? The least you could do is help me out a little!"

"Whatever! I don't know. It's not an exact science. It depends on how strong your bond is. It's just like what you did with Les."

"You aren't going to get another boyfriend, are you?" Jack asks from his back.

I grip his hand tighter. "No! No, of course not, baby."

"Yes. Yes, she will. She'll have scores." Deanna grins, looking down at him.

"Shut it, bitch!"

"Hey, hey." Jack holds my arm so I won't tackle Deanna. "No need to fight. I'm not going to remember any of this anyways."

"Then why the fuck did you even say anything?" Deanna gives him a hard kick in the shoulder.

"Bitch," I shout as I try lunging at her, but Jack's iron grasp keeps me in place again. "He isn't Les! You can't touch him!"

Jack gives a soft laugh. "It didn't even hurt. She probably broke her toe. Come on. Let's get this over with." He puts my hand on his chest and gazes up at me with deep golden-brown wells that assure me things are going to be all right. "Don't hold anything back. Say it like you mean it."

I swallow the lump in my throat, peering into his eyes as my hand rubs his chest. "Jack, I, uh…I want you to forget this whole morning. You're going to forget everything that happened today."

His serious eyes relax, and a small smile slides across his lips.

"You won't remember anything we spoke of. You're going to close your eyes, and when they open, you're going to think you just woke up."

He nods slightly and then closes his eyes. They open, and he jerks up to his elbows. "Whoa!" He looks around for a moment and then to me. "What happened?"

"You slipped and hit your head," Deanna says quickly. "There was ice on the floor."

"Shit. Really? Oh, man. I don't even remember coming over here. I remember, I was texting you to find out why you weren't texting me back. I was…I thought you were breaking up with me," he looks at me with so much fear in his eyes. "I don't remember coming over at all. Damn. I'll have to report this." He sits up on the bottom step of the stairs as he pats himself down.

"Report?" Deanna' eyes widen on me. "What do you mean report? You're fine."

"Yeah. Just to my coaches. It's dumb, but I have to report any serious or 'possibly serious' injuries. It's just a formality." He pulls his phone from his back pocket. He starts typing but then looks the phone over several times. "How in the hell did that not break? That's crazy lucky." His thumbs flash around the screen before he pockets the phone. "Well, I texted coach, so on Monday they'll do some cognitive tests and I'll be cleared. It's happened before."

"Yeah, glad you're not dead," Deanna says. "Mom would have been super pissed to have a dead body on her hands," she adds looking at me.

"Jack, are you sure you're okay?" I hold his face in my hands and search his eyes for the parts I erased.

"Yeah." He gave a shrug and then adds, "Well, it's funny, I don't have any head pain. On the other occasions where I had a concussion, I've felt a little dizzy, had a mild headache. All that hurts is my shoulder." He rubs the shoulder that Deanna kicked. "I mean, it doesn't hurt that bad. Feels like a child punched me or something. Was that you? Did you hit me for something I said?" His jovial, innocent eyes sparkle with life. They say nothing about the fact that I just robbed him of his memories. "Hey, hey, it's all right." His hand graces my cheek as he wipes a tear with his thumb. "I'm sorry if I'm making you repeat yourself, but why weren't you responding to any of my texts? What were you doing?"

"It was a girl's night," I answer, holding back the majority of my tears for Jack and my seething rage for Deanna. "And Deanna kept my phone from me."

"Well, that wasn't very nice." He pretends to scowl at Deanna. "I was genuinely worried."

"Well, I'm a fucking bitch, so get used to it." She flashes a mocking smile. "I'm taking a shower, if anyone falls on the stairs again, I'm not helping."

"Fair enough. And what about you, my frightened rabbit?" He pulls me into his lap. "What about our date? If you were up all night, how are you going to be able to stay awake let alone sing?"

It's like nothing happened. This whole morning hasn't happened in his mind. He's saying things over again that are new to him. It wasn't an accident that took that from my Jack. I did that.

"Ah! Did I just say sing? Oh man! I must have hit my head real hard to spoil the surprise." His big smile fades into a smaller version as his eyes soften. "Hey, I'm okay. You won't even remember this in a couple weeks." He gives my arm a quick peck since it's right next to his lips. "Are you still up for tonight? A little karaoke?"

I nod since I can't get words to come out of my mouth. My eyes are like faucets and the lump in my throat feels bigger than my head. *How could I have done this to you?*

"If I remember correctly, you've said, several times now, that good boys get rewards. Yet, I have not received these implied rewards. If it's all right with you," he pulls me deeper into his lap and inhales. "I'd love to see your room again. Maybe we can take a little nap together."

"Uh, I'm still here," Aub says. Her face, as best as I can see through my watering eyes, is torn by hurt and shame, just like my heart. "I don't think you want me taking naps with you."

"Oh hey, Aubrey, didn't see you up there, sorry. I don't mind, though," Jack says, looking back at me. "Or, maybe we could all stay awake. Good boys get rewards after all. Just as long as she keeps her hands off you, because you're all mine."

"Wow, fucking gross," Aub turns from the banister and goes back into my bedroom.

Jack laughs and picks me up to carry me up the stairs. "Good thing my shoe dried, I could have slipped and we'd both be tumbling down the stairs."

Deanna walks from her room in nothing but a towel with her change of clothes in her hands. "If you get tired of the little girls, you can join a real woman in the shower."

Jack restrains me from murder once again as he carries me into my room and sits me down gently on the edge of the bed next to Aub. He takes a step back and smiles at the two of us. "I think some music is called for."

The shower water starts just as he finds the play button on my CD player. Slipknot's *Duality* pour out of the speakers. I haven't turned it on in months. It's funny to hear what I'd last been listening to but even that can't put a smile on my face after what I've done.

"That will do." He mouths the words as they play. He walks to the door, gives a quick peek out into the hall and closes it quietly.

Wait… He doesn't really think something's going to happen with the three of us, does he?

"You don't have super hearing, do you?" he asks, the playful smile on his face a distant memory.

"What?" Aub and I ask in unison.

"You and your sisters, do you have super hearing? Could she hear us over all this?"

"No. Why? What are you talking about?"

He kneels in front of me. "You were supposed to tell me I had a concussion during your compulsion. If you're going to control minds, you'd better learn how to do it." A sly smile. "As much as I wish you had some kind of mental power over me, you don't."

Chapter Nineteen

"Wait, you remember?" I throw myself on him, knocking him to his back, kissing and crying the whole way to the floor.

I haven't hurt him. I haven't erased part of him. He's whole!

"What if your bond isn't strong enough?" Aub asks. "I mean, what if you do have control over him, but not enough to make him forget stuff."

"I don't know." I can't take my eyes off my wonderful man. I cup his sweet face between my hands and let myself fall into the honey of his eyes. "I don't know how any of this works."

"Focus," Jack says in a smooth tone. He places his hands on my waist and raises me slightly, just so I'm not smothering him. My hair still drapes around his face, keeping us in our own little world. "How long do her showers typically last?"

"Deanna's? Why are you asking about my sister's showers?" Fury explodes in me. I flick my hair back since this mother fucker doesn't deserve to be in a private bubble with me. I slide my hands from his face to his shoulders and I prime my knee to slam into his crotch.

"Just trust me."

Those words fall on me like a warm blanket. They wrap me up, making me feel so safe and secure. None of the monsters of my life can reach me with Jack at my side. I let my knee relax.

"Like, twenty...thirty minutes," I guess.

"Wow, that's more time than I thought," he says. "How do you feel about searching your mom's things?"

"What?" Aub and I ask in unison again.

Jack smiles up at me, such a warm smile, at first, but it slides into a wicked grin. "From what I've gathered, you two didn't have much luck last night figuring out whatever all this is. It sounds like your mom told you about it, which means, while we have the chance, our best bet to learning more is by searching her room. If you don't want to, we—"

"I fucking love you, Jack Billard!" I grab his face and plant a massive kiss on his lips. "When we're done with this, I'm going to fuck you so hard. Come on!"

I step over Jack, hurry out of my room, down the hall and into Mom's office. Jack and Aub come in right behind me. We split up, searching for what exactly, I'm not sure. I sit at her desk, Aub searches the bookshelves while Jack moves behind the wet bar.

"Jack! What the fuck?" I hiss. Now is not the time for a fucking drink.

He crouches and disappears but a second later he calls out. "I found something."

Aub and I both crane our necks to see but he stays hidden.

"Nope, never mind. It's a love letter." A few bottles clink around and then he moves on to search the couch.

Love letter under the wet bar, noted. I'll have to come back for that later, but it makes me realize that whatever we're looking for won't be sticking out on top of a drawer. We're looking for some wild shit and Mom would have taken precautions. *I need to think like a psychotic narcissist who hides her ability to mind fuck men. Where would I put shit?*

Her bedroom comes to mind. Maybe she has a safe hidden somewhere. She certainly doesn't have one in the open. Deanna and I raided her closet on multiple occasions over the years, first for Christmas presents and later for clothes. Still, best to clear this room as while we can before moving on to her bedroom.

When I pull her bottom drawer out to see if something might be hidden behind it, the weight shocks me. I pull out the two books and folder to find it has a false bottom. Under the thin wood lining, sits a leather journal, a stack of papers that look to be torn from old books and two handguns.

"Holy shit! I got it," I shout, unable to restrain myself.

I pull the journal and papers out just as the shower shut off hard enough to make the pipes jump in the walls.

What the fuck? Of all days not to use the massage setting!

I hand everything to Aub who runs back to my room as Jack gets to work on setting the bookcase right. I put all of Mom's things back in the drawers as best I can remember and run for the door, but Jack catches me by the waist and pulls me to the couch.

He lays me on my back and pulls my leg to wrap around his hip. His lips crash over mine and his tongue finds its way easily past what little defenses I put up.

Point-two seconds later, Deanna breaks things up. "What the fuck are you doing in Mom's study?"

Jack backs off me but positions himself between me and Deanna like a human shield. "*Mom's* study? I thought it was just *a* study. Wow, that is a very nice towel," he turns to me. "It would look great on you."

"Please, get him under control, Abby. You know you can't be in here without Mom's permission. If you're going to fuck, just do it in your own bed."

"Aubrey's trying to sleep," Jack says.

"With that loud as fuck music?"

"I said trying." Jack shrugs.

"Fuck her." I grab his hand and storm past my sister. "Come on, babe. We'll wait till Aub is asleep and we'll fuck right next to her."

"I like the sound of that," Jack says with a smile.

I lead Jack back to my room as my heart thunders in my chest. *Did she buy that?* There's no way of knowing for now. We just have to continue to play our parts.

Aub lays on her side in bed with her back to us. When I close the door, her head pops up and she slides out from under the sheets. "You two aren't going to actually have sex, right?

"Well, if we're going to keep the story up, I think we're going to need to make some noise." Jack puls me by the hips to him. "And to be honest, I don't think anyone could actually sleep through the two of us having sex. I have every intention of making you wake the dead in China." He smiles wide and his eyes slip to Aub. "So, it would only make sense that you would wake up and leave, which you won't be doing since we're sleuthing, making staying your only option. But since you can't just sit and watch…"

"Jack," both of us shout.

He holds his finger to his lips. "She might have heard both of you shout my name, I mean, I think we're past the point of no return now." He shrugs and grins.

"I said we wouldn't be doing anything, Jack." I whisper the words as though I'm trying to stab him with them.

"Ah, right. That was before you wiped my memory. I forgot."

"You're being bad, and you'd better stay soft."

He raises his hands up in surrender. "I'm only joking. Come on, let's see what you found."

"Where is it, Aub?"

She goes to the head of my bed and pulls out the journal and papers.

I hold out my hand. "I'll read the journal. You two go through the papers."

I open the leather-bound book to see my mother's handwriting.

10/14/1982

I've found more information on my lineage today. A strange account going back to second century Rome. I'll go back to the library tomorrow to steal the pages I need.

For now, I'm continuing with my tests. Two men have gone to the gay bars and had anal sex even with the current outbreak of AIDS. They will do anything! And everything! I have two attending me now. One at my feet, the other between my thighs. Both with rubber bands tied tight around their cock and balls. Nothing I do deters them. I took Joe into the cellar and had his balls cut off, yet he still begs to please.

02/17/1987

I received a letter last week from a lawyer stating I was named the sole beneficiary in a will. It was Billy. It turned out that he had a semi-successful career as a racecar driver. He always was a fun ride. But without my care he withered away and died. I went to the will reading. I was named in the beginning but was then to be referred to as Goddess throughout. After liquidating his assets, it will be just over a million. This morning, in the dead of night, Kyle and I went to his grave. I called in Lenard and Peter. The three of them dug up his fresh grave and I pissed on Billy's dead body for old time's sake. I'm sure he was cumming in heaven, watching me give him one last shower.

10/19/1998

My abilities are slowing somehow and at the same time growing. With new men, I find it harder to coax them, but the men who call me Goddess have grown new abilities to help them please me. Justin seems to know what I am hungry for or thirsty for well in advance. Dimitri has grown three inches since I last slept with him only two days ago. Ivar's muscles have expanded to rival that of Schwarzenegger in his hay day. He beats people to death for my amusement.

I put the book down. After reading nearly half the thing, a sick swirl in my gut wars against the invigorating flow of Power that wants to dominate Jack. My once large room has become oppressively small and stale. I go to the bathroom just in case, but the walk shrugs off the sickness and the open air of the house goes a long way.

"So, what did you two find?" I ask when I return.

Aub took to sitting at the top of my bed next to my desk where Jack sat. Once she finished reading a page, she'd hand it off to him to read.

"Well, to be honest, not much. Most of this is just documents of what you already told me," Aub says. "It's like family tree shit."

"That's called genealogy," Jack chimes in. "This *family tree shit* is very important."

While reading the journal, I looked over to him every few minutes to see his reactions, but they'd all been head nods, lean backs, scoffs, even a laugh at one point.

"What do you think?" I ask.

"Well." He hesitates, scratching the back of his head for a moment. "You have to understand, from my point of view, I see all ancient religions to be satanic at the end of the day. The Romans worshiped their gods, but they were likely fallen angels, a.k.a. demons. This woman Augustia, I'd say she's a fallen angel that's just given over to her lustful desires."

"And you don't?" Aub asks with a smirk.

"I certainly do, but I don't have superpowers. Angels were made separate from the world, that being the universe. They were made for Heaven. They're multi-dimensional beings with abilities that seem godlike, hence the worship. But while they were made for Heaven, meaning, they weren't meant to die, age, grow sick, they also weren't meant to reproduce. The Bible says they have offspring with the women of Earth. So, clearly, they did somehow. I've sometimes wondered if in their casting out of Heaven and subsequent corruption by sin, they, perhaps through genetic modification, managed to give themselves a way to reproduce or maybe they just made test tube babies."

"Demon test tube babies?" Aub laughs. "Do you hear yourself?"

He shrugs. "Well, the music is a bit loud. But we're talking about beings who watched the God of the Universe *do things*. Please let that sink in. They are so far ahead of us, I wouldn't rule out anything. This woman obviously had children, the genealogy shows that. I'll be honest though." He frowns and shakes his head. "This looks like it might be fake."

"Fake?" I question.

Jack hesitates again, his eyes shift to Aub momentarily. "Well, I did my genealogy and this…well, it looks different."

Why is he holding back from me? When his eyes flick to Aub for a second time, it dawns on me. "I told her. She knows about you."

I brace for anger or resentment that I shared his secret but it's just something he's going to have to deal with. I'm not going to lie to Aub.

He sighs. "Okay, good. That makes this way easier to explain. So, yeah. I did my genealogy to see if I could find out where things changed for my family. I'd already done it in my past life as well, so I had a head start. I followed my family tree, and while the people were the same, the professions were all different till I got back to tenth century."

"What was that profession?" Aub ask.

Jack's eyes slide to her as his sly grin spreads. "Viking raider. My point is, I think these might be fake because they don't look like real documentation. It wasn't very much. Here's Tabatha's mother, Gwendolyn and here's Gwendolyn's mother Mariella. There's no mention of sisters or other daughters. Hell, only some of the documents even talk about husbands. When I did my genealogy, I found *everyone*." Jack leans forward and presents three fingers. "I see three options. One, these women only have one daughter at a time. But, you have two sisters, so it's not that." He lowers a finger. "These could be one-hundred percent fake, maybe your mom made the whole story up and then has this, I don't know, planted for you to find. That seems super odd. Or the last option is that this isn't fake exactly but might be edited to only show the lineage that leads to your mother. Maybe that's all she cares about. That idea made me wonder if there could be other family lines with women of the same origin. Potentially stronger lines."

"Stronger lines?" I ask, but the Power has another question in mind. "You think Deanna might be stronger than me?"

"Inheritance is something that we think of as legalistic, but in truth, the first child of each sex often has stronger DNA ties to the same sex parent. So, it would stand to reason, that the first daughter of each generation might be a stronger lineage than that of the second or third daughter. Now, that's all theoretical in this, because I have no idea how magic powers get passed on, but I do know that Satanist prize first born children, particularly boys though, for their rituals. So maybe there's something there."

"Why the fuck do you know so much about Satanists and their rituals and genealogy shit?" Aub asks.

Jack gives another shrug. "Know your enemy and all that."

So that's how he's looking at it. "But what do you *think*?" I ask again.

"Oh, I mean, I believe it. We're in a spiritual war. This is kind of like knowing that rocket launchers exist, and they're normally used so far away that I never have to worry about it. Only now someone just shot one at my girlfriend. It's dangerous, you know? But it's not like we can't figure it out and handle it."

How can he be so calm and rational through all this? He almost seems flippant about it.

"And the fact that I'm controlling you doesn't affect you at all? You're not worried about that?"

"I can tell you with one-hundred percent certainty; it doesn't work on me."

My heart jumps for joy, though a hot rage creeps in. *How dare he defy me?*

"What?" Aub laughs. "She wrapped your dick in a bow."

"And I told you to get soft and you did," I add to remind him who's in control.

"Those things are both very true, but neither needed special powers. Look, I'm not super big into swimming, but if you remember, my last girlfriend was captain of the swim team. I went swimming all the time. I don't hate it. It wasn't like I did it against my will. I was allowing myself to change for her, but there was a limit. When she said I should join the men's team, I told her I didn't want to. Same goes for you. Granted, I'm willing to do *way* more for you than I was for her, but I've only done things that I'm *willing* to do for you. If you told me to kill Aubrey, I wouldn't do that. She's too cute to die so young." He taps Aub's nose, making her crinkle her face before slapping his shoulder.

I stare at him, completely dumbfounded. "So, you—you willingly did those things?" There's no possible way. He has to be delusional, some effect from the domination magic. "You've kept yourself soft for over a week now just because I told you to."

He scoffs. "You said your mom only told you this a couple days ago. You wrapped my dick in a bow last week. You didn't think you had special powers then. You believed it was possible on its own up till now." He stands and holds my hands, looking down on me with that warm smile like the sun in spring. "It's just us. It's our chemistry together."

"That seems hard to believe," Aub says.

"She tried to take my memories and it didn't work. I think the only way to know is to do tests. If the deciding factor is a sexual bond, then we need to strengthen that bond and test the limits of what I'm willing to do. I'm already willing to do a great deal for you, but there are plenty of things I wouldn't do."

"You did hurt that boy in wrestling," I said.

"I did, but that's who *I* am. That match might have gone the exact same if you hadn't been there. I let loose as much as I'm able when I'm on the mat. Anyone who's willing to step on it with me is risking their health. I've ended wrestling careers before and I'll do it again. I'm vicious on the mat and that's all on me." He tilts my chin up to look at him. "But I certainly liked showing off for you by manhandling Kirk." His lips cover mine in sweet, warm delight.

Tinges of Power snake through me to meet those lips. The fact that he's so strong yet so bent to my will is thrilling, but in spite of the invigorating sensation, I sigh as the sudden weight of being awake for so long hits me.

"You okay, hun?" Jack asks with a knowing smile.

"I'm just so tired. We were up for so long and now I don't think I can go on anymore."

Aub stifles a yawn and rubs her eyes. "I'm super tired, too."

"Bed, now," I order them both. I jump into the bed and turn out one of the lights. "Turn off the music," I tell Jack, since he's standing next to it.

Aub slides under the covers and turns off the light on her side.

The music disappears and Jack comes over to the bed. "I'll let you get some rest."

I shake my head. "Good boys get rewards." I hold up the sheet for him to climb in. Even though we'll be going to sleep, the Power flowing in my veins wants to play. "Your clothes look dirty, take them off."

His eyebrow rises as he stares at me.

"Abby," Aub says nervously. "Don't you think that's a bit much?"

"No. It will be good for him." I challenge him with my eyes. "He can't get hard. It's a good test."

As Jack unbuttons his waistcoat and then shirt, I looked over to Aub as Jack's shirt comes off his muscled shoulders. Seeing her jaw drop at the sight of my man is surprisingly a turn on. Is it because she's my best friend and not just some random girl? Something about her lusting over him doesn't seem as threatening. The Power doesn't explode in anger at her hot gaze on him. She said that if it wasn't her, she'd want it to be me. Could I be the same? Moreover, will I ever let her have a taste? She's been crushing on him just as long as I have, both in school and as an author. *Maybe a birthday present someday.*

"Pants," I order as I look back to him.

Jack undoes his belt and lets his pants fall to the floor. His cock pushes up against his boxer-briefs, not overly tight. I'd guess he's at quarter-mast, but even that's too much.

"Jack," I admonish. "I want you soft. Do as I say."

I turn to Aub as Jack does his breathing exercise. Her eyes are locked on his cock, wide and full of promise and fear. I can't blame her. I'm still scared of it. Maybe keeping him soft is a subconscious defense of what I'll eventually have to deal with. *Or maybe it's that forcing a man against his nature is true domination,* the darker side of my mind whispers. I can't deny the Power that blossoms inside my heart, to then surge through my veins. Just the thought of controlling him gives me a rush of the delectable sensation. It's like a hurricane of fire mixed with arctic winds tunneling through me. Heat that can burn my mind away and cold that can harden my heart. My eyes slide back to my man to find the bulge has lessened.

Once it's limp, I scoot over to the center of the bed as I continue to hold the sheet. "Get in."

As he lays next to me, his scent of citrus and spiced wood washes over me and that flow of Power coursing through me pulses between my thighs. I reach over to grab his soft, bow-tied cock through his black underwear. He throbs in my hand, and I give him a sharp tug.

"Don't you dare get hard. You stay soft for me."

He grunts and looks at me with hard eyes that made me think I've gone too far. All this time I've wondered what he would do for me, what his limits are. I haven't stopped to think what he would do if I ever went past those limits.

He turns to his side to face me, never pulling himself from my hand. His arms wrap around me, pulling me into a deep kiss that makes the pulse in my legs quicken. His tongue dances over mine with a mesmerizing rhythm.

I find my hands sliding along his muscles, first his arms, then his back and finally landing on his solid chest where I feel so warm. He's a soothing hearth to my over-stretched soul. This week has been the most turbulent in my life, and it's only a shadow of things to come, I could feel it somehow. Yet, laying here, next to him, letting the heat of his body wash over my skin, his lips crashing over my own as his tongue sends shockwaves through me, everything else fades away, as if he's already taken care of it.

When he finishes, he slides me back into my place on the bed. "Dream of me." He smiles with a wink.

He rolls to his back and shut his eyes, so I do the same, only when I roll to my back, I bump into Aubrey.

My heart breaks as I realize she's still here. I'd completely forgotten. As Jack's heat washed my problems away, she disappeared with them.

I roll over to face her and bring her into a hug. "Thank you for being here," I whisper. "I really need you."

Her hands remain limp for a moment but then snake around me till she's holding me just as tightly as I am her. "I need you, too," she whispers back. "I love you, Abby."

Her words slam into my heart, in a way that Jack's can't. At least not yet, not till we can be sure that my family magic doesn't work on him. Aub's words are real. Her love is real. That, I can be certain of.

Chapter Twenty

I walk into a room I'm not familiar with. It's in the shape of a large diamond with the door I stand in at the bottom tip. The old wooden floors are well-kept, and the vaulted ceiling stretches at least thirty feet up. A couple of feet in, draped red curtains pull back and expose the bedroom that's easily three times the size of mine. To the left sits a computer with three screens, just past that are two doors. To the right, a collection of bookshelves wrap around to the far wall and stop at a full-sized refrigerator. A warm and inviting loveseat waits in that corner beside a small table with a couple of books. In the far corner, a four-post bed with black curtains tied back dominates the room.

Jack come through one of the doors to the left, completely naked and wet, with a towel draped over his head and steam billowing around him. When he see me, his eyes shoot wide.

"Abigale. What are you doing here?" He shakes his head. "I'm sorry. I didn't mean it like that. I'm just surprised."

He slings the towel to the floor and walks over to me, full of confidence. When he pulls me into a deep kiss, I'm shocked by the sudden skin-on-skin contact of our bodies.

I hadn't noticed I'm naked, too.

My nipples harden against his thick body as my thighs become slick with my desire for him. I reach down to grab his hardening cock, but notice my ribbon is missing. My need to discipline him overtakes my need to taste his tongue.

"Jack," I snap. "Where is my ribbon?"

He looks down between us, though there's no way he can see his erection with my heavy chest in the way.

"Oh, I don't know. I'll put it back on." He turns around, pulling his long cock from my hand quickly jaunts to his computer. He types something in as I stare at his cute butt, then instantly turns around with the ribbon wrapping his limp member. "Better?" he asks with an apologetic smile.

"What the fuck? How did you do that?" It's like some sort of magic trick. There's no way he could have put it back on so fast when he was typing.

He shrugs and wraps me up in his arms again.

His kiss enthralls as his hands slide down to grab my ass cheeks. It takes nearly everything in me to push him back.

"Down boy," I command, causing him to take a step back.

He puts his hands up in surrender and smiles like a cocky bastard, making the Power flowing through my veins flare.

"I said down," I snap, pointing to the floor.

Jack's confident smile takes a hungry edge as he lowers himself to his knees. Like a machine in total control, his movement is as seamless as it is precise. I can just imagine it moving over me in a perfect rhythm, but that will have to wait. He needs a lesson first.

"Crawl." I place my heeled boot forward as his goal.

I'm somehow standing in my white dominatrix outfit Deanna gave me. Before I can think of how it's magically on me, Jack's crawling captures my attention.

Like a tiger stalking his prey, his muscles flow like liquid steel, sliding from one position to the next. He presses his lips against the side of my boot, then runs his tongue up, up, up, till he slides along the skin of my inner thigh, heading straight for my blooming flower.

I want it so bad, but my hands strike out, grabbing his head by the hair and yanking him back to look up at me. My desire for Power far outweighs my desire for his love.

"I didn't say you could have that!" I smack him across the

face while still gripping his hair, tilting his face up and locking him in place. "I own you, Jack! You do as I command!"

"Yes, Mistress." Jack moans. A haze falls over his eyes as if he's drunk or drugged.

I spit into his gaping mouth. "Who do you belong to?"

The haze lifts, and those honey-brown eyes hone in on me. "I belong to—"

I wake in my bed with a start and a hunger between my thighs. Jack lays on his side with me buried in his warm chest, his scent so strong I taste him. Jack's thick arm wraps around me, his hand ending in a tangle of mine and Aub's black hair, hugging her head to my shoulders.

Aub's arm droops around my waist, her fingers dipping into Jack's waistband, giving his soft cock an escape that it declined to take.

I'm sandwiched tight between them, my thighs practically melting and my lungs burning to the point they threaten to incinerate me and both these fuckers in my bed!

I fight off the urge to scream at them. The need balls in my throat, but I swallow it down as if swallowing a whole god damn ostrich egg. *Jack was simply holding me, and Aub was there. Simple mistake, that's all. Aub is reaching for me, and her hand went just a little too far, nothing more than that.*

Aub is getting in the way of all the rewards I have planned for Jack, but I can't be mad at her. I'm desperate for her right now. My life is too crazy for her not to be here.

I sigh, letting the anger dissipate with the breath. I tap Jack's granite chest and whisper, "Time to wake up."

He rolls to his back and falls off the bed. Catching himself with his foot and hand, he manages to spin upright as he groans. "Oh, fuck." He instantly starts his breathing exercise as he turns away from me.

I look back to Aub and give her a few taps on the hip. "Come on Aub, we have to wake up."

Aub rolls to her back as well but with enough bed for another two people, she sprawls out and yawns. "Shit, what time is it?"

After one last exasperated exhale, Jack answers, "Seven-thirty. We could still go on our date if you want."

I drink him in with my eyes. He's quick to put his pants on, but I see that he managed to remain soft. "I'd love to, hun. I just don't know with everything that's going on."

He crouches down next to me. "All of your problems will be here when we get back."

What the fuck is that supposed to mean? "That's exactly what I wanted to hear."

"And we'll be here, too," he adds with sincerity. "We're not going to solve this today; we won't solve it tomorrow either. We might not even solve it over the next five or ten years, but we're going to graduate, you're going to study law with Aubrey, you're going to have a career, a few babies," he adds with a smile. "We can't be consumed by the demons in our lives to the point that the angels beside us don't recognize us any longer." His hand comes to rest gently on my cheek. "You can't let your problems get in the way of your life. You need to be able to put them to the side, to have fun from time to time. We can solve these problems. We can take our time, be diligent about it and we'll come out on top because have gotten through it together."

Confidence swells inside me. He's right. I can't put my life on hold for this. I'm planning a life of fighting crime in a courtroom, I can't slow down now. Aub and I have worked too hard for this magic bullshit to derail us.

As I sit up, I reach over to take Aub's hand as I ask Jack, "You mean it? All of us? Together?"

"I'm your man and she's your best friend. You couldn't be set up for success any better."

Aub squeezes my hand, giving me another shot of confidence.

My heart bursts with love. "God, dumb-dumb, how are you so smart sometimes?"

"As long as it's not math, I do all right." He grins.

I sit there between the best two people in my life. Aub has been a pillar for me seven years running, and Jack has come along at just the right time. I reach out to Jack to take his hand.

"Together?" I ask, looking between the two.

"Together." Jack smiles.

Aub hesitates for a moment but then smiles and nods. "Together. But I need a boyfriend. I can't sit around and watch you two fuck all the time."

"Just some of the time?" Jack suggests with a sly smile.

"*Ew!* No," Aub laughs.

I laugh along with her, but a tinge of that seductive Power whispers that I'd enjoy her watching me with Jack. *How will she react watching me break him?* I wonder for a moment before I shake the thought. *I'm not breaking him, so there's nothing for her to watch!*

"So, which one of you wants to take me home?" Aub asks, pulling me from my thoughts.

"No, don't go." I realize she's not meant to be on this date, but I'm not ready to be without her. One day Jack will be my rock, but for now, that's Aub. "When can you come back? I really don't want to be apart."

"Well, I feel pretty rested." She shrugs. "So, I'll be up all night. If you want to come get me after your date, I'm up for more digging. And I mean *after*, as in the whole date. I don't want you to pick me up after you get done singing but still want to bang."

Jack roars with laughter. "If you're wanting to wait till we don't want to bang, you'll be bones in a grave."

"Wow, okay." Aub rolls her eyes as she slides from the bed. She looks back just as her feet peek out from under the covers. She scowls at Jack for a moment before she points to the opposite wall. "Turn around."

Jack turns. "Look, why don't I take you home. I'll wait while you get ready and then I'll bring you back and we can all go."

Oh, I love this man. "Are you sure? I've made you wait for so long."

"What's another night?" He shrugs, the muscles of his back ripping like steel cables under his skin. "I could wait a thousand years for you."

"Then you'd be bones in the ground." Aub chuckles as she slips into her jeans.

Her plump ass holds the pants at bay for a moment till her pale cheeks slip under the black denim. Jealous doesn't even begin to describe how I and most other women feel about that ass. Mine's decent, sure, I have very nice hips to give me a wide set of cheeks, but her ass is that perfect, top tier, peach ass. They say God gives you either an ass or tits and a surgeon gives you the other.

"Bones," Jack echoes softly. He looks at me with tender eyes and places my hand against his cheek. "Just waiting."

"Should I vomit now or wait till I'm in your car?" Aub asks.

I push Jack away with a playful smile as I slip out of the bed, but he grabs me off my feet into his arms and I scream in delight. He spins around before falling back onto the ruffled sheets. He kisses me with lips like silk pillows laid over steel. His fingers tickle my thigh and ribs, making me squirm in his arms.

"Okay! Headed to your car to puke. Thanks," Aub says, leaving the room.

"Be back soon." He kisses me again, then springs to his feet but turns at the door. "Think of me when you're in the shower." A quick wink and he's gone.

I grab a change of clothes and head to the bathroom, but an idea dawns on me.

Me: You should invite Derrick.

Aub: Genius! Hope he's free.

Aub: Fuck yeah! He's down. Double date!!

After taking a nice long shower, including a little time imagining Jack with his shirt open and cock out, I step out and wrap my hair in a towel while applying my moisturizer. A minute later Deanna comes in, closing the door behind her.

"Knock much?" I ask.

"So, it worked right? He doesn't remember anything?"

"Yeah, you saw him. He doesn't remember anything from before this morning."

"He freaked me out when he started questioning the story. Like his phone and his shoulder." She looks to the side and her jaw shifts. "I felt like he was faking it."

I bark a laugh and then cough to try to cover it up. *Shit! Jack, you cocky bastard!* Why did he have to be so literal? "I...uh, did it over again. He was asking too many questions about how he fell. So, he wasn't asking about anything after that."

She sighs in relief and nearly falls back against the door. "Thank god! I was so fucking scared."

"Why?" I start to brush my teeth, the vibrating brush buzzing in my head as I look at my sister through the mirror.

"Because, you stupid bitch, Mom would literally kill him. Fuck. I wasn't just saying that shit to sound tough. I nearly pissed myself when he stood between us. He's fast as shit! And I don't want him dead. He's hot as fuck."

I scowl at her reflection as fire explodes in me.

"Ah, I see you're getting territorial. Good! That's how you should be. Our men belong to us, don't let any other bitch get close. And don't worry, I'm not going to try anything. I'd never do that to you. It's nice to have a cute guy around, though. More than that, he's rich as fuck, apparently, so that's good for you." She shrugs. "At least you won't have to worry about money."

"But you would tell Mom that he knew shit and let her kill him?"

Her jaw hardens along with her eyes. "I'd have to tell her. It's our lives on the line, Abby!"

Shit. Abby, not bitch? She really believes it and she's worried for me. "You're worried that if people found out we'd be burned at the stake or something?"

"Yes! People won't want a few women running around with the ability to control others. They'd fuck us raw then cut our heads off."

"Wait. What if we told them about it but also told them to never tell? That way we can be open with them and they aren't allowed to talk about it."

"Quit trying to find a loophole. Mom will fucking gut him if she thinks for a second that he knows."

"What does it matter?" I shout. "If we just mind fuck them, they won't know!"

"I don't know if it works like that!"

My brain fails to function for a moment as it processes what she just said. *What the actual fuck?* I turn to her and shout, "Wait, what? What do you mean?"

"I've never made a guy forget things," she blurts out. "There, happy? I only said that shit to get you to listen."

"What?" I cry out. *What was the purpose then? Why would she even think to say it if she's never done it?* "You—You've never done it?"

"No! Mom told me that it's possible, but she said it takes years of taming."

"I've had Jack for a week! Why would you think that it would work?"

"Because Mom's a fucking liar and I was desperate for a solution! God, insufferable bitch! I'm serious about not wanting to see Jack die. I can see how happy you are and I don't want you to lose that."

Well, fuck. That's one way to kill an argument. I hug her, pulling her close. "Fucking dumb bitch. I love you."

"I love you, too," she says, before pushing me off. "Now get off me, you're fucking wet."

"Jesus, I'm trying to have a moment. I guess not. Are we done then?" I move back to the sink to finish brushing my teeth. "We're going on a date when they get back. I'd like to be halfway ready."

"Oh? You've decided to bring Aubrey in on it? Let her suck his balls while you ride that big cock." She teases with a smile.

The Power stirs in delight at the image Deanna places in my mind but I quickly push it down. "No. I'm not fucking sharing him with anyone. Now will you get out?"

"No," she states, dropping the playful banter shtick. "Not till you tell me what Aubrey knows."

The toothbrush slips from my hand. I try to catch it, but I fumble it till it slaps the mirror and falls into the sink.

Deanna scoffs. "Smooth."

I pick up the brush and start rinsing it off as I glare at her through the mirror. "You wouldn't hurt her. She's like a fucking sister to us!"

"I will beat her ass, just like I beat yours…" She pushes off the door and leans over my shoulder to add, "*sister*. What does she know?"

I turn around and plead with her. "Please, you can't say anything to Mom. Aubrey's not going to tell. She swore to me, she swore to you."

"Enough begging," Deanna snaps, stepping in closer, making me lean back over the sink. "We Augustia women don't *beg*! We make others beg! Now tell me what you've told her."

"I told her everything," I whimper.

Hearing myself sound like that sickens my stomach and makes the Power recoil in disgust. It shoots through me with scorching fury and suddenly, not only am I not afraid, I'm pissed!

I shove Deanna off me, her back slamming into the door. "You will *not* hurt her. I won't let you!"

"Fuck! Stupid bitch," Deanna groans as she rolls one of her shoulders. "I'm not going to hurt her. I love that girl. But I need to know what she knows so that I can make sure she doesn't learn anything else."

"What else? What are you talking about? I already told you, I told her everything. What else is there for her to find out?"

"Mom hasn't told you everything yet, fucking idiot. She hasn't even told *me* everything. I told you she's a lying bitch. She has some grand plan she made up when we was younger on how she's going to tell us everything. I've had six talks so far."

"Why? How many talks are there?"

She smiles as she shakes her head. "I don't know. She's never told me."

"So…what, then? Is there more? Do we have more powers?"

"Yes, there's more. Mom didn't tell you about erasing a guy's memories, but I did. She told me that the day she told you about our lineage. I haven't even had a chance to use it on one of my guys, I've been so backed up in the lab. That's why I wasn't sure it would work this morning. The thing is, Mom won't let me tell you and Mom is fucking psycho, so you better act surprised whenever she tells you something that I already have. When I joked about building a harem, or as Mom *insists* on calling it, a Collection, I'm really building a fucking army."

"An army? Why? She has twelve men, Dad be—" *The bitch is fucking lying to me.*

"There's my ridiculously smart sister. Glad she's finally come to the party. I knew you'd need some time to get your feet under you, but now you see. Twelve is a fucking joke for someone who's been doing this as long as her. She says she 'threw men away,' fucking bull shit."

Her diary said that she had given men over to AIDs and had men kill themselves just to see if they would. I consider telling Deanna about what we found, but then decide I should get as much out of her as I can first.

"So, you're building an army, to what? Go to war with Mom?"

"No, dummy. I'm making an army to defend me from her. She's all out of juice, or so she says, but I remember a time where she got this bell boy to do everything she said. At the time, she told me that's what a little flirting will get you, but now I realize that it was our Power. I was thirteen and mom was pregnant with Zest."

"Meaning she'd had sex with the third guy. So why lie about it?"

"She's trying to slow us down. Fucking is the fastest way to get a guy and she wants us to keep our numbers down."

"Why? Because she doesn't want us to make armies?"

"Power, bitch. It's not just power over men, it's just straight power. She loves making anybody, *everybody,* her little bitch. She can't get enough of it."

"Okay, okay. So, tell me this; you think she has more guys

and you're going to fuck around till you have more. Why haven't you then? You only have two guys."

She stands there looking at me like she expects better.

"*You* have more guys." I groan. I should have seen that coming. God, I'm being so stupid about this! "So, what? You know that the three-guy rule is bullshit or something?"

"No. I'll admit, I've been a little bitch. I've only had sex with Micha." I feel like she's bullshitting, but I can't call her bluff without risking that she's not. "But I have a few toys around town and when you brought Jack home, I decided I needed to find some higher quality men. Does he have a brother?"

"No," I growl.

"Geez, fine. But we need to work together. I'm scared shitless of Mom. She's going to turn on us eventually. I can fucking feel it. Maybe it was just the two of us being back-to-back or something. Maybe she'll chill out before Zest gets her Power, but I don't think she will. At the beginning of summer, she talked to me about telling you everything. She was having doubts at first, but I calmed her down. I thought she was just being dramatic. I mean, I've been waiting for her to tell you this shit for over a year now. When she first told me, bitch woke me up at fucking midnight on my eighteenth birthday."

Eighteen? She's had the power for three years? I wonder exactly how many guys she has around town.

"She told me that the Power hits on our eighteenth, but when yours was coming up, she changed he story and said it can be different for different people. A fucking whole year later and she bailed a week before you turn nineteen. She said it was another business trip, but they really went to Europe. I was snooping around and I found their itinerary. London, Berlin, Rome. I thought it was fucked up she was waiting to tell you about it and she wouldn't let me do the honors, especially when

Jack came into the picture. When she was home last month, she said she was going to tell you and the day before she left, she told me she had the talk with you. Then, as the bitch was walking out the fucking door, she pulls me aside and tells me the truth just so that I wouldn't slip. She's very, *very* serious about being the one to tell you and Zest. She's laid down some creepy veiled threats of what she would do if I ever told either of you. So, listen to me and take my words seriously. Do not tell Aubrey anymore! And make sure Mom doesn't find out. Mom *will* kill her. She won't let *anyone* know about this shit but us."

"If you want to work together then you need to tell me what you know. I can't help if I'm in the dark."

She looks at me with considering eyes. "Fine, but under one condition. You have to promise me with Thing One, Thing Two."

"Are you serious?" I can't believe she's asking to revert back to when we were five or six. We loved the *Cat in the Hat* and Mom called us Thing One and Thing Two so much that we made pacts named after the erratic little helpers. If we ever made a Thing One, Thing Two pact, it was sacred. "We aren't little kids anymore."

"I'm dead serious, and I want you to take this promise as seriously as any of the Thing One, Thing Two pacts we made in the past. If you're not willing, then you can just wait till summer for Mom to tell you the next bit."

"Fine." I sigh. "But I'm not doing the stupid dance."

"Me neither, idiot. We're not fucking five." She holds out her hand. "Thing One."

I grab her hand. "Thing Two."

"I promise to keep my fucking mouth shut about all of this," Deanna says.

"I promise to keep my fucking mouth shut about all of this," I repeat.

We shake hands three times and release, letting our hands raise over our heads with our fingers fluttering. A dance on nearby furniture would have ensued if we were still two feet tall.

"You want to finally know how Jack gave you a squirter in the hall?"

Chapter Twenty-One

Deanna's smile mocks me from skin to core. I'm tempted to throw her through the wall.

"What do you know about it?" I nearly scowl but I won't risk her holding it over my head any longer than she already is.

"Two things. One, it was from the Power. Mom hinted at the fact we have *way* better orgasms because of it, but what she left out was how our pets gain powers as well."

My jaw drops. "So, I gave him the power to give orgasms with a lick?"

She raises a finger as her brow lifts. "Hey. Big sister talks, little sister listens. No, because two; the sexual act could be something as simple as a kiss or a touch, as long as it was enough for the Power to react. He probably doesn't have powers yet. It takes a while, but the orgasm is the Power's way of telling us that the man is capable of gaining powers. If you don't get some orgasm the first time, he's not going to develop anything. The stronger the orgasm, the stronger the powers."

"What kind—"

"Big sister talks," Deanna interrupts. "Powers can be anything from physical growth to mental growth, extra sensory perception, even telepathic communication with his mommy-dommy. Mom said there are others, but never went down a comprehensive list so I've been trying to figure out more on my own.

"Kurtis gave me one decent gusher. That's why he's my main squeeze. So far, he's shown signs of extra sensory and telepathic powers. He's always by his phone when I'm about to call because he knows it's coming. He picks up the perfect take-out, shit like that. A couple of my other guys have had some results but so far, it's been very small improvements. I've kept logs if you want to look, but it's honestly not that much because Mom only told me about it back in April. I don't get why she's being such a fucking Nazi about telling us about this." She huffs in frustration as she leans against the sink. "It's like she thinks that because she had to figure it all out on her own, we should, too. But it's like, her mom wasn't around to tell her and she's here with us, so why be a bitch about it?"

"So, Jack will get superpowers or some shit?" I can't wrap my mind around the idea, but then again, this seems to be the week for it.

"Yes, some good one's I'm guessing. Just a lick? Jesus Christ! The gusher Kurtis gave me was from a finger blast behind the Staples he worked at. I'm guessing Jack will get something really good if he managed something so strong with so little."

"How many do you have?"

"Eight. Others," she adds with a hungry grin.

"Not wasting any time." I match her stance against the counter. "How easy was it?"

"Like, easier than saying my own name. I just look them in the eyes and tell them to follow me. They always do. I lead them somewhere private and then kiss. Game over."

"Do you have to keep it up or something? Or is it permanent?"

She shrugs. "Kinda both. End of the day, permanent as fuck. I left one guy alone for nearly a year to answer that very question. When I came back, he was on his knees crying, but he's a fucking loser, just like your Les."

"What?" I wonder out loud. "What do you mean, like Les? I didn't have the Power till a few weeks ago."

"It's not like an overnight thing. You were probably slowly gaining the Power when you were dating him. You said Les was finger banging you? You probably didn't have enough juice to dom him with a kiss, but I bet he sucked you off his fingers and that would have been enough. He's been thinking of you nonstop, but too scared to approach you. The guy I left for a year; it was Mark. He told me everything," she purrs with a sadistic smile that coaxes the Power to spread through me. "He told me how his every fucking thought was about me. How he couldn't eat unless he thought I might possibly come back for him one day, that I might have need of him, that he needed to stay alive just in case I wanted him back. He sobbed tears of joy as I had all my guys run a train on him while he licked my feet."

The Power shoots straight to my clit like a bolt of lightning, striking me with a pleasure that threaten Jack's fingers for supremacy.

I do my best to keep my face as passive as I can manage. The last thing I want to do is come in front of my sister because she's talking about having her boyfriends fuck each other. "Are you serious? You really did that to Mark? You're not just saying it like you did with the mind erase shit?"

"Yeah, yeah," she says with a dismissive wave. "I lied about the memory wipe shit, but it worked out. That's all that matters."

"So, what else?" I need to keep the conversation moving in order to get the image of Mark licking feet while getting drilled out of my mind.

"If you get into a guy's head enough, you can enter his dreams and really fuck him up."

"And you've done that?"

"Only to three of my guys, the rest I'm not close enough, but I'm working on it. But if you're able to compel Jack to forget things, I'm betting that's close enough to visit him in his sleep."

My dreams of Jack over the past couple weeks flash through

my mind. *Am I already in his dreams?* "Are the dreams super realistic and go straight to sex?"

Deanna's mouth pops open in a scandalous shock. "You've had them! I fucking knew it. You've got Jack nailed to the ground if you're in his dreams."

But he doesn't think it works. Is he lying? Or maybe he's just making excuses. Maybe he's just as dominated as Mark, but he can't tell.

"Anything else?" I ask, afraid of the answer.

She nods with a satisfied smile. "So, like Mom said, we get our looks, our brains and our athletics from our bloodline. I don't know about you, but that made me feel like shit. Like none of the hard work I put into myself counted. It's more, though. Our pets aren't the only ones to get powers. Again, it takes a special pet, but they can give *us* powers as well."

"Like?"

Like this, she says in my mind.

I scream at the top of my lungs and would have fallen backward into the shower if Deanna didn't catch my arm.

"Calm down, bitch," she says as she drops me.

My ass hits the tile with a padded *thump*, thanks to the towel. I look up at her, too stunned to get my feet under me.

"Cool trick, huh?"

"Can you read my fucking mind?"

"No." She frowns. "I wish. And before you ask, I'm guessing Mom doesn't have that power either, given some of the shit I've done, but she can speak in your mind like I can. You try."

"Me? I can't do that." I scramble to my feet while keeping the towel wrapped around my body.

She shrugs and places her hands on her hips. "Maybe you can. Give it a shot. Just look at me and think something."

"That's all there is to it? You just look and think?"

"Well, when I say think, I mean like, intend. Be intentional. Force the words into my mind."

I stare at her forehead and think, *Can you hear me? Hello?* "Nothing?"

She frowns and shrugs. "Maybe you need more time. Given your experience with Jack, I thought you might have more abilities already. That's interesting. Keep me posted though. If we combine our tests, we could learn a lot."

"I'm not preforming tests on Jack."

"Yes, you are. Even if you don't want to use the scientific process, you're still experimenting. All couples experiment. They find out what works and what doesn't. We just happen to have a few more variables and possible results." She ends with a sweet smile. "I assume you've heard the Power in your head? Had a few darker thoughts, maybe you find yourself short with other boys."

I smile as Jack's words fall from my mouth. "I'm done wasting my time on boys."

"Just wait. Jack is good, don't get me wrong, but he's not the end, little dove. Not by a long shot. As good as he might be, he's not going to be enough. I thought the same thing with Kurtis, but it will never be enough. As long as the Power is in us, we'll always want more."

The idea that I'll want more after Jack makes my chest tight and my blood boil. I don't want to be forced to want others. I don't want to be forced to want anyone. A sudden chill creeps up my spine like dead hands climbing up each vertebra.

"Do we ever want a guy because of the Power? Can it make *us* attracted to someone?"

Deanna thinks for a moment as if I've given her a difficult test question. "Mom's never mentioned that. And I don't think I felt pushed toward Kurtis. I don't think so," she concludes with a shake of her head. "The Power drives us to get more, but not specific men. Otherwise, I think I'd have a better stable."

I sigh in relief. "So, who are these other guys you've been taming?" I start at the fact that I just said taming so casually.

"I've just been picking up guys I think are cute or that no one would miss, you know? I don't want to have to deal with family or they might start asking questions about why their son is suddenly doing my bidding. That was my thought process till you brought Jack home. Seeing his profile pics didn't do him justice. I need to be more selective. I need men who have position. I need guys with guns. Lots of guns! Mom told me about this guy she had for a while, killed himself for her, yeah right. She said he was in the army and knew how to stab a guy fifty different ways with a spoon. I bet he's still alive and I bet she has others who are super dangerous killers."

The doorbell rings but then the door opens. "We can just go in, dumb-dumb," Aub says.

We come out of the bathroom, and I look down at them from the banister. Jack still stands outside. "You can come in, silly."

A grin stretches his face. "I knew you'd look amazing in a towel."

"You're not ready?" Aub asks, as she stops halfway up the stairs.

"I'm working on it, bitch." My eyes fall back on my big, beautiful man. "What do you know about guns?"

"That depends, how old are we talking?"

How old? "What? Whichever you know about."

"Well, the 1712 Bulvachav musket was really decades before it's time," he says with a level of enthusiasm that worries me. "I mean, this thing was able to shoot an eight-ounce shot up to twenty-five yards with a high degree of accuracy."

"Nice," Deanna says. "He knows about muskets. That's super useful."

"I'm kidding." Jack laughs. "Why would I know about muskets? You girls are way too gullible. Why are you asking about guns?"

"I was telling Deanna how much you kick ass and she said you couldn't fight off a gun." I'm much better at making shit up after some sleep.

"She's right," he says. "Bullets beat hands every time, but I have a few guns. Did you know, fully automatic weapons are banned except ones that were made before 1978? Which is interesting for a whole other reason. But I don't have one." He frowns.

"Then what the fuck is your point?" Deanna snaps, leaning over the railing as she spat her words.

"I don't have *one*, because I have three of them," he shouts, as he shoots imaginary bullets with his fingers. "Ha! Got'em!"

"What a fucking idiot," Deanna sighs. "Please, stay gone." She walks to her room and slams the door behind her.

"I'll be down in a minute." I open my towel to quickly flash him before I head to my room with Aub.

He groans as I shut my door.

"What have you been doing this whole time?" Aub asks.

"I was cornered by Deanna."

I turn on the stereo and explain the first half of the conversation as I put my outfit together. I tell her we made a Thing One, Thing Two pact so the rest of the conversation is off the table. Like the best friend she's always been, Aub understands. Still, I manage to elaborate on some of the things I read in Mom's journal that make more sense after Deanna's enlightening conversation.

Aub went with one of her spikiest outfits, so I decide it will be cute to match. I pair my red and black corset with red and black arm sleeves. I also slide on several wrist bands, topping them off with spikes. For my bottom, I wear a black tutu with black thigh high nylons and my new knee-high boots. With their steep but sturdy heels, they're quickly becoming my favorite. I grab my two oversized spiked belts, each one wraps around my waist and hangs off opposite hips to push the bushy tulle skirt down so I'm not exposed. More spiked bands go around my ankles before setting to work on my face. "Jack," I call as I apply my lipstick, black with a crimson line down the center. *A dark geisha.* Just one more thing to set the outfit off.

Jack comes into my room and shuts the door behind him when I motion him to. I point at the floor in front of me and he moves to it smoothly, like a natural born predator. His goofy smile's gone, his eyes look at me with a hunger and readiness that makes the heat between my legs rush up through my chest just as the Power slides down between my thighs.

"I need my ribbon," I say with my hand out.

If there's any hesitation, I don't see it. He unbuttons his pants, never breaking eye contact, though the corner of his lips curve into the faintest of smiles.

"Okay, I'm out," Aub says, as she starts to leave.

"Stay," I say, my eyes locked on Jack's. "If you want. I don't mind. Do you, Jack? Do you mind if she sees your cock?"

"Not at all." He pulls it out, mostly limp with a good amount of chub to it.

Power flares through me, lighting my nerves to the point I can feel even the faintest movements of air from Jack's hot breath and the cool breeze that Aub's hair sends when she snaps her head to the side to block her view. She even blocks her face with her hands, how cute.

"You're both fucked." She looks at me from the corner of her eyes. "Do you really want me here?"

Her words only serve to embolden the Power in me. I motion to Jack's cock. "I thought you might like to see it. Am I wrong? I saw how you looked at him this morning. Go on, take a peek," I add with a wink.

I pull the bow of the ribbon loose and it slides free. His cock thickens but with his increased breathing, it stayed mostly soft. I put the ribbon to my nose and the light shudder of a near orgasm ripples through my spine.

Aub lets her head turn and her mouth drops as her eyes pop. "Holy fucking shit," she breathes.

As I put my hair up with the ribbon, I ask, "Do you have more of these?" I flick the tiny pink condom on his dick that looked to be quite full.

"In my glovebox."

"Good. Make sure to bring one with you next time you come inside." Once I have my hair up, I squat down to his cock and gave it a kiss, leaving a black and red lip print across his thick meat.

Aub's mouth hangs ajar as her tongue traces her plump upper lip.

Oh, Aub, if only you could taste it. The savory spice, sweet citrus and thick musk has my mouth watering. *I'm going to stick you down my throat tonight*, I promise his cock. I raise my hand to him. I can get up on my own, but I feel like being pampered.

Once he pulls me up, my puffed chest presses against him and I give his cock an aggressive squeeze. It bounces in my hand, eager to match me.

"Not yet, my love." I reach up to him and pull his head down to kiss him.

His lips are like fire, scalding me with his desire. My mind boils, my heart burns, and my soul is a raging inferno that wants to crush this man under my heel! I push him back just to survive, but I also push him back to save him. To save him from me.

"Stay soft," I breathe. Once a few more breaths have cooled my lungs sufficiently, I add, "When we get home, you can get hard. Not before. Now put it away."

He slips it back into his underwear, a large vein throbbing angrily at me as it falls behind his black undies. He fastens his pants and then pushes his hair back as he exhales.

"Good." I place my hand on his chest and gave him a quick kiss. "Are you mad at me, baby?"

"Never," he answers.

"But is that because of her Power?" Aub asks, her eyes lingering on Jack's pants.

Jack smiles. "No. It's her scent surrounding me." His hand presses mine harder into his chest. "It's her touch, edging me on. It's the look in her eyes that tells me she's happy. It's her kiss."

He strikes like a viper, his lips snatching mine up, reigniting the whirlwind of flames inside me. I want to push him off, not because I don't want it, but because I didn't initiate it, but my hand pulls on his tie instead.

"Whoa! Calm the fuck down," Aub shouts.

When I pull back, I realize my legs are around his waist and his hands are cupping the bare skin of my ass.

"Put me down." I growl. *How dare he do that without my say!* Once my feet are on the ground, I pull his tie again to bring him eye level. "And don't do that again, unless *I* tell you."

He nods with a smile, but an energy pours off him as if he's primed, as if he's about to launch himself on me. A tingling thrill spreads through my spine, but I'm not going to let him get away with it.

"Down boy," I command, snapping my finger and pointing to the ground, cracking his tie like a whip.

He lowers himself like a panther, his eyes never leaving his prey. When one knee touches the floor, his lips tilt into a grin and my heart jumps, thinking he's going to tackle me.

I growl his name to show him my displeasure, but his eyes only widen in anticipation.

When his other knee hit the floor, he leans back to sit on his haunches, bringing his tie taunt in my hand.

"You two are serious freaks," Aub says, sitting on the edge of my bed. "But the fact I really wish I had popcorn right now tells me I might be, too."

I smile at her joke as my gaze slides back down to regard Jack. His eyes are still on me, but they've lost that immediate intensity. He's simply waiting for his next command, hungry to appease.

"Who's in control?" I ask.

His smile says a witty remark is coming but he shrugs. "You are, of course."

"Can you really make him do anything?" Aub ask.

"She can," he answers, his eyes never leaving me.

"Quiet, Pet."

He gives a deep bow of his head.

Oh, I like that.

"What are you going to make him do?" Aub asks before she swallows hard.

There's a hunger in her eyes, too. Her tongue flicks across her lips.

She wants to taste him so bad. I wonder if she can taste him in the air. Remorse slides around my heart and squeezes. I shouldn't be playing with Jack in front of her. It's not fair unless I share, and that might not be something I could ever bring myself to do.

"Nothing more for now. I just wanted to remind him of his place."

That smile reemerges on his face, as if he's winning, as if he thinks he's in control. A hunger of my own simmers inside of me, a hunger born of my Power that needs to prove him wrong.

"Kiss my boot," I command, sliding my foot forward just a touch. "And then we'll leave."

He leans forward, placing his hands gently on the sides of my boots and presses his lips to them as if he was kissing my cheek.

I can't feel the physical pressure of his lips through the thick leather, but the energy of that kiss runs through every nerve of my body, as if his lips are everywhere at once. I'm so glad I didn't let Les taint these boots. These are for Jack's lips.

I throw my head back in pleasure and laugh.

"Oh my God," Aub exclaims with an awkward laugh. "Who the fuck are you? You, like, really get off on this, don't you?"

I sigh and smile. "*Ugh!* I love it, Aub. I can't imagine any drug getting close to this." A shiver spirals down my spine that I shake out. "Okay. Enough playing around. We should get going. Are you going to behave?" I ask, looking down at him.

He nods and stands when I point up and pull on his tie.

"Go start the car," I say before giving him one last kiss.

He walks off with a smile and I fall back on my bed with a sigh.

"I love this."

"You're fucking glowing! Oh my gosh, did you come from that?"

"No, but I feel like I did. *Ugh!* That man! He makes me go crazy."

"Is tonight the night then? You're going to sleep with him?"

"If you find us fucking in the bathroom, will you guard the door?" I joke.

"If you fuck in the bathroom, I'm taking his keys and leaving!"

I make a pouty at first but then ask, "What about Derrick? A double date might turn into both of our first nights."

"Derrick has a lot more work to put in before I let him in, but I'd be willing to give him a taste."

The thought of both of us with men on their knees between our legs flashes in my mind. I shake the thought and stand, we need to get out of my bedroom if I have any hope of getting my mind out of the gutter. "Let's go. I need some air."

"Don't wake me up when you get home," Deanna says from the living room as we leave.

Jack has backed the car up into the driveway, so the passenger door is closer to the front door. He opens both doors for us, Aub sitting in the back and me in the front.

When he sits down, I say, "So get this. Deanna told me a whole bunch more shit."

On our drive over to the bar, I tell Jack what I can. Leaving him in the dark didn't hurt as much as the thought of keeping things from Aub, and I wonder if that's just because he's a guy and Aub is my best friend, or if it's because the Power that flows in my veins sees him as nothing more than a pet, one that only needs to know how to please his... *What did Deanna call it? Mommy-dommy?* The Power drools at the thought of hearing Jack call me his mommy-dommy.

My mind fails to escape the gutter as it floats between thoughts of Jack on his knees, pleasing me with his tongue, to Jack on his back as I ride him, pinning him helplessly to my sheets.

Chapter Twenty-Two

Jack coaxes me into singing *Licking Crème* by Sevendust with him. Lucky for him, I have a few drinks in me, otherwise there's no way I'm going to pull off Skin's portion. Aub and I already sang the shit out of *Helena* by My Chemical Romance, while Derrick and Jack had done a Green Day song. I find not jumping him progressively harder as the night goes on.

Jack's money trumps our age, but Aub and I still snag a few drinks from the bar top when no one's looking. We always have fun sneaking drinks behind a bartender's back. Not sure how, but those drinks always taste better, maybe it's the splash of victory mixed in. After several rounds of shots, it's near impossible not to fuck Jack right here on stage as he sings to me with his intense eyes and devilish grin.

Aub and Derrick wait for us at the dimly lit booth, making out as if no one can see them. When Jack and I get back from the stage, I pounce on him, knocking him backward onto the large seat. After a few minutes of kissing, I push his face to the side and lick his ear. "Time to go home, baby."

He grabs my chin and turns my head, so I see under the table with him. On the other side, Aub's hand disappears down Derrick's pants while his goes into hers. The pair play with each other to the beat of the music, some Poppy song a couple of girls have chosen to sing to.

"You like that?" I whisper as I continue to lick his earlobe. "Do you want to do that? Does Aubrey get you hot? Do you want to fuck her?"

His head slowly turns to me with his brow knit in confusion. "Do you?"

I put a soft, but also not-so-soft, knee in his groin. "Oopsie!

Clumsy me," I say with all the sugar of a cute cartoon character. I stand and turn to Aub. "You ready, Aub?"

Aub pulls back from their kiss and gives Derrick a pat on the face. "Oh yeah. I'm ready."

Derrick's face slouches like his limp spine and he tips forward into Aub's breasts.

"*Ah!* Wait just a little bit, baby," Aub cooes.

Jack stands and leans on the table. "Aub, what is he on?"

Aub rolls Derrick's head in her tits. "He's drunk, Jack."

Jack reaches over and lifts Derrick's hand, it clatters on the table. "He's fucked, Aub."

The rattle of the plates and glasses shock Aub out of her sex haze as her eyes shoot wide and she jumps in the booth. She lifts Derrick's head up as drool falls from the side of his lip. She pushes him back against the wall and scurries out of the booth.

All the shoving wakes Derrick to the point that his loose lips turn into a dopey grin.

"Holy fuck, I didn't know! I fucking swear to God." She shivers as if someone dumped a cold bucket of water over her. "That's totally fucked. He hasn't done anything. We've only been drinking."

Jack moves around the table to sit next to Derrick, checking his eyes even though Derrick lazily pulls on Jack's waist coat. "Well, given that he was playing with you under the table, I'd say whatever it is just set in."

"Wait, you saw that?" Aub looks at me with wide eyes. They shift around for a moment then she steps close and whispers. "I'm literally on fucking fire, Abby. I swear, I didn't know he was fucked up, and I wouldn't have even done that shit in public if I wasn't wetter than the fucking ocean right now."

The Power roars in me that Aub's date is fucking with my plans, but I whip the beast back into its cage for Aub's sake.

Seeing the fear in her eyes pulls my arms around her. "It's okay. You didn't know. No real harm done. We'll take him home and that will be the end of it."

"This is fun," Derrick shouts. He lifts a half empty beer and sloshes it while Jack checks the other drinks on the table.

"I don't know." Jack shrugs. "I don't see anything in them, but I don't know if I would. A dissolved pill maybe but if it was something clear, there'd be no way of knowing. Are either of you feeling anything?"

Aub shakes her head. "Just a strong buzz, which is fucking long gone now! You think someone roofied him?"

Derrick's eyes light up. "Yeah, let's go to the roof! I want to see the stars! They're so cool."

"Who would drug *him*?" Jack asks. "It's more likely it was meant for one of you two, but the drinks got switched. There was that loud crash about thirty minutes ago, right before we got our round. Maybe it was some switch up then and his drink was meant for another table."

"We can't take him home like this," Aub says. "His mom works third shift but has the night off. We can't take him to my house." Her eyes dig into mine and I can almost hear her pleading with me. *I can't, Abby. I'm burning up.*

"We can go to my house," Jack says as he throws several hundred-dollar bills on the table. "I've got a room he can sleep in." He pulls Derrick from the booth but when Derrick's legs prove to be limper than wet noodles, Jack picks him up and flings him over his shoulder.

"Holy shit," Derrick shouts. "Fucking room is spinning, man! We're fucked!"

"Your dad and sister won't care?" I ask.

Jack laughs. "I own my own house."

Of fucking course, he does, I seethe. *You didn't think that was something you should have told me?*

He looks back at me as he pushes through the exit door. Warm honey swirls in his eyes almost as if apologizing.

I open the back door for Jack, and he puts Derrick in, fastening his seatbelt for him.

Aub stands at the door and shakes like a leaf. She looks up at me, tears brimming.

I can't. I can't sit with him. I imagine her voice quivering, which is odd since she isn't normally scared, but it just comes so easily to my mind.

I look in the back where Derrick holds that dopey grin. *Fuck…* "Sit in the front, Aub."

Before anyone can protest, I slide into the back seat and shut the door.

Aub's relief crashes into me and when she gets in the front, she looks back at me to mouth, 'Thank you.'

Jack had made the sacrifice to not drink at all so he can be our designated driver. We drive for about twenty minutes before we reach a gated neighborhood.

I get a text from my sister with a picture attached. It's of her in the same dominatrix outfit she bought for me but with a red inlay. Curtis is on his hands and knees with a leather mask on his face. I can tell it is him by his shoulder tattoo, *Property of Deanna*. Her boot is on a pedestal, and he licks it while she holds his leash.

Deanna: There's an eight-inch dildo in his ass too. Beat that bitch!!

I don't like how the Power surges down between my legs from seeing my sister dominate her boyfriend, but just thinking of that picture being me and Jack makes me squeeze my legs together.

I nearly leap from my skin when Derrick's fingers touch my

arm and in the dark of the car, he leans toward me like a fucking zombie.

"Don't!" I shove his head back, but he looks over at me again. "Just fucking go to sleep."

He slumps in his seat, his head laying back against the plush headrest.

Aub's eyes grow wide as she looks at her date then to me.

Did you do that? I imagine her asking.

I shake my head, not sure if I really did or not, but I hope not.

We both turn away. Best to forget about it.

We pass larger and larger houses, the land between them expanding till the houses disappear altogether, replaced by driveway gates and tall trees.

"Are we almost there?" I ask.

"Yeah. It's a bit off the beaten path. I wanted a house that wasn't technically in the city. I want to have horses on the property someday."

Aub laughs. "Why have horses when you already have a horse cock." She goes rigid as her shock slams into me, mixing with my own. "I—I don't know why I just said that. I'm—I'm sorry. I…"

What the fuck was that? I imagine her panicking.

Why the fuck am I imagining her talking so much tonight? I've never put words in her mouth before. We can often talk to each other with just a look, but I don't imagine her voice in my head. I just understand her, nothing more. What the fuck am I doing?

"Hey, you're okay." Jack reaches a hand over to her shoulder for a quick squeeze then places it back on the wheel. "You're just a little drunk. Don't worry about it."

Relief radiates from her. "Please tell me you have coffee."

"We have coffee," he smiles. "Jake drinks the stuff, so whatever he has is all that's there."

"Oh, I don't want to take someone else's. Wait, you have roommates?"

I press my lips together, so I won't shout his head through the fucking windshield. *Deep breath. You can do it.* I take two *very* deep breaths and even smile in my mind before I speak. "Jack, baby, don't you think that's something you should have told me about?"

His eyes peer through the rearview mirror to hit me with another soft and warm apology. "Yeah, I probably should have. I just never thought to bring it up. I'm sorry. It's a big house and it helps them out. They don't have to pay for a house or apartment so they can save money right now." He smiles at me through the mirror. "Don't worry. They're not staying forever."

"They? Just how many people are there?" I ask.

"Four. Jake, who probably isn't home. He races cars so he's likely off doing that. Quinn and Peter. They'll be there. They're always there. They get stoned and write music and stream all day. And then there's Devon. He has a girlfriend, Wendy. She might be there with him, but she doesn't live there."

I try to think of the people he's talking about, but I can't bring any faces to my mind. "Do I know any of them?"

After a moment, he shakes his head. "I met Jake and Quinn through my martial arts classes years ago. Quinn brought Peter to our tournaments, they all went to Jackson, though. I've known Peter now for about four years, but I've known Jake and Quinn for about ten. I met Devon in first grade. He went to our school, but he played Magic in the hallways. So, unless you were in with that crowd, you probably didn't meet him." He stops at a gate, and it opens on its own.

We drive on a dirt road for another minute. Enclosed by tall pine trees on both sides till it suddenly opens on the left to a field of grass. A house sits further up that looks like an old plantation home with wide pillars and multiple chimney stacks. There are lights in the first-floor windows but the second and third floor are dark. Jack parks next to another three cars, one of which is his old blue shitter. The cars sit in a line in front of a barn of some sort, it's hard to see in the dark. Half a second later, a blinding floodlight blasts us.

"Oh, shit!" Aub writhes in her seat and covers her eyes. "Fuck! Fuck! Fuck!"

"Calm down," Jack laughs. "Just look away."

The light is as strong as the sun, but I manage not to be blinded. Besides illuminating the north-west hemisphere, it also brightens the barn. A massive open door reveals a woodshop with a large buzzsaw on one of the tables, piles of wood and a few half-built projects.

I open my door and step outside. The smell of fresh cut wood hits me and I realize it's exactly how Jack smells. *So, this is why he smells like wood.* "Is that where you cut up all the bodies?"

"Yeah." Jack laughs as he reaches into the car to get Derrick.

"Why is your light so bright?" I shield my eyes with my hand, but even that seems to only be a half measure.

He holds Derrick by his side and an arm thrown over the back of his neck. Derrick's legs move sometimes and drag at others, but Jack's stride doesn't change either way. "Because it's dark and if there's someone out here that's not supposed to be, we need to be able to see them. Can you walk, Derrick? It'll be good for you if you can."

"*Buzzzzz.*" Derrick's head lulls and he stumbles but Jack just walks on toward the house.

I take Aub's arm, and we follow behind the men.

Upon closer inspection, the house is definitely an old

plantation house. Ten large pillars rise from base to roof in the front, framing wraparound porches on both the first and second floors. Dual stairs spiral down from the second story with accompanying flower beds following the railing, filled with herbs of all different types. The bottom porch, decorated by a few rocking chairs and a patio table, house numerous potted plants that either sit on the wood porch or hang from above.

As we walk up the porch steps, Jack taps his phone a couple times, and the double doors unlock automatically.

"No way," Aub and I say in unison.

"I told my friend about an app that doesn't come out for another few years, so he made it."

"They know about you being…" I glance at Derrick and whisper, "from the future?"

Jack looks at Derrick slouched like a melting gummy bear. "He's not going to remember any of this. The guy that made the app, Mark, he doesn't know. He made the app after I gave him the idea. Only Devon and Quinn know."

I feel a little less special since someone else knows, but I guess Aub is my confidant; it makes sense that Jack would have some guy friends to confide in.

When we go inside, the house looks like the beginning of a horror movie where the old house is nice and clean, and the dead bodies haven't started thumping in the dark just yet.

Stairs spiral off to the left, and a closet waits to the right. A long and wide hall, so large it reminds me of a ballroom, stretches to the back of the house with double doors mirroring the front. The ceiling goes clear to the third story and two catwalk hallways wrap all the way around the second and third floors with several doors lining the halls. Four wood pillars stretch from floor to ceiling on both sides of the massive hall. On the foyer's half, two doors on each side lead to more rooms, but beyond that, light spills out from large openings on both sides, enticing me to dive deeper into my man's house.

"What's in here?" Aub asks as she pulls on the door closest to the entrance. While the other doors match the house's updated but Victorian inspired look, this door is solid metal.

"It's a gun safe."

Aub's hand shoots off the handle as if it bit her. "Holy shit! Like a gun safe room?"

Jack puts Derrick down on a bench across the foyer from the death door and walks over. He presses a button on his app and a loud *clunk* comes from the door. Jack pulls it open and my mouth drops.

"You asked if I have guns. I have guns."

All sorts apparently. Multiple handguns, revolvers, hunting shotguns, tactical shotguns, hunting rifles, assault rifles, a fucking LMG! *Is that a tube for a rocket launcher?* Then there are swords, bows and arrows, throwing stars. All neatly displayed on the walls and racks, surrounded by crates of ammo. *What in the fuck?*

"Wha-What's all that for?" I ask.

He fucking shrugs like it's nothing. "It's mostly just for fun, but it's also for protection. We live far enough away that if there's a problem, the cops aren't going to get here till it's already a situation."

"So, you intend to fend off a burglar with an LMG?"

A smirk slides across his face. "That one is purely for fun. I'll show you how it works sometime, if you want. I own about a hundred acres, so we go out and shoot at a range we built. I'm a certified gun safety instructor. I know what I'm doing. For protection, it's really the handguns and shotguns. That's why they're closer to the door."

Well, if Deanna's right about Mom having guys with guns, I guess this is for the best. As nervous as a fucking armory makes me, I can't deny that it's a little hot to know that Jack can use a gun if he really needs to.

He closes the door, taps his phone and the *clunk* rings out, again. "Let's get that coffee, yeah?" He picks Derrick up from the bench, this time just throwing the unconscious man over his shoulder.

As we walk forward, the room to the right reveals itself to be a kitchen, fully updated with white marble counters and subway tile backsplash. The dark cabinets match the wood flooring, while the stainless-steel appliances show two ovens over top one another as well as a gas stovetop.

A man sits at the island table in a loose robe, his dirty blond hair is a mess as if he's just woken up. When he looks over to us, a grin spread across his face slowly as if he's moving at half speed. His blood shot eyes, and reeking smell of weed explain his slow reaction.

A woman grabs a pitcher of water from the refrigerator that matches the cabinetry, her blonde hair swishes across her finely sculpted back. She wears a plain white tank top that highlights her strong muscular build and grey sweatpants that showed off her shapely ass. She doesn't look like a body builder, but she's certainly more than the average athletic type.

"Quinn, Peter, this is Abigale and Aubrey. Oh, and the guy on my shoulder is Derrick. We think he drank something that was spiked."

Quinn is a woman? My jaw clenches as my eyes slide to Jack like a knife to a throat.

"Damn, man," Peter says. "That's jacked. Did you get the guy who did it?"

Jack frowns and shakes his head.

"That's fucked up." Quinn says. She reaches her hand over the island toward me. "Nice to meet you, Abigale."

I take her hand and grip with ferocity, but if my handshake hurts or even bothers her, she doesn't show any sign.

"Call me Abby," I say with a forced smile. "Jack just told me about having roommates."

"That's Jack." She shoots him a disapproving look. She shakes hands with Aub as well. "Saying things he should have said a long time ago. If you ever want embarrassing stories, just ask," she says with a smug smile.

"If you want the best stories, you should ask me," another man says from behind us.

"Abigale, Aubrey, that is Devon."

Across the wide hall, a massive living room sprawls outward and down to a tv big enough to be in a small movie theater. The sunken room made of a large couch and big chairs perfect for spooning. In front of a pool table, just on the edge of the room and the hall, Devon sits at a computer with three screens.

He's small for a guy, probably my height, with slick, long dark hair that looks like he hasn't washed in a while. "It's nice to finally meet you. I'd get up to shake your hands but we're about to pull this boss any second if our raid leader would take his head out of his ass. Jack won't shut up about you, so I feel like we've met before, but you're way hotter than he let on."

"Oh, is that right?" I raise an eyebrow at Jack.

Devon smiles. "Yeah, he made you sound like you were like, nice, but really, you're like, whoa. You know? It—" He turns to his screens begins furiously pressing buttons. "Fucking little bitch! Ha!"

"Okay, he's gone for a while," Jack says.

"What are you going to do with the guy," Quinn asks

"I'll put him in one of the empty rooms."

Her eyes slide between me and Aub.

"Could you get some coffee going?" Jack asks. "I'll take care of Derrick and be right back."

"Yeah, sure." Quinn pulls some coffee and a grinder from a cabinet.

Jack walks back to the foyer and heads up a spiral staircase to the third floor with Derrick over his shoulder.

"Tasty little snack," Quinn says as she watches Jack take him, grinding the coffee to dust with the grinder and her bulging biceps.

My own muscles tense, ready to jump over the island and smash her face into the sink if she's talking about my Jack.

"Too bad he's fucked up." She shrugs before she pours the ground beans into a coffee maker. "At least both you girls look delicious." Her eyes fall on me, and I can see why she and Jack are friends. Her green eyes hold that same confidant hunger that Jack's do when he looks at me. Predators. They're both top of the food chain predators.

The Power swells in my defense, keeping me from trembling like a frightened rabbit.

"Well, no free samples," Jack calls as he opens a door on the third floor. "Put on some coffee, please."

When he goes through the door, even with Aub at my side, standing across from Quinn suddenly feels dangerous. Those predator eyes of hers seem darker, almost as if she's been playing and is suddenly turning serious.

"Don't fuck up Jack," she warns. "No offence. I'd say it to any woman. He's my best friend."

The swelling Power deflates slightly at her admission. I look over at Aub and know exactly how Quinn feels. I'd say the same thing to any guy she brought home.

I raise my chin to let her know talking down to me isn't

going to fly, but I smile as well to show her we aren't enemies. "Don't worry. I'm going to take good care of him."

Quinn's brow lifts and as a cocky smirk spreads. "Peter and I were about to watch a movie, but we couldn't decide between a comedy or action. What do you think we should watch?"

My smile matches hers. "Something loud, with lots of explosions."

She nods and turns back to the coffee pot. She pours two cups and slides them across the island.

"That was fast," Aub says.

"Expensive machine." Quinn shrug. "Jake, for all his gruffness, likes his coffee to be premium."

I take a sip. I don't agree with coffee's bitter bite, but I want to encourage Aub since she needs a couple shots.

She takes a few more sips than I do but doesn't drink a lot. "I'd better not have too much. I think I should just get some sleep."

"You could watch a move with me and Pete." Quinn offers. "I don't bite. Then again, looking at your outfit, maybe you'd like it if I did."

"You fuck everyone Jack brings home?" I ask.

She laughs. "Have you seen these two?" She flicks a finger at Pete and then Devon. "Jack doesn't bring home scorching tens every day. I was just offering her a little fun while you and Jack go at it."

Heat explodes between my thighs. No matter what response I choose, I can only see this conversation getting out of hand, ending either in a fight or with me running to Jack so I can fuck his brains out. I decide to cut to the end.

I grab Aub's hand, not about to leave her with that tiger, and pull her to the stairs. Jack comes down as we go up and we met on the second floor.

"My room's this way." He smiles. His eyes flash to Aub and then back to me.

"She's going to sleep."

He nods and I can almost feel his shoulders relax. "Okay, there's a free room just down the hall here."

We follow Jack down the catwalk hallway. This part of the house seems to be stuck in the turn of the century with creaking wood, long hallway runners, gold light fixtures and paintings that looked older than America.

My eyes lock with the Quinn's once again. The extra distance doesn't seem to do anything to lessen the intensity of her stare. She smiles and gives me a wink before we turn into the last room on the hall.

It's decently decorated but looks like he ordered a room from Ikea. Not a bad idea, but it does look a little generic.

"There's a bathroom right there, but it's a Jack and Jill, so just lock the door on the other side if you go in there, but remember to unlock it when you're done. She'll do the same."

"She?" Aub asks. "As in Quinn?"

"Is she into women?" I ask.

"When she's high." Jack scoffs. "Or at least that's what she says. She and Peter play around, but...I think she's looking for someone who can keep up."

"What do you mean?"

"Peter's a nice guy, real good guy. He'd take a bullet for a stranger. But he's high all the time."

"You said they get high every day. Was that not an exaggeration?"

"For him, no. It's every day, multiple times per day. Quinn, probably every other day, or a little less. She usually gets high and works out then rides it out while they make music and post videos online."

"Yeah, that's great and all but what about her coming into my room at night?" Aub asks.

"She's not going to do that. Aub, I promise you. She's not as scary as she lets on. She'll respect your privacy. You have my word."

Relief floods me and Aub's relief proves palpable.

She turns and hugs me. "Don't forget a single thing. I want all the details," she whispers.

"One more thing," Jack says. "You'll find PJs in the dresser. Quinn thought it would be a good idea to have something for guests, and this is the girl's guest room, so, take your pick."

"Okay. Thanks, Jack." She let go and walks into the bathroom with a wave goodbye.

Jack leads me across the balcony portion of the hallway to the other side of the house and then down the hall, placing us back at the front, directly over the death closet.

He opens the door but then turns and offers me his hand. "This room is home to me. That is, whenever I'm not with you."

I take his hand and he pulls me into him. "Am I the first girl you've brought into this room, Jack Billard?"

"You are, and don't make fun, it's not as broody as yours."

Strong hands reach low to grab my ass, sending a shock of energy through me.

I grab onto Jack's broad shoulders and jump, wrapping my legs around his waist. I lay a soft kiss on his lips. My jarring pulse says that we're going to get rough at some point, but I want to make sure he knows how I really feel. If the Power comes out and starts barking orders, I need him to know that I love him.

He shuts the door behind him and walks into his room.

I look over his shoulder as we pass draped red curtains pulled back to the sides that he quickly loosens to let fall and block the door. My head spins around to take everything in. The computer, the two doors, the corner of bookshelves and the fridge. It's just like my dream. Then he lays me down on his bed. The massive four-post and black curtains spring up around me while the black comforter rolls out beneath me. Did I really invade his dream?

"I had a dream of this room." I push his chest and he backs up, watching me as I keep looking around the room. I point to the door closest to his computer. "You came out from there with a towel on your head."

The honey in his eyes sparkle with surprise. "That's the bathroom. How... Did you really have a dream about my room?"

I nod and scooch to the edge of the bed to put my feet on the floor. "It's exactly like my dream. Did you have a dream like that earlier? It was today."

He raises an eyebrow as his eyes shift. "I remember having a really hot dream, but..." His face scrunches in playful concentration. "Yeah, I can't remember what it was. When I woke up, I remember we were making out, or maybe I was going down on you. Fuck, I don't know."

"Yes! You were going down on me. You really can't remember?" Is that normal? Deanna didn't mention if the guys remember. Then again, she probably doesn't tell her guys they're under her control or that she enters their dreams.

"Hey. What's going on?" He gives a little tap on my side but makes no move to reinitiate what we'd come in here for. "You okay?"

"It's the Power. There's no way I could have known about your room and I think I was in your dream."

His smile spreads. "Can't deny that's a little hot you can jump into my dreams. Imagine all the impossible hijinks we could get up to."

"But that means the Power works on you, Jack! That means that—"

"You jumping into my dreams is not the Power working on me. Just order me to do something you know I won't do and then watch me not do it."

"And what if it's just a matter of strengthening the bond?"

His smile grows wicked. "Then we'll know after tonight, won't we?"

When I don't smile back his fades.

"Oh, I really thought that line would work." He rubs the back of his neck and looks around. "Well, ah…we can do something else. We can sit and cuddle. I could read to you, if you like, or give you a massage. I could make something for you if you're hungry."

"*Ughh!* All you want to do is serve me." It's just like what Mom wrote and what Deanna said; the men want to serve. "Does that sound normal to you?"

"What if that's how I love you? Maybe my love language is Acts of Service." He grabs one of my hands and smiles with warmth that I don't deserve. "Hey. I'm not under your spell. Well, technically, I am." His sympathetic smile turns hungry as his other hand wraps around my waist. He pulls me against him and sways his hips, moving mine along with him in a slow dance. "I am completely enthralled by you, every moment of the day, but it has nothing to do with your Power. Only you."

The Power burns with rage but my heart jumps at the thought of him loving me for me, and not because of the Power. I need to stop focusing on whether or not Jack is immune and start focusing on how not to use the Power on him. I need to take control, but not over Jack, over the Power.

"What about me serving you?" I ask.

The Power recoils in displeasure but I don't give a damn. Jack is my man, not the Power's plaything.

"You want to do something for me?"

No, the Power whispers. "Yes."

He sits on the edge of his bed and pats the sheets. "Lay down and let me give you a massage."

"Jack, that's not fair. That's not for you."

"How is me getting to rub oil all over your naked body not for me? You know what happens at the end of a full body massage right? While my fingers are nice and slick?"

My legs wilt from the nuclear heat of my blooming flower. *Fuck! What am I doing turning down a full body massage?* "That's also for me."

He unbuttons his shirt and waistcoat with his honey-brown eyes looking me up and down. "And what about after the end? When I use the oil on myself and I plunge into you? Is that just for you?"

My muscles tense as I restrain myself from running to his bed and jumping in. When his shirt comes off, I force myself to turn from him. "Damn it, Jack! I want to do something just for you."

He laughs for a moment but then the sheets ruffle from his considerable weight. "The second door, that's my closet. Go in there."

My mouth opens to ask why, but I shut it. *I just need to trust him and do what he says.* "There better not be a present or something waiting in here for me." I open the door to find immaculately organized shirts, jackets, pants and shoes. "Looks pretty nice. You have Quinn keep it neat for you?"

"Quinn's not my type." His voice rumbles.

"And what is your type?"

"Down at my shoes, at the far end, pull the carpet back, and you'll see a small notch in the wood. You can pull the board up. And my type is any good woman who's not blonde."

I go to the back and pull back not carpet, but a gorgeous rug that feels brand new. I lift the wood up to find a small cubby hole with an ornately carved wooden box and a handgun. "Another gun?"

"Leave that and bring me the box. Don't open it."

Fuck this, the Power rails. *Make him bow down on his face for giving you orders.*

I swallow a bitter taste that grows in my mouth. *I'm stronger than this magic shit!* Mom and Deanna probably never even tried to beat it. They don't have a Jack to try for.

I pick up the box, which has some serious heft to it. My fingers slide along the top carvings of mostly scroll work but in the center is a heart with a sword through it.

I come out to find Jack sitting in bed, his back against a padded headboard and his legs under the sheets. His pants lay in a heap along with the rest of his clothes.

He pats the middle of the bed next to him. "Come on. Oh, you might want to take off your belts and boots. All the spikes might not feel so great."

I've been imagining Jack kissing my boot all night and I hoped to get him to take them off for me, but I swallow my pride again. I kneel down, placing the box on the floor and unlace my boots, leaving the spiked ankle bracelets on them as I step out. I unclasp my belts and let them fall to the ground, allowing the tutu to rise some.

Jack's eyes stick to my thighs as if he's having a staring contest with them.

I toy with the idea of crawling over him, but I don't want him to grab me and start pleasuring me. I need to do whatever he wants, whatever this little show is that I'm performing for him. The Power rails against taking orders but my resolve to conquer this beast hardens as I look at Jack. Jack is my key. I need to break the Power with Jack, not break Jack with the Power.

I walk around to the other side of the bed and crawl in. I stay on top of the sheets just in case he's naked under there. He holds an arm up for me and I curl up next to him.

He takes the box as his other arm wraps around me. "Thank you for bringing me my box. Wasn't too hard, yeah?"

"If this is the box you keep your massage oil in, I'm going to be pissed."

He chuckles and jerks a thumb to the nightstand where a tall bottle of body massage oil stands. "I already have that taken care of." He opens the box to reveal a red velvet interior with a leather-bound book and a smaller black box. "We're going to do a little reading." He pulls the book out and hands it to me. "I want you to go to March 28th, 2008. I start a new journal each year, so it's all in order."

My heart shoots straight through the vaulted ceiling. This is his diary?

I open the book to a random page.

August 20th, 2008

I kind of botched—

I close the book, but keep the page marked with my finger. *My fucking birthday? Really?* I wonder in astonishment. Is this a cosmic joke?

"Yeah, read that one." Jack gives my side a little push of encouragement.

Fine, why not? I open the book back up and look over the beautiful blue calligraphy handwriting.

August 24th, 2008

I kind of botched it. I thought getting a present would be coming on too strong, but I should have gotten her a card at least. I don't know what I was thinking, but I do know exactly what to get her. I hope she loves it.

Things went decently well. Aubrey let me sit with them, but

Abigale seemed irritated. She doesn't know me yet. I'm going to change that. It was rough though, not going to lie. These two are dangerous alone, put them together and I'm surprised I made it out alive. Smart, witty, drop-dead gorgeous, and a little mean to top it all off.

My biggest concern is that Abigale didn't show much interest, which I guess makes sense. She likes them dark and brooding. Kind of makes me wish I had my mohawk still. She might have responded better. I don't know.

I can make it work. I have this feeling deep down that if I pursue this, it's going to turn out right. It just feels so odd when I look at her. I feel like I'm in love but maybe it's just been such a long time. Rebecca was a lifetime ago. She'd want me to be happy. And this woman…she doesn't make me happy, she makes me joyous, she makes me gleeful, she makes me excited to see what happens next. I'd take a bullet for her and she probably doesn't even care enough to remember my name. I can tell this is going to be a problem if I'm already head over hills like this. She deserves a man, not a puppy dog.

I wiped the errant tear from my cheek. "This just makes me think it's the Power. You were head over heels the first day we really met."

"Now go to March 28th." His hand rubs my back and ends on my hip, pulling me in closer to him.

With nowhere left to go, I lay my head across his marble chest. As I flip through the pages to the right date, my eyes drift down his body. His smooth, hairless chest is in stark contrast to the thick happy trail that comes up from under the sheets to circle his navel and spread out over his lower abs. My eyes drift lower to check for signs of the lurking monster beneath the black covers, but nothing shows.

March 28th, 2008

Dear fucking Diary, I'm super fucked! I just read this piece by someone and I'm not sure who she is but I need her. I fucking need her!

Abigale Charleston. Who is she? I just scoured the house for my year books but I can't find them. She's not in class the period that I'm there so I have no idea. I'm terrified to ask around, and honestly, it's not because I'm scared Vanessa will find out. I'm scared Abigale will find out.

I consider myself a very loyal person but after reading this absolute work of art, I feel nothing for Vanessa. I feel like shit writing that. She's a great girl, and I'd be lucky to have her, but this other woman, whoever Abigale is, she exists somewhere out there, and I'm never going to feel that strongly toward Vanessa. I'll have to break up with her today.

Reading her words was like seeing into the future. She's one of The Ones, I know it. Kids, if you're reading this, I'm talking about your mother, this is the day I fell in love with your mother.

"What's one of The Ones?" The lump in my throat from his silly but heartwarming writing muddles my words.

"I don't believe in the idea that we have only one perfect match, the idea of there being 'The One.' I think that there are multiple people that we would gel perfectly with, so, earlier in my journals, I explained that, and how I one day hoped to find one of The Ones meant for me." His arm squeezes me against him. "And I think you're one."

It's just the Power making him say that, the dark side of my mind whispers. What if it's right? All his feeling for me that sound so good, but what if they're all forced on him. He's no different than Derrick. *He's basically drugged.*

I sigh in defeat. This wasn't going to work. "Jack."

His eyes are as soft as the pillows and his smile is inviting as a warm hearth in the middle of winter. "Tell me not to love you."

I blink in shock. "What?"

His charming looks pull me in only for his words to shove me away.

"I told you, there are a great many things I'd do for you, but there are a few things I'd never do. If you *really* have power over me, you can tell me to stop loving you, and I should. As long as the Power is what really controls me."

Could that work? It seems so simple. It's like cheating the system somehow. Mom and Deanna certainly wouldn't have told any of their men to stop loving them. At most, they told them to stay away. *But what if it works?*

You'll lose Jack, the Power warns.

"Just say it."

You can't lose him! He's too good to let go.

"I don't want to." I wrap my arms around him as best I can and cling to his chest.

His laugh shakes me as if riding a wild bull.

He takes the box from his lap and places it on the nightstand, then stores his journal in it. "What's the worst that can happen? If I stop loving you, that means you've been controlling me this whole time and I never loved you in the first place. You wouldn't want me like that, would you?"

Who cares? All that matters is that he belongs to us!

I shake my head but refuse to release his tank of a body.

"The only other option is it doesn't work, and we can get past this mess." He pulls me by my hip, pressing me against him till I slide over his massive stomach. It's like mounting a horse. He lifts my face up by my chin to look at the swirling honey. "We're doing things for me, remember? Now say it. Say it like you mean it."

How dare he command you? We give the commands. Put this slave in his place. The Power flares at being given a command, especially one I don't want to do. It threatens to overtake me. My grip turns sharp as I bite my nails into his skin, my jaw clenches in anger and my chest burns with fury.

Jack is mine, the Power claims.

No! He belongs to me!

I grab Jack's face and pull him into a deep kiss. The slick heat of our lips fights down the fire in my chest, beating the Power back into the cage of my heart like a bloodied animal.

"I love you, Jack." My forehead rests against his as our lips still touch. I close my eyes, unable to say the words while looking into those beautiful honey maelstroms. "Stop loving me."

Nothing happens. I wait, my pulse pounding in my head. I open my eyes like a five-year-old peeking out from behind the safety of a blanket to see if the monsters are coming.

His eyes look at me like two barrels of a shotgun. The soft, warm honey, replaced by hardened, dark eyes. He whispers back, "No."

His lips snatch mine and he rolls me over to my back. My legs curl around him, pulling his waist into me. The heat of his lips helps evaporate my fearful tears. My heart pounds in my chest with glee.

He is mine, not the Powers!

His erection thumps against my ass like a battering ram, knocking some sense into my brain.

"Woah! Hold on, hold on, baby." I swallow to help catch my breath. I pat his chest, hoping to calm him as well but my heart still races with what feels like a thousand pounds of muscle over me. "We're going to do a few things for me now, okay?"

An eyebrow rises at that. "And what if I don't want to? Saying no to you felt pretty good."

"Jack." I grip him, digging my nails into his arms.

Of course, he doesn't flinch. "I'm teasing. You know I'll do whatever you want. We didn't need the Power for you to be in control before. We don't need it now."

"Good boy." I give him an approving smile and rub the dig

marks I made. "I think I should be on top. You're just so big, I'm a little scared you might get carried away."

He smiles and nods. "Fair enough."

He lifts me with ease and sits back against the headboard. His cock touches by back and I turn to look at it.

"Where was he this whole time?"

"I had him trapped under my legs."

I grab him and we both gasp. His cock radiates heat like a nuclear rod. I shudder as its heat seeps into me, just imagining how it will feel inside me.

My flower blooms and I open for him. *Oh, God, Jack. I need it now.*

His hands slide up and down my thighs, disappearing under the tulle for a moment before he unties the string and throws it off to the side.

My free hand spreads out on his smooth chest as wave after wave of heat slams through my body till it pulses outside of me, no longer capable of being restrained. It melts my skin and simmers my brain till it consumes me.

I am heat.

The Power rises in me like a phoenix from the ashes, but we're finally not at odds.

Chapter Twenty-Three

I lay over him and take his lips with mine. While one hand cups my ass, the other stretches out to his nightstand. Music blares and a hard driving beat pumps into me as guitar riffs rip through the air.

Jack's hands squeeze my cheeks and pulls them apart making my heart jump. Despite my body arching my back to lift my ass up for him, the thought of taking him still scares me. I let the fear fade into the back of my mind as I pull his face into mine, deepening our kiss. Our tongues dance in perfect rhythm as if they've done it a million times.

His hands slide up my body to my corset. Fingers move over the strings but the knot catches and won't budge.

Rip it, Jack. Rip it off my body!

A growl resonates from his throat that turns into a roar. His hands grip the corset and in a horrifying display of strength, he tears it off me, jarring my body and stopping my heart.

He freezes in place with his arms outstretched, holding the two pieces of fabric in his hands. His shoulders and biceps look like a fucking heaving mountain range as his heavy breaths raise and lower the muscles. He tilts his head back and huffs a growl before throwing the corset pieces away. His eyes land on me; the honey glowing as hot as a raging fire.

Holy fuck, I'm about to get mauled!

His hands lash out and pull me onto his chest. Fingers dig into my exposed skin with a fierce need, gripping me by the ribs at first before he goes to my breasts. His lips take mine again and the Phoenix pulses, spreading her wings past my body. His lust and need for me become clear in that moment, as clear as my own desires. His cock behind me roars with need, but I swoon when I feel the roar of his heart. He needs me more than just physical sex, he needs my love.

Even still, one hand grips my ass while the other reaches past. His cock head presses against me and my repressed fear jumps back to the forefront of my mind.

"Wait!"

He stops but his iron grip on my ass doesn't change.

I put my hands on his chest and sit up. The extra foot of space from his hot breath does wonders for my ability to think straight. "Slow down. I'm in control, remember?"

He squeezes his eyes shut and huffs a couple times like a snorting bull. When he opens his eyes, the fire has dimmed but not died.

"Sorry." He shakes his head and gazes into my eyes as his hands softly cup my jaw. "You're in control." He pulls me forward and kisses me with sweet, tender lips. He holds his hands to his side. "I won't even touch unless you say."

I smile. "I doubt that."

Here we go, Abby. You can do this!

I look back at his throbbing cock. It pulses like a mad dog on a taunt chain. Maybe keeping him soft for so long was a mistake. A few stroke sessions throughout the week could have made the big boy less angry.

The Phoenix spreads her wings in my heart, sharing her resolve. When she speaks, she isn't angry like the Power had been. If anything, she's strong, determined, and most of all, hungry. *This is exactly what we're meant for. Don't just jump on him. Make him wait. Make us wait. It can be so much better.*

Good things come to those who wait, I think in agreement.

When I lookback to Jack, all those thoughts fall away.

His massive chest dwarfs my hands, and his eyes radiate his

maddening hunger for me. *That look, oh, absolutely to die for.* It fuels the smile that grows on my lips.

"I need to take off my panties," I say, pouting my bottom lip. "But I don't want to get off you. Rip them."

He grins like a wolf and sits up, pressing our chests together. He grabs one side of my panties. The fire grows in his eyes again as he pulls, ripping one leg free, and then the other.

It's too bad, I really like them, but they lived a good life and died an even better death. I push Jack's face into my heavy tits and shake for him before shoving him back down on the bed.

I slide down his body, letting my black nails bite into him, leaving red tracks that read: *Property of Abigale Bethany Charleston.* Maybe Deanna is onto something with her little tattoo. I move as far back as I can till Jack's erection points at the ceiling, I slide my lips up his shaft as I stand, using my hands on Jack's chest to keep my balance. Luckily, I'm as wet as the Amazon Rain Forest, I practically glide along him.

"I'm so wet, baby," I coo. I take one hand off his dense body to pull at my ribbon. I let my hair fall over my shoulder to spill onto him as I keep raising my legs and hips up his seemingly unending shaft.

He grunts like a bear as my lips slide over his cockhead. His eyes squeeze shut and his hands grip the sheets hard enough I sure he'll rip holes in them.

I hold him there, perfectly primed. A centimeter up and he'll spring loose, a centimeter down and he'll enter me.

"Are you ready, baby?"

I'm teasing myself just as much as him. My flower pulses for his cock, the head pressing past my lips feels like a rumbling rocket before liftoff, but the Phoenix gives me the strength to hold back. To make it better.

"I am." His whole body flexes under me.

I slide down and he enters me like I'm a glove; an undersized, stretched to the limit, bursting at the seams glove.

Heat flushes through my body, melting my joints and my knees buckle.

It's like the tower of terror carnival ride, a free fall plummet, but without my legs, I have no breaks to stop me before I crash. As I plumet down his girth, the hours of practice with my purple dildo seems to have been for nothing as his cock stretches me so much, I'm sure I'm going to rip.

A nasty snap makes me suck air in and Jack's hands flash to my waist, stopping my freefall.

He groans and squeezes his eyes shut. "Are you okay?" He swallows a light curse before asking again. "Hun? Did I hurt you?"

"Didn't keep your hands off for very long." I grip and pat his wrists as thanks.

Some noticeably thicker fluid runs down my vagina. His cock penetrates me while a long slash of red rolls his length. *Oh fuck! I'm not even halfway and he fucking broke my hymen.* I'd been able to maneuver around it with my toys and hoped that I'm one of those lucky women blessed with a more elastic hymen, yet he snapped it without even trying.

The Phoenix dulls the pain and whispers of more pleasure to come. *You just need to be brave enough to take it.*

"Abigale? Should I stop?"

"No." I take a deep breath and reposition my legs under me.

I continue down him but this time no pain touches me. He becomes a hard caress over each of my nerves. It's not exactly pleasurable, but it doesn't feel like I'm in danger of dying at least. His molten rod presses and pushes against my walls, resizing me to fit him. His long grunts and painfully desperate moans tell me the sensation of coming alive is not mine alone.

I understand why Deanna has been so insistent that I fuck him. Taking him in feels like planting my flag in his flesh, like climbing an impossible mountain and staking my unending claim. Ironic, since he's the one impaling me.

I delight in seeing him struggle against his nature. His hips twitch as if to rise to meet me, but his muscles tighten to hold himself back. I delight in feeling every vein, like a pulsing range of mountains pushing into the clouds of my tender flesh. Most of all, I delight in the constant slide. It's as if he never ends, and I don't either. The two of us infinitely entangled.

When my butt touches his thighs, I shudder as the orgasm runs through me like a freight train. I gush hard, fluids soaking Jack's bush until it quickly spills over his hips and down my legs. I shout something but my brain can't make heads nor tails of it. My eyes roll in my head, and my legs melt into Jack's skin. I barely feel my fingers gripping those blocks of stone he calls abs.

The faintest sensation of my lips being rubbed reaches me, but Jack's overbearing cock stops the sensation from becoming anything more than a fleeting whisper.

I ride that wave of pleasure to its peak several times before I truly come back to my senses. I move over him in a rhythm that I don't remember starting. Every time my cheeks slap against his thighs, I smile more and more till giddy laughter pours from my throat.

"Yes, Jack! Yes! Just like this. All night, baby. All night."

Both of his hands rub his face as he groans and grimaces. "Oh, Abigale."

"Touch me." I grab his wrists and pull his hands to my aching breasts. "I want to feel you, feeling me."

His hands grip my breasts too hard at first but then relax. "Fuck, Abby. I… I'm—" He squeezes his eyes shut as his jaw clenches.

I take a couple of breaths before I managed to say, "What's wrong, baby, don't you love it?"

"I…" He grunts again and pounds the bed with a clublike fist.

His grunts and desperate moans tell me exactly what's going through his mind. *I want to come, but I can't.* I can practically hear him say it.

"Good boy, don't come." I smile.

He lets out a strained huff and his hands go to my waist.

I giggle as I place my hands on his abs and lift my butt to slide up him. Every millimeter sends an explosion of pleasure through me, ripping out from my core as the Phoenix radiates beyond my body. Fingers swirl around my clit but vanish as soon as I look down.

Jack groans. "Wait, please. Fuck!"

"Don't come, Jack." I lick my lips and add, "Momma comes first." I've already come several times but making him wait is good for him, good for both of us. The Phoenix is right, the tease makes it better.

"Oh, fuck! Fuck," he shouts as his hips jolt and his cock drives into me, rattling my mind.

I press my hands into his abs firmly and he settles. I'm not fooled into thinking that my strength subdued him. If Jack really wanted, he could flip me and turn me into a pretzel while dicking me down. It's his need to serve that overpowers him. His obedience is stronger than his thirst for pleasure. Seeing him in such agony, for my sake, makes my heart swell. He's walking through the fires of Hell for me.

"Did you like when I said Momma?" I coo as I wiggle my ass over him.

He bucks again with another loud curse before he settles, taking deep breaths.

I guess that's a yes. I like it, too. Maybe better than Mistress. It's like the equivalent of a man being called Daddy. I guess I'll have to try it out to be certain.

"Say it." I fold my legs under me so I won't have to stand. I place my feet over his thighs and squeeze his rips with my knees.

Jack moans as I slide up his shaft.

"Say it," I huff. The Phoenix wraps me like a warm blanket, and I find myself at Jack's tip.

His rigidity threatens to pop him loose, but I squeeze him tight.

"Say it, Jack." I swivel my pussy around his head.

Jack's mouth hangs open as he struggles for air. His hands cup my face. The honey hardens and he smiles. "Momma comes first."

"Yes, she does. Good boys get rewards," I say as I take all of him back into me.

The tip of his dick punches my brain. I take a beat to gather myself. I'd naïvely thought I would go straight back up to his tip and tease him some more but taking twelve inches of cock quickly drives the air from my lungs.

The sensation of a hand moving over my mound comes again, this time much stronger. I look down but there's no fucking hand, just Jack's cock stretching me to the point my pussy's beat red. I look away. It certainly looks much worse than it feels. *Best not to think about it.*

Once I regain my composure, I ride up and down on him for a few minutes. I'm not able to go from tip to base without pausing, but four to eight-inch stretches at a time seem doable. It's not long before I fall into a pleasing rhythm, lifting up and plopping back down with a satisfying *smack*.

"Fuck!" he shouts. He places his hands on my waist to slow me down. "Wait, I'm going to come if you keep this up."

"Oh, you mean this?" I lift my ass to run my body up his length. Slamming down on him makes me wince but I push through and go back up him. "You want to come?"

I slide back down on him with force, ramming him into me. Pressure builds around my flower, spreading out to my belly and down to my knees, tensing every muscle along its path.

I lowered my top half to his chest to get my lips as close to his ear as I can without ruining my momentum. "Come for Momma."

Jack's hips buck, and his massive arms hug me to his chest.

The Phoenix sweeps up the mounting pressure as she rises in my chest, making my heart sing. *Oh, Jack.* I dive into him, letting his scent roll over me, more hot musk than orange or wood but still intoxicating, maybe even more so. The Phoenix crashes down on my clit like a fucking collapsing star. My legs jolt as the orgasm rips through me, lancing through every cell in my body, from the tips of my toes to the end of each strand of hair.

Jack's body flexes in glorious fashion. His arms tighten around me, and he whispers, "Abigale." He grunts as his cock grows thicker inside and he shakes. "Oh, my sweet and wonderful Abigale."

I kiss his chest since I'm pinned to it. His arms relax and he tilts my chin up. My eyes don't have enough time to focus before his lips take mine. Such a sweet and warm embrace.

The invisible hand rubs my clit with desperate need, and I shake as I come again, an aftershock of the earthquake Jack gave me.

What the fuck is this? Is it the Phoenix? No... She rests in my heart like a well-fed tiger.

When I move to look down, I shiver as Jack's cum sloshes inside me. The gushiness is a little gross, it feels like he shot a whole bottle of lube up my core, but at the same time, it's as sweet and warm as the honey in his eyes.

I close my eyes to relish in the moment, and the win. I beat this fucking Power. I've tamed it into something beautiful and majestic. Jack wasn't tamed by some magical bullshit. He was tamed by *me*! It's *me* he can't resist.

He sighs and runs his hands up and down my back. "You ready for that massage now?" He laughs.

"I want to go again." I'll probably have to let him take charge. My exhausted heart kicks up at the thought of Jack drilling me, but with the question of whether or not I can take his dick answered… "Good boys get rewards."

Chapter Twenty-Four

Jack's back rub puts me to sleep, and I wake laying on him. The sun isn't up but I don't see a clock anywhere to know what time it is. Cotton balls fill my throat, so I go to his fridge and open the door as quietly as I can manage. It's stocked but mostly with protein drinks. There's a jug of water and some sports drinks, so I take a red bottle. At the bottom, a bowl of oranges brings a smile to my face.

So that's your secret. If this is really how he smells and tastes so good, and he's done it on purpose, the man's a certifiable genius.

I walk around the room, just to get a feel for it. I'm sure to be spending a lot more time in here from now on. *This won't just be Jack's room, it's going to be mine, too!* My heart leaps. *He's not a little boy living with his parents. This is his fucking house.* My house one day. It could use a woman's touch, but honestly, Jack has style. His room isn't covered with posters of cars or sports teams. He has bookshelves and fucking oil paintings in his room. Jack is a man, with a man's taste.

I look at him in the bed, his large frame taking up so much space. He makes the massive bed look normal.

After a few more swallows of my drink, I sit it down on the nightstand and climb back into his…*our* bed.

He stirs, his eyelids fluttering open over hazy eyes. "Hey."

"Hi." I smile.

I crawl into his arms and turn around so he can spoon me. I turn over my shoulder to kiss as he pulls me against him. His cock grows hard against my butt, so I reach back and put him between my legs, letting him grow against my lips.

"You fell asleep before your happy ending."

I laugh and rub up against him. "Oh, no. I had a very happy ending."

His arms wrap me up and his lips rest just above my ear. "I didn't say it before because my mind was shot into space. I love you, Abigale." He repeats the phrase a few more times in between kisses to the back of my head.

I turn over my shoulder again so I can get those strong lips on mine. "And I love you, Jack."

"I have to admit, I was really scared it wasn't going to work out."

"What? Why wouldn't we work out?" I squirm in his arms so I can turn and slap some sense into him. We're perfect together! There's no reason we won't work.

"I meant the sex." His arms coil, stopping me from ruining our positioning. "I was worried I'd be too big."

I sigh in relief that he's not talking about personality. The Phoenix stirs and spreads her wings, unfurling waves of heat. Jack's need seeps in through my skin and I bite my lip knowing exactly what I'm about to do with him.

"You are too big." I pull on him between my legs till he oozes a little to get his head wet. I push him down and back to line him up with my salivating flower. "*Augh!* You're lucky you found me."

He slides into me, and I nearly squeal from how tight he makes me. Pushing from behind is a new sensation, and all the pressure of his powerful cock rolls against my clit.

A deep, lusty moan rips from my throat as I throw myself back into him.

Another loud moan echoes from the other side of the house. *Aub?*

I smack Jack's thigh in panic, and he pulls out delicately, thank God.

I run to the door but then realize I'm stark naked. I turn and

Jack's already in his closet, reaching in and pulling out a large fluffy bathrobe that he tosses to me. It slams into me like my mother's fur coat it's so big. I slip into it and bolt out the door.

A dim glow from below comes from Devon's screens. The large TV screen is on, but the Windows XP screen saver bounces around. Quinn staggers out of the dark and into the long hall. The glow of Devon's screens highlight her muscular legs since she doesn't have any pants on.

She rubs her eyes and sees me hustle down the hallway. "You okay?"

What does she care? "Yeah. I'm fine."

She nods and shakes her head before walking to the kitchen. I glance back just as I get to Aub's door to see her guzzling a glass of water.

I turn the doorknob, but it doesn't open.

"Door doesn't open without a key," Quinn says.

"Where is it?"

"I have it," Jack says. He holds his phone up as he walks the hall in a tight pair of boxer briefs. He taps the screen a couple times and the lock slides in the door.

I swing the door back and find Aub sitting on the floor with her legs spread, completely naked.

"Oh, God! Aub!" I hop in the room and close the door. "Are you okay?"

I stand facing the door for another moment, collecting myself to look at her again. Aub and I are close, but we've never crossed the line of seeing each other's privates.

"Abby, what did you do?" she whines. Her breaths are hard, laborious actions, each one sounding more desperate than the last. "I could feel it."

"Feel what?" I kneel next to her and grab her messy sheets, pulling them down to hug her shoulders. "Aub, what happened?"

"I felt everything." She gazes up at me, her dark blue eyes like whirlpools, begging me to jump in. "I felt Jack."

Felt Jack? What the hell does that mean?

"Is everything okay?" Jack asks from the other side of the door.

"Yeah. We're fine. Just, go back to bed."

"No, water," Aub pleads, grabbing me by the bathrobe's collar. "I'm so thirsty. Please." She turns to the door. "Jack, I need water."

"Yeah, no problem." Jack responds.

"Aub, what do you mean you felt Jack?"

"It was like I was you, everything you did, Abby, I could feel it. Before I could even tell you, my knees gave out and I've been on the floor ever since. He rubbed my shoulders and I fell asleep."

What the fuck?

Aub pulls me close. "Abby, I fucking need him. I have to have him. I need that dick breaking me!"

"Calm the fuck down!" I pry her hands loose from the robe. "Aub, that wasn't you! I don't know how you felt that shit, but that wasn't you."

"Could it be the Power? Is that one of your powers?"

My mind spins as pieces fall into place. *The Power pulsed outside of my body, even when it turned into the Phoenix. I sensed Jack so much better. We had one mind. I needed water, Aub needs water... Oh fuck!*

I leap to my feet and dash out the door. The sturdy railing holds as I slam into it, nearly pitching over the hard wood.

Jack holds a glass to a large container of water in the refrigerator downstairs, pressing on the spout to pour. He shrugs and then says something to Quinn who's leaning against the sink next to him with her own glass. The harsh light of the fridge shows off her white lace thong between her crossed, overly muscled thighs. Is that how Jack likes them? A feminized version of his own bulky size? She's so close he can reach out and touch her. He closes the fridge and hurries over to the stairs.

"Why didn't you get water from your room?" I whisper when he returns.

"I don't have a glass in there."

"What did she say to you? What were you two talking about?"

His wolf's grin appears but it bursts with pride. "She was asking when the wedding's going to be so she can pick out a dress."

Heat splashes my face so hard it reaches my ears. "What?"

"She was joking." Jack's smile widens. "Here, give this to Aub."

I take the offered glass of water and go back into Aub's room, shutting the door behind me.

She downs half of it before coming up for air. "Abby, I didn't mean what I said. I'm sorry. I'm fucking out of my mind. I had dreams and all sorts of shit."

"You're okay. Don't worry about it. I guess I should ask Mom or Deanna about it."

"Did they ever mention domming women?" She polishes off the rest of the water.

"No. But they also didn't talk about subduing the Power either."

"Subduing? I don't know if there was anything subdued about what happened tonight."

I explain to her how I fought down the urge to completely control Jack. How he gave me orders and the simple but painfully difficult task of following them allowed me to kill the Power, and how she rose as my Phoenix. In between all of that, I give her a play-by-play of losing my virginity.

"Fuck. That's pretty cool." Aub smiles as we sit on her bed. "I'd like to have a flaming spirit animal. I'm more of a lizard kind of girl.

I hit her lightly with my pillow. "You are not. Besides, it has to have wings. You're a dragon."

"Reptile it is." We laugh but then she sighs. "I guess this means I'll need to be far away whenever you guys have sex. Not that I want to be close, I just mean, you know, road trips and shared vacations might be out of the picture."

"No, I don't want that. I just need to learn to control it. Now that I know it's a thing, I can practice."

"Well, if you plan on practicing more tonight, mind either knocking me out or letting me join? It wasn't fun being in here alone."

It can be better, the Phoenix whispers. *Bring her along. You know you want to.*

No! I'm not crossing that line with Aub. It was a fucking joke. She's really asking me to *not* go back to Jack's room and fuck. She just doesn't want to hold me back. A feeling washes over me that if I go back to Jack's room, I'll probably not be able to resist.

"I can just sleep in here with you. Might be for the best. I think I'm going to fuck Jack every time we're alone in his room, so, I think I'll stay here."

She laughs and turns over in bed. "Be the big spoon?"

I turn off the nightstand lamp and hug her waist. "Yeah."

We lay in the darkness for a time, shifting slightly every now and then. Her soft hair smells of fruits and aloe. Even knowing the smell of her shampoo, having even used it a time or two myself, I still fall into it. What waited for me beneath the products is even better, her natural scent has always reminded me of the way dark cherries taste. *Maybe I could finally taste her.*

"Abby?"

Her voice snaps me out of my ridiculous haze.

"Do you think Jack knows you're staying? He—he's not going to get worried and come in here, is he?"

Come in here? What is she talking about? "I don't think he's going to come in here."

"Won't he be worried? Shouldn't you go tell him?"

"I guess…"

"Should I go with you? You said if you were alone…"

"Aub, are you trying to get in bed with Jack?"

She rolls over and gazes up at me. "His bed is bigger than this one, right? You said it's a king."

"Aub!"

Her brow knots. "I'm sorry. I'm super fucking horny and the man of my dreams is right in the other room and you're all that's in my way, but you're my best friend, so maybe you'd let me join in?" Her rant ends in the tilt of a question and a hopeful smile. When I don't say anything, she pouts. "You made me watch you toy with him earlier. That shit was super fucking hot and I thought I'd fuck Derrick, or maybe just let him go down on me. I don't know, but that fell apart and after feeling what you felt… Oh! Abby, I know this is fucked. I can't believe I'm even stooping so low as to ask you."

Her head drops and she cries on my chest. The robe soaks up her tears and I pull her in. My heart cries out for her. If our roles were reversed, wouldn't I do the same? If I'd been given a taste of what we had I'd beg from my knees. *Just how much did she feel? How much did Quinn feel? Quinn!*

"Come on!"

I shoot out of bed and run down the halls with Aub following like a specter with her sheet flowing in the dark behind her. If Aub's desperate for Jack, Quinn has to be wanting him, too, and I'd left Jack alone for at least half an hour!

I burst through his door and past the curtains. Empty. No Jack, no Quinn. A soft glow pours out from under his bathroom door and the downpour of water on tile muffles voices. *There's no way, right? He wouldn't say he loves me then fuck behind my back.* I open the door as quiet as I can. If they're fucking, I'm going to kick his balls so hard they'll come out of *her* mouth.

The bathroom is astounding. White tile sparkles on the floor. On the wall, back tiles join in to swirl up to the ceiling. A large, double sink, marble vanity spreads out along one wall that ended with two doors. One looks like a linen closet while the other looks like a door to another room. At the end of the room, a claw foot tub sits like an island unto itself under a skylight window. On the wall to my left, a small wooden door with a window appears next to the tub and right next to me, steamy glass obscures who's inside the massive stone shower.

I clench my fists and open the glass door.

The shower would fit another ten of him easily. A three- or four-foot-long rainfall showerhead pours down over his rippling muscles. He turns and smiles. The voices continue and I finally see his phone in a Ziploc bag tucked into a tiled cubby hole.

"Hey there." He turns, exposing his erect cock as he tilts his foamy head back into the water.

"Jack," both Aub and I shout, though mine has more shock in it while Aub's is more delighted surprise.

"Aub is right here!"

"You didn't bring her?" Jack askes.

"Not for this. I thought you were fucking Quinn!" *Oh shit! That's going to take some explaining.*

Jack raises an eyebrow at me. "Quinn? You thought I was fucking Quinn?"

"It's... The Power, Aub felt us. Everything we did. And when I woke up, I was thirsty and horny. Putting you in me woke both of them up. They were both thirsty and horny, too. I saw her flirting with you downstairs, don't even try to deny it."

He nods and then his eyes slide to Aub. "You mind shutting the door to the bedroom? The heat's escaping. As for Quinn," he adds, looking back at me while Aub closes us in. "You're right. It was weird. She wasn't begging for me to fuck her or anything, but she was talking some."

"What did she say?" *That fucking lying bitch. Just friends, huh?* I take a deep breath. It might not be her fault exactly. The Power's more to blame.

"Can't hear you." Jack steps back into the water with his winner's grin. He leans back and flexes every muscle of his gorgeous body.

Watching the water cascade off his chest and abs makes my breath catch, but seeing the stream run over his cock makes my mouth water.

"Why don't you come in here so we can talk about it? Acoustics are way better."

Get wet with Jack? Yes, please.

I turn to Aub, not sure of how I'm going to tell her to leave. Her eyes are glued on Jack's tantalizing cock. What if I was in her position? What if I'd been worked into a frenzy and then brought face to face with it? *What if I let her join?*

Told you, the Phoenix says.

There's no going back if we do this. Our relationship will never be the same. What we have is so special and looking at those big blue eyes makes me want to call it off.

The Phoenix massaged the tension in my chest, making the decision easier to see. *You can either let your love grow or show her where your love ends. Either way is fine. She'll respect your boundaries. You're best friends after all. But you can be more.*

I bite my lip and close the door to the shower. When I snap my fingers at her, she blinks, and her slack jaw rises. Her eyes dart around as if she just woke up.

I take her hands in mine and whisper, "You know I love you, right?" Not sure of the best way to start this little talk, some reassurance is probably for the best. We need to be on the same page if we're going to do this and not get hurt. "Both of us fucking Jack is going to be fun, no doubt about it, but we made a pact to never let a guy get between us, right?"

"Yyeah. Of course. Never." Her hands squeeze mine. "I love you, too, Abby." Her eyes slide to the foggy glass and then to the floor. "I swear, I'd never try to take him from you. And I won't ever ask again. I promise. Just this one time."

"I'm not saying this is a one-time thing. This isn't going to be something we do and then forget or pretend it never happened. I mean, let's be real, this is going to change *us*. I…" I think for a moment about how jealous I'd been about Quinn, but that jealousy doesn't reach me when thinking of Aub. Aub can steal a man if she wants, but in my heart, I know she won't do that to me. "I trust you."

Her eyes glisten and her lips quiver. "Thank you." She swallows hard and gasps. "I don't know why I'm getting all emotional." She laughs and brushes away a tear. Her deep blue eyes hardened as she looks at me. "We can do this."

The Phoenix rises from her perch in my heart to swell my body with heat.

Aub's eyes shoot wide. "Did it just… Your Power?"

"Yeah. You can feel it?"

She bites her lip and closes her eyes as she nods. "Yeah. It's like a soft hand caressing me."

"I'd like to be caressing you," Jack says. "Water's going to get cold if you keep chit-chatting out there."

"Jack," Aub shouts.

"Damn it, Jack. We're having a fucking moment."

When he doesn't respond, I return my attention to Aub. Her eyes are still closed, and she smiles.

Can I share the Phoenix with her? Is that an ability Mom and Deanna never knew to try? *How would I even go about it?*

Her wings unfurl and Jack's frustration reaches me. An image of him in a void comes to my mind. He stands naked and in the dark, pulled to his knees by taunt chains around his wrists and neck.

They won't hold much longer. The Phoenix warns.

I give Aub's hands a squeeze. "Come on. Let's go take care of Jack."

I shrug out of my robe as Aub lets the sheet fall to her feet. My heart rate shoot through the ceiling. I've always found Aub gorgeous, but at a distance. Standing in front of her like this, steam pouring over us from the shower, heat rises inside me, and given her lingering gaze on my body, I suspect it's rising in her as well.

We step into each other, tentatively at first, but as soon as our bodies touch, our lips collide like over charged magnets. Her soft skin sinks into mine like it belongs there and a thrill races up my spine at the taste of black cherries and whipped cream. The Phoenix soars through me and into Aub.

Holy shit! This is what it's like? she thinks in my mind.

I nearly scream in both panic and elation.

Aub? Can you hear me?

Her fear spikes in my heart and she pulls back from our kiss. My hands stop her from leaving our embrace, massaging her skin in hopes of calming her.

"It's okay." *It means we're close enough to have this together. I can't even do this with Jack yet.*

So, you can hear me? she asks, her eyes searching mine.

I grab her chin with my finger and thumb to pull her in for another firm kiss.

Yes. I hear you. I say in our minds. Her soft lips mold around mine as our tongues slip over each other's.

The Phoenix grows between us, melding us together. An urge grows in me to push Aub to her knees so her lips can grace my mound, but I resist.

You both want it. The Phoenix says. *Let her.*

I pull back and open the door. My hands shake on the handle as I restrain myself from shoving her to the floor and sitting on her face. "Get in the shower, Aub."

Domming Jack is one thing, but I can't do that to Aub. If we're going to survive, we need to be equals. She steps in and freezes. I step in next to her since the door is large enough for the two of us.

Jack leans against the far wall, slowly stroking his cock. Water splashes over him, trickling down his body. The long rainfall shower isn't the only source of water. The section Jack leaned against has a bar several feet above him that cascades water over the stone surface like something from a swimming pool feature.

"Took you two long enough." He opens his arms for both of us.

Chapter Twenty-Five

I grit my teeth. *We have to share.*

I mean the thought for myself, but Aub looks at me and nods with hard determination in her eyes. She grabs my hand, and we walk to Jack, passing under the rainfall shower together. Jack takes our free hands, and we stand in a tight triangle.

"Abigale. You know I love you and I know you love me. The two of you love each other. It's clear you have something special together." He looks at Aub and bounces her hand in his. "That leaves you and me, Aubrey." The honey in his eyes melts as a smile forms on his face. "I'm going to take care of you just like I do Abigale. I don't want you to ever think I'm doing this as a favor to her. I'd never have sex with a woman I didn't love."

Did he just say he loves me? Aub gasps.

Despite the steam surrounding us, I suddenly feel very cold, like being left outside on a winter's night.

His eyes return to me. "Loving her won't make me love you any less. Just like loving her won't make you love me any less. We're in this together."

He treads a very fine line, but as the warmth of the shower reaches me again, his words stoke a fire inside me. I smile and nod in agreement. "Together."

Aub's smile borders frantic as she bounces on her toes. "Together."

Jack pulls both of us in, squishing all three of our bodies together.

Heat explodes against my skin, blasting through me. A duplicate heat blasts through Aub that runs through my body as well.

Jack's hand reaches down to grip my ass and a ghostly hand grips my other cheek.

Did you feel that? I ask.

Holy shit, yeah! It's what I felt earlier, but stronger. Is this going to ha— Her thoughts fizzle as Jack's fingers slide into both of us.

His hands move like mirror images of each other, causing me to feel not only what he's doing to me, but the inverse since that's what he's giving Aub. He pulls us against him, and we rest our heads on his massive chest. We reach over to each other and kiss as Jack continues to grip and finger us. A good warm up to a main course that my heart cries out for.

Jack pulls us apart and lifts us with his fingers, causing us to gasp as we raise to our toes. His lips strike Aub's. They sizzle on mine like a recent memory. After a few moments with Aub, he lashes out at me like a viper, taking my lips with his. His offers no escape, though I wasn't looking for any.

The thrill of Jack taking control comes as a surprise. I've become so used to dominating him I haven't considered how much I might love him taking control. My pulse races thinking of Jack using his raw strength over me.

He pulls back and smiles, taking a deep breath. His hands loosen and run along our asses and then backs.

He starts to lower himself but both Aub and I press our hands against his chest, pushing him into the shallow waterfall behind him. His back *smacks* against the stone and he grunts a laugh.

Can I suck his cock? Aub asks.

I can see Jack's plan: give us both the same in the beginning to set the tone that we're equals. It's important that we keep that up, at least during the appetizer. If I stand with Jack while Aub gets on her knees, even if I keep quiet, which I almost certainly won't be able to, it will unbalance the delicate dynamic he established.

Yeah. You don't have to ask, Aub. I grab her arm as we lower to our knees. *Let me join you.*

I let her take the head since she hasn't gotten anything but her own fingers tonight. I kiss and lick his girth closer to the base since Aub can't make it all the way. She makes several very impressive attempts though, pushing herself far enough that our cheeks touch. Feeling Jack's cock touch the back of her throat as if he's in mine forces me to pull back and reset a couple times but after a couple minutes, Jack's long arms reach down to grip our hair.

He bends at the waist and pulls Aub off his cock. She laughs as his eyes glow like an animal in the dead of night. A gleeful fear shoots through her heart and into mine before Jack pulls her in for a rough kiss. He turns to me and gives me the same rough kiss with a hard press of his lips and strong flicks of his tongue. His hand grips my hair to the boarder of pain before he shoves me down his cock.

Aub kisses his shaft and licks his balls but also reacts when Jack's large head slips down the back of my throat every other thrust.

He lets go of our hair and straightens up as his hands push his wet hair back. "Fuck!" His deep shout rumbles through the stone tile like a roaring bear.

I pull back from his cock, stroking his head in the hopes that it will calm him. "Jack, baby, you okay?"

Aub kisses and massages his balls, hoping right along with me.

He stands there for a moment longer, before he pushes off the wall with his shoulders. "I want both of you in my bed, right fucking now." He turns off the water and points to the door.

"First door next to the sinks. Grab some towels if you want, or I'll fuck you soaking wet. I'll give you a ten second head start."

Aub and I stare at each other in pure shock. Excitement ricochets up our spines like electric bolts running through powerlines.

We both rush out the shower door, holding onto each other to keep from slipping, then run into the bedroom. We hop into his bed and hide under the sheets. One of these days we'll need to kick everyone out for the night and play 'hide and fuck our brains out.' His house is perfect for it, though, I'll probably just hide in his bedsheets anyway.

Aub and I huddle together, frozen and breathless, listening for his footsteps, but after a moment of holding each other, our hands start to explore. I'm very familiar with Aub's body after seeing it for years, but getting to touch it like this is all so new. Soon, we're tangled up in each other to the point that the shift in the bed as Jack climbs on startles both of us.

A long muscular hand reaches under the sheets and blanket to snatch Aub by the waist.

I wrestle with the covers for a moment before I fling them off. "Jack! She's mine!" My mouth drops when my eyes land on them.

Jack has her under him on her stomach. One hand grips her hair, pushing her head into the bed with an iron beam of an arm while the other grips her jiggling ass so hard I shout from the ghost hand on my cheek, though Aub only growls. Veins throb along his cock, hungry to enter her from behind. Poised over her like a silver back, Jack's eyes challenge me with a bright glow.

"Come and get her."

Deep blue eyes look at me through messy strands of wet hair. *Let him break me.*

You don't fucking mean that! I scramble across the bed. I get to my knees and hold onto Jack's shoulder, gently rubbing the large expanse of his chest. "Go easy, Jack. It's her first time, too."

He chuckles and pulls my chin by a steel finger. "I'm going to break her in half, and then I'm going to do the same to you."

"Jack!"

"Yes, please," Aub moans, lifting her ass up more for him.

"It's what you both want." He smiles and kisses me. Sweet and tender lips remind me of his kindness. "I'm exaggerating. Calm down." He points to her head with a devious grin. "Take a seat, let her moans rattle you."

He gives me a light pat on the ass, and I do as he says. I sit in front of Aub but wait before I have her between my legs. I want her to experience Jack clean with nothing else to distract her.

"Aubrey, this is going to hurt some." He leans forward, and I feel his head press against her lips. One hand goes to the bed, while the other massages her back. "Just say stop if you want it to stop."

His hand grabs her hip, and he presses forward. His head dips inside and his shaft stretches her. A sharp pain hits me and I know he's taken her virginity.

Fuck! Aub shouts. A hard gasp is all she manages out loud. *Oh fuck!* She arches her back further to tilt her ass up more. When his hand moves to the small of her back, she simply nods.

Jack slides that same hand to her ass and he grips one of those firm cheeks before going even deeper.

"*Ah!* Fuck," she shouts. "Jack. Yes! Keep going. Fuck!" She grips his pillar of an arm while her other hand reaches out to me, grabbing my thigh.

Jack slides further in and I gasp. Is this what she felt earlier? The bumps of his skin and the veins press into me as if he's moving inside me. The only sensation missing is his considerable weight.

The Phoenix sings with how good Jack's cock feels. The fact that she gets to feel it twice between me and Aub only unleashes her further.

Abby, Aub moaned. *I want more. The Phoenix...she...*

Jack's cock delves deeper, cutting her thought short when his thighs smack her plump rear.

Jack growls something but it comes out too guttural to understand.

Make it better, the Phoenix whispers.

I slide forward and spread my legs for Aub as Jack falls into a slow rhythm. Even with how wet and open she is for him, a tinge of pain still reaches her. I don't want that pain any more than Aub, a nice massage will rid us of it.

She lifts her head as I scoot forward and she sets straight to work, swirling her tongue around my clit. I refrain myself from humping her face. I brush her hair out of her face so I can see her better. The soft curve of her jaw fits in the crease of my thigh perfectly. She looks up at me for a moment but then blushes and closes her eyes.

Look at me, I say softly. I need to watch my tone, even in our mental link. We're riding a knifes edge between who's in control. Aub's getting fucked by Jack and giving me head; her only control is that she can say stop if she wants. I have to make sure I don't tip the balance any further.

Her eyes open right as she sucks on my clit and those blue eyes, darker than the deepest ocean waters, challenge me. *Fuck me.* She demands.

The Phoenix turns my heart into an inferno, sweeping away hesitations. *This is how she likes it.*

I push her face into my mound and grind my hips against her smiling lips.

"Give it to her, Jack! She wants it rough. Ow! Fuck!" My hand lashes out to slap her as she bites my clit.

She growls a laugh as she holds me in a light grasp between her teeth. Her hips move in tandem with Jack and her hands grab my thighs to squeeze her head.

Freaky little slut, I chuckle. I take over squeezing her head. I've crushed watermelons in the past. *Let's see how long you can last.*

I count to ten before she pulls on my legs, and I let her go. She gasps for breath before letting out a sultry moan and kissing my flower.

The sensations of Jack's thrusts and Aub's lip service melt my brain, and it isn't till Aub starts grunting that I realize she isn't between my legs anymore.

At some point in my haze, Jack pulled her up to stand on her knees as his massive arms snaked around her neck and head.

Aubs little hands hold onto the bend of Jack's arm. A constant slew of garbled words spews from her mind into mine.

Aub? Are you okay?

She's better than okay, the Phoenix whispers.

Pressure builds in my core and my weak knees shake as the orgasm washes over me.

Aub's sapphire eyes sparkle a dazzling radiance as she comes.

I pant for breath but with Jack's continued thrusting and light choking, I can't seem to get enough.

He thrusts hard and deep one last time and my eyes are pulled by the Phoenix to his spasming cock. His grip around her neck loosens to the point that it merely holds her up. His fingers interlocked with hers and they rub her belly together. He whispers something to her, and she nods with a limp, euphoric simile.

He pulls out, lets her down gently on the bed, and then crawls over to me.

Too tired to move, my legs are still splayed wide for him. He folds me in half, and I watch with bated breath as his cock dives into me. Covered with his and Aub's cum, it slides all the way in without issue.

It doesn't take long before another orgasm rips through me, lighting up my nerves like a Christmas tree. His next three thrusts press against me so perfectly my legs lock, my toes point, and I come in glorious release.

"Oh! Abigale. *Ahh!*" Jack looks down on me, the honey dripping with lust and satisfaction as he fills me again.

Fuck. I'm going to need birth control. It may be too late with how much he's come.

Fuck that, Aub says. *I want his babies.*

The image of both Aub and I swelling with Jack's children forces my legs to wrap around his waist and hold him in me. I swirl my hips, feeling his mass inside me.

I caress Jack's face and then point over to Aub. "Put me next to her."

He lifts me with ease, and I hold to him with my legs to make sure he doesn't pull out.

You don't really mean that. We're not even old enough to drink and you want to start popping out kids? Her eyes remain closed as if she's sleeping peacefully. Hell, maybe she is asleep. Do we need to be awake to talk in our minds?

"Spoon me." I curl my shoulders toward Aub to offer my back. As he pulls back, I firm my weary legs as much as possible. "No. Just, get behind me. Don't leave."

He chuckles and moves one of my legs over his chest and then falls in behind me. His softened cock twists in me, sending a shiver up my spine.

Why not? Aub asks. *It's a big house. Plenty of room for plenty of kids.*

We're in fucking college, Aub. We want to be lawyers.

We can do both. Best to get used to it early on.

I guess that's one way to look at it.

What if I don't want to yet?

Her eyes open and she scoots into me, letting her head rest on my chest. *Don't worry. We'll do it together.*

Wrapped in Aub and Jack's arms, I sigh. "Together."

Chapter Twenty-Six

The next morning, Jack wakes me with his morning wood, and I wake him by sliding up and down it. After another round of soul warping sex, we take a shower that actually consists of washing. I'm grateful that his shower has a built-in bench since Aub and I can barely stand.

When we come out of his room, the house looks and feels twice as big with the sun coming through all the windows. I'm swathed in the comforter since Jack demolished my corset, while Aub stands next to me wrapped in Jack's bathrobe since her clothes are still in her room.

Aub bundles the fleece around her and inhales deeply. *We could fill this whole house with little ones*, she sings.

You have baby fever or something?

Jack comes up from behind and hugs both of us to him. He looks so good in his grey plaid suit and white shirt with the top buttons open. He gives Aub a kiss that makes my mouth water and then one for me that makes my mound water. "It's all yours." His eyes peer out over the house, and he smiles. He pats our butts and walks off. We're both quick to follow.

I have big dick fever, she thinks as she watches Jack, *and I know what comes after getting fucked raw every day.*

We walk to Aub's room while Jack goes up to check on Derrick. The house seems hollow without anyone downstairs, but I'm glad to see what the house will look like when it's just us. We open the dresser to find women's pajama bottoms and tank tops.

Fucked every day, huh? I pick a red tank and some matching bottoms that cover little more than my ass. These are definitely Quinn's size. Even with her muscular frame, the woman doesn't have half my ass.

It's so fucking cool we can talk like this. Aub puts on the same red top and bottoms. *Twinsies!* She does a twirl, giving me an eye full. *You don't want to fuck every day?*

I don't like being teased.

Yes, you do. You fucking love to get teased. She wiggles her ass and I move to pounce on her but Jack calls from down the hall.

"You girls good? We going?"

Yeah, be— Fuck. "Yeah, be right there," I holler back.

Aub and I both laugh as we come out of the room and walk down the hall. Quinn's door is open, so I stick my head in to see her sleeping with Peter snuggled up in her chest.

She's a mommy-dommy for sure, Aub says.

We go downstairs to find both guys waiting at the door. Derrick apologizes for anything he might have done but we assure him it wasn't his fault. We take him back to the bar so he can drive his car home and then Jack takes us to my house.

Inside, Mom and Dad's luggage is at the foot of the stairs. They must have gotten home literally minutes before us if Dad hasn't taken the suitcases upstairs yet.

"Pack your things," Mom says from the upstairs' hall. She strides down the hall and into her office, so I bound up the steps to follow.

"What are you talking about?" I ask when I get into her office.

She flicks a finger at the door. "Close it."

I do as she says and before walking to her desk where she holds a hand out to me.

She takes my hand and frowns. "I'm really sorry about his, hun, but I don't have a choice. I was hoping you wouldn't manifest your Power till after this year, which is part of the reason I didn't tell you earlier, but it's out of my hands now. You'll have to bring Jack."

Can you hear her? I ask.

Holy shit! Yeah! Aub replies. *Why does she want Jack?*

"Bring Jack? Where? You're not making any sense."

"I'll explain on the way, but it's an Augustia thing. Deanna is taking Zest to your grandmother's, so she'll be staying there for the time we're gone. Do you have any others besides Jack?"

"Mom. What the fuck are you talking about? I have school tomorrow. Same with Jack. Where are we going and for how long?"

"Damn it, Abby!" She shoots to her feet, attempting to tower over me but failing. With my boots' height and the Phoenix soaring, no woman will ever be above me again. She recoils a little when her outburst doesn't work. Her eyes narrow and her nose flares. "You fucked him. Well, good for you. I *am* very proud of you, but just because you've had a dick in you doesn't give you the right to be a dick to your mother. I said pack! You don't need to ask where or why, just go pack."

"I don't need to do a fucking thing you say."

Tell her, Abby! You fucking run this show now.

"You live under my roof, don't you?"

"I could change that in less than ten minutes."

Fuck yeah!

An eyebrow lifts. "Is that so?" She stands poised like a defied queen, ready to give the order to lop off my head. "Looks like that young man did wonders for you." She lifts her hands to show she means no harm. "You've outgrown me. Now that, I'm *very* proud of. Fine, I'll tell you. Unlike your sister, you've earned it. The Augustias have a multi-stage trial every thirteen years that culminates on All Hallow's Eve and into the Day of the Dead. Happy?"

Okay, what the fuck? A trial? Like a fucking sex tournament? Aub asks.

"No! I fucking barely got half of that. The Augustias? Plural?"

"Yes, there's more than just us. You found my stash here in the *hidden* compartment, didn't you?"

Oh shit!

"When did you find out?"

She laughs. "Just now, since you admitted it, but don't worry. I left it there for you and your sister, but I don't think she ever thought to look."

Holy fuck! She planted it!

"I left the juicy bits for you, but there's many more of us out there, and every thirteen years, we get together to perform some rituals. I won't say what till you start moving your ass to get packed, but I will say that it's mandatory. If you don't come willingly, one of the higher ups will bring you. Same goes for any of your Collection. *Anyone* subbed to you must appear. They have ways of finding out who's subbed. If you cause trouble, you'll be penalized, and this is not a competition you want to be at a disadvantage in. Not to mention, you're already at a disadvantage."

"What? How?"

"You only have Jack, right? If you had none, it would have made it so you'd get passed over, but claiming Jack means he's your only entry while everyone else will have six."

My mind spins but Aub keeps me focused. *We need to leave.*

"Whatever Mom." I step out of the room and into the hall just as the front door opens and several men with guns enter the foyer.

Holy fucking fuck, Aub shouts.

Jack jumps in front of Aub to shield her as panic blooms in my heart.

"Remember what I said?" Mom's heels *clack* on the hard wood behind me. "Those higher ups won't take no for an answer." She leans back against the railing, smiling up at me. "I'm one of those higher ups. Now get your fucking shit packed. Too bad about Aub."

I start down the hall, but Mom's words freeze me in place. "Wh-what do you mean?"

"I have to get rid of her," she shrugs. "If only you'd done what I said from the start, I wouldn't have had to show my hand. Now she knows, and she has to go."

Fuck! What are we going to do?

"No, wait! She's mine, too! I can read her thoughts. That means she's mine, right?"

Mom pushes off the banister and scowls at me. "Did Deanna tell you about mind reading?"

Shit! I can't throw Deanna under the bus. Who knew what Mom might do to her. "No! It happened last night. We all had sex and I could hear her thoughts."

Mom tilts back and laughs while clapping her hands. "Oh, my sweet little angel! You didn't! That's very impressive. Women are much harder to tame then men. There's ways to know if you're lying," she warns with a wag of her finger. "Magic, Abby. We *will* know if she's bound to you or not. If we take her there, and she's not bound to you, she'll be taken by one of the women there. A permanent slave."

"She *is* mine!"

"Oh, there's that fire I saw a minute ago. Good, you'll need it. Prove it. Aub, dear, hold up your hands to my men, any number of fingers you like. Jack, be a good boy and use those big shoulders to block her from Abby."

They do as she says, Aub trembling while Jack's eyes stay as hard as his jaw.

"Good. What's the number?"

It's seven, Aub says.

"Seven."

One of Mom's guys nods and Mom throws her hands in the air. "Oh my God! You really can read her mind! Ah! I'm so proud of you Abby." She wraps me in a hug, but I push her back. She frowns and brushes her dress. "Fine, be that way. It's nothing personal, dear."

Her men all lower their weapons and stand like guards on duty.

Oh, thank fucking God, Aub sighs.

"See?" Mom asks. "I mean no harm. I don't want to force you, hun. I didn't have advanced warning my first time, so I was found and brought there. Plucked right out of the street. That's how I really found out about it at all. That's how I really found my mother. Look, I put you in a bad spot, and I'll take the heat for that. You'll see, I promise. I've got some pull and I'm going to do everything I can to make up for not telling you sooner. Now, go get packed. Everything will be provided, but I know how you get with hotel towels. Bring whatever you want. Good?"

"Yeah, great." *Come up here.* I go to my room and shut the door once Jack and Aub are in.

"What the fuck are we going to do?"

Jack holds a hand out to me, his other already holding Aub's. When I take it, he says, "I told you, guns beat hands every time. We're not getting out of this."

I take Aub's other hand and look at the two people I care most about in this world.

"We have to ride the storm." Jack continues. "If we find a better place to make a break for it, we will. Otherwise, we'll play whatever little game they have in store." His grip firms. "We'll do it together."

Aub smiles up at Jack and then over to me. "Together."

I give them a solid nod. "Together!"

About the Author

T. A. Kemons is an American author living in Appalachia. Writing and storytelling has always been a passion for them. They write steamy contemporary and salacious paranormal romance novels in the hopes of igniting that same passion in others.

More from Deep Desires Press

Prey

Britt Collins

Most people learn after the first mistake, two at the most. It took Lucas Ford three and now it might cost him his life.

Mistake number 1:

At eighteen years old he saw the unthinkable, a vampire. She told him her name is Victoria. He followed her through the woods and enviously watched as she drank from another. He fell in love.

Mistake number 2:

He told other people what he saw. From that moment on Lucas was labeled as crazy. After years of therapy and joining the army he was cured and beautiful, exotic Victoria—and his love for her—it all became a fading dream.

Mistake number 3:

He let twenty years pass, thinking she was a figment of his imagination. Now she's here and very real and needs his help.

Vampires are under attack by a new kind of predator. They are no longer at the top of the food chain. Lucas is determined to find this twisted executioner before Victoria becomes the latest victim.

He's more than willing to lose his life for her.

Wolf Heart
Dorian Flynn

It's been years since Elias has seen his childhood rival and friend Julian. The last time they were together, Elias kissed him, sending Julian running away. And by morning, he was gone. Since then, Elias has kept his secret close to his chest, hoping Julian would do the same.

But Julian is back now, and simultaneously a string of mysterious animal attacks have struck the town, rousing superstitions about a Beast that swept through before Elias was even born. A Beast that was only stopped by Elias's grandmother.

Elias may have been keeping his own secret, but as he and Julian reconnect, what secrets will he discover about Julian's family…or his own?